PRAISE FOR E.M. POWELL

'The author skilfully builds tension and excitement as the crimes escalate and the pool of suspects narrows. A very enjoyable read.'
—*Historical Novel Society*

'E.M. Powell has created an immensely likeable pair in Stanton and Barling, in this exciting new medieval mystery series. Action-packed and laced with sly humour . . . I was completely riveted by *The King's Justice.*'
—Mary Lawrence, author of *The Alchemist's Daughter*

'E.M. Powell's medieval murder mysteries are like mead: sweet, potent, and seductively addictive. One sip and you won't be able to stop reading.'
—Jane Holland, bestselling author of *Girl Number One* and *Lock the Door*

The Canterbury Murders

OTHER TITLES BY E.M. POWELL

Stanton and Barling Mysteries

The King's Justice
The Monastery Murders

The Fifth Knight Series

The Fifth Knight
The Blood of the Fifth Knight
The Lord of Ireland

E.M. Powell

The Canterbury Murders

A STANTON AND BARLING MYSTERY

Crosshaven
Press

Published by Crosshaven Press

ISBN-13: 9798682187768

Cover design by Ghost Design

For Judy Bailey, who always said I should

Chapter One

If God could grant a perfect close of day, it would be this one.

Benedict, prior of Christ Church, Canterbury, walked alone in his garden, his silent steps on the paved stone path as slow as the calm beat of his own heart.

The peace of Vespers coursed within him. He had joined his fellow monks, as always, to sing and pray the Divine Office as the sun had set on a glorious spring day. Now came the quiet hour of early night, to be spent in solitude and contemplation.

Dew soaked the meadow turf of his lawn, the grass smooth as the finest carpet. Neatly trimmed shrubs filled the borders, the evergreens a pleasing contrast to those covered in soft, unfurling buds. In the beds, clumps of bright yellow celandines glowed in the dusk. White wood anemones could be candles waiting to be lit. The sweet scents of sage and rue hung in the still air, mingling with the sharpness of the box hedges. Unseen birds sang themselves and the world to slumber.

He looked up at the vast, cream-stoned cathedral nearby, its towers reaching high into a clear sky that held the last vestiges of light to the west and a low-hanging sliver of moon. It should have been a sight that filled him with serenity: the resting place of the body of Saint

Thomas Becket, the blessed Martyr. The place of a multitude of miracles for the sick, the lame, the infirm, where pilgrims flocked from all of Christendom for the saint's intervention.

But as ever since that terrible afternoon two and a half years ago, to look upon the cathedral filled Benedict with breath-robbing anguish, an anguish that at times threatened to rip out his heart. Much in the same way as the heart of his beloved cathedral had been ripped out. It bore the evidence of its near-fatal wounds still, the jagged scaffolding cloaking it in ugliness, an ugliness obvious even in the concealing shadows of the advancing night.

The cathedral's wounds had not been inflicted during the hours of darkness, when murderers and robbers and others bent on wrongdoing often chose to be abroad. It had been an afternoon. A September afternoon, unseasonably hot and humid, with the sun glowing a dull amber and a blustery gale that brought no freshness to the air.

Benedict could feel the pull and flap of the strong, warm wind on his black habit, though the garden around him remained quiet.

It so often happened like this. He could be perfectly content one minute. Or busy with his unending list of tasks as prior. Or having his face shaved by one of his servants. Or breaking bread for a meal. It mattered not.

He would be back in those fateful autumn hours.

The commotion from outside the south wall of the cathedral grounds. Three cottages, all on fire.

Outside. Not of my concern: his dismissive words to one of the monks who had come to alert him. 'Make sure you keep the gate clear,' he'd said to the monk. 'We cannot have pilgrims delayed in their entry.'

The townsfolk had merged on the threat, making such a commotion and clamour as only townsfolk could. Not to mention the loudness of the excited mob of pilgrims and hawkers that followed

2

them. After more uproar and shouts and soil and water and hooks to pull down burning walls, the flames had been vanquished.

Order has been restored. The monk's report to Benedict.

Benedict had nodded and gone back to his work.

Such fuss at so very little. People did like to make a great happening of nothing. No doubt they crowded into the town's alehouses, using the thrill of danger that had caused no actual harm to them to tell stories and exaggerate their own part in it. A danger that was safely past.

But it was not.

For the powerful wind, the wind that Benedict often thought of since as having blown from hellmouth, was doing its unseen, wicked work, silent as a serpent and equally intent on evil.

As the townsfolk beat down the flames of the burning cottages, as they tackled the flaring thatch, sparks and embers flew up. Up, up on the violent gusts of wind, cloaked in dust and yellowing leaves ripped from the trees. Up, up over the walls of the cathedral. Up over the very tops of the trees. Up to the roof of the cathedral, where the buffeting gale forced them between the gaps of the lead, like a shower of smouldering hail.

No one saw. No one knew.

On the ground, people proclaimed victory.

In the roof, the sparks met the rafters, the bone-dry, rotting wood that had held up the mighty edifice since the time of Saint Anselm.

On the ground, people cheered and raised their ales.

In the roof, the rafters were afire, feeding the crackling flames that jumped to the beams and the braces to greater life.

On the ground, people clapped their hands and sang.

In the cathedral, the lay brothers polished the carved wooden seats of the choir, as the lead-lined, brightly painted ceiling high above them hid the inferno of broiling heat and flames.

In his chambers, Benedict amended an account to order some extra grain for the monks.

On the ground, people sang on.

In the roof, the flames grew to such a height that the leaded roof began to soften. Melt. Dissolve.

The first smoke poured out in a white, billowing cloud.

And on the ground came a shout: 'Look, look! God's eyes, look!'

And another: 'The cathedral's on fire!'

The same shout at Benedict's door, the shout that had him race outside, following the frantic monk's lead. That had him jostle for position in the heaving crowd, staring aloft in disbelief, his heart thumping in his chest.

All around him, horrified faces. Gaping mouths. Pointing fingers. Cries and calls of shock.

'May God help us!'

'It's all of the roof, look!'

'It's afire, afire!'

Benedict willed his voice to shout for his brethren, his feet to run back. He could not. His tongue stuck to the roof of his mouth and his feet could be nailed to the stone path on which he stood. Only his heart had life, thudding as if it would break from his chest.

The first jarring alarms to summon help pealed out from the cathedral bell tower.

Then bright yellow flames shot up from the roof in a huge burst of roiling black smoke, roaring into greater life in the devil's gale.

Screams and yells of horror, of terror surrounded Benedict.

'It's the end of the world!'

'By the holy paternoster, we are done for!'

The nearest churches took up the cathedral's call. The bells of Saint Mary Magdalene, Saint Andrew, Saint Alphege rang out in wild discord.

A fresh roar from the wind sent charred wood and burning cinders raining down to lamentation and wails of dread.

Some people fled, others sank to their knees with tears and prayers to the Virgin, to Saint Thomas.

Benedict's heart pounded harder, harder. He thought he might faint, he thought he might fall. He drew in a desperate breath.

And then there was peace once more. No fire raged through the cathedral. No showers of embers rained down. Nothing broke the quiet, except for the gentle chorus of birdsong and the distant sounds from beyond the garden walls of the city of Canterbury moving to the end of the day.

Benedict wiped the sweat from his face with an unsteady hand. He needed to become calm. Must become calm. The hour of Compline drew near, and he would be amongst his monks again. He had to be their strength, their guide. He would make another couple of circuits of his garden, would pray to Saint Thomas for aid in steadying his mind.

The Martyr would help him in his need, for he was working without cease for the glory of Thomas. The cathedral had, by the greatest of miracles, been spared from total destruction. Thomas's bones had been safe in Anselm's crypt. Now, Benedict's burden was to rebuild: not just to replace what had been destroyed, but to even greater glory. He looked up at the disfiguring scaffolding again. His was a heavy cross to bear, and one he must bear alone.

He turned at the squeak of the iron garden gate opening.

One of his monks hurried through it. 'My lord.' Breathless. Not like Benedict had just been but as if he'd been running.

'What is it, man?' Benedict did not mean to sound so harsh. He simply was not yet restored. 'The bells have not rung for Compline.'

'My lord prior.' The monk's face showed ashen in the dim light. 'You must come at once.'

'What do you—'

'There's been a murder.'

Benedict feared he had fallen back into one of his episodes. 'A murder?'

The monk nodded. 'In a terrible way, my lord. Terrible.'

'Steady yourself,' said Benedict, wishing the same for his own heart. 'Which of our brothers has lost his life?'

'No, no. It's not one of the brothers.'

Benedict clutched with gratitude at the small mercy. 'Then why is it of such importance that I attend?'

'Because it's one of the stonemasons. From here. From our cathedral. He . . . he's been stabbed. There's so much blood.'

'Then it will be a robbery, or—'

'No, no.' The monk's words came out as a low moan. 'No robbery. He has all his possessions. Something far worse.' He swallowed hard. 'The killer mutilated him as well.' His voice dropped to a petrified whisper as he explained.

Benedict listened in horror. No, this was no episode of his own mind.

The monk's terror was as real as the hard paving beneath Benedict's feet. As the liquid ripple of birdsong. As the scent of the box hedges.

And as the shadows of the scaffolding above him that held the beauty of his beloved cathedral in a hideous, unyielding grasp.

Chapter Two

For almost as long as he could remember, Hugo Stanton had loved horses.

The way their swift hooves could eat up the long miles of a journey. The way their height meant he could see far ahead in open country or over the tops of those who scurried about on foot in a busy town street. The way they could get him out of trouble, which they'd had to do more often than he would've liked.

But on this showery, breezy Palm Sunday afternoon, he missed the strength of their broad backs.

He loosened the straps from the bulky, heavy bundle that plagued his own spine. With a grateful groan, he slid it down onto the damp, flattened grass and the discarded evergreen branches of the day's procession. At least the pack made a decent seat for his backside, and he could rest his aching legs and feet.

Noisy pilgrims flocked around him, entering and leaving the grey-stoned church of Saint Dunstan like so many ants, back and forth to their nests. Unlike ants, they didn't seem to have any mind about where they walked. A man without use of his limbs lay on a bier on the ground nearby and had already been stepped on twice.

'Oi, watch where you're treading, fool!'

Three times.

Stanton took his leather water pouch from his belt and drank a mouthful. The Lenten fast, with its scarce meals of salted fish had his thirst up more than the hottest midsummer day. Usually, he'd welcome that. For thirst meant ale, and ale meant an alehouse. He'd lost count of the number he'd passed during the last three days, on the long road from Southwark to Canterbury. Not just alehouses. Likely-looking inns. Alewives at the side of the road with sweet-smelling barrels. All calling to him with the promise of respite from a throat drier than if he'd swallowed a fistful of sand.

A call that had had to stay unanswered, because Stanton wasn't travelling the pilgrim way alone.

He was travelling with Aelred Barling, the King's clerk, who viewed ale as if it had been spat straight from the mouth of a serpent.

At first, Stanton had been cheered by Barling's unexpected announcement to him in the clerk's Westminster solar that they would be going on pilgrimage to the tomb of Saint Thomas Becket at Canterbury, a trip that would end with celebration of the great feast of Easter. His cheer hadn't merely been because it would help to pass the last of the long, hungry, dreary days of Lent: Stanton had heard great tales of pilgrimage from several of the other young men at the court. Inns. Singing. Drums. Dancing. Bands of young female pilgrims who were out from under the eye of parents and priests. He knew full well that he'd have to escape the clerk from time to time to make the most of it all. He'd find a way. He always did.

But he'd also hoped that their friendship could be rekindled. He and the clerk had become closer than ever at the Yorkshire monastery where they'd been summoned to solve a series of the grisliest murders just last January. Impossible to think of now, but it had been a time of bone-chilling cold and even worse terror.

Yet, on their return to the court, the closeness between them had disappeared far faster than the winter snows had. Barling had shut himself away with his legal manuscripts, emerging only to send Stanton to chase down this witness or deliver that document with curt orders that held no warmth.

Any attempts Stanton had made to get Barling out and about – to take a walk along the river or a trip to join a game of skittles – had been met with a shake of Barling's tonsured head and a claim that he was far too busy for such frivolous nonsense.

Stanton was reminded of the sea-mushrooms on the rocks on the beach near his childhood home in Norfolk. Shiny-red, smooth and still, they looked as if they had no life to them. He could poke and prod them with a stick, and nothing would happen. But he knew full well that they opened up in a mass of busy tentacles when the tide covered them again. As things stood, all he had was a stick.

He sighed and finished the last drops of his water.

Barling's pilgrimage announcement had been followed up with one of Barling's written plans. 'Stanton, we will travel from the court through Southwark and thence to Dartford, and then on to Rochester. Our journey will be on horseback.' The clerk presented this to Stanton as if it were a normal occurrence.

Stanton hadn't commented. The chances of the awkward clerk managing to stay on his animal and not end up in a ditch weren't good. At least the pilgrim road would be packed, so their pace would be slow. Even Barling could stay on at a walk. Mostly.

Barling carried on with his plan. 'We will be accepting the hospitality of virtuous houses along the route. These people have answered God's call that they provide charity to pilgrims.'

That had Stanton sending up a quick prayer. *By all that's holy: please let these folk be of good spirits and have full dishes and brimming cups.*

A prayer that went unanswered.

Stanton could only sit opposite morose faces and scrape his meagre chunks of hard black bread around bowls that he'd emptied of salted herring in half a dozen mouthfuls, his hunger from the fast still gnawing at him after the one permitted meal of the day. A few dour remarks would break the heavy silences, with complaints about the clamour of drunken pilgrims on the road setting the dogs barking being a favourite.

But Barling had kept the last part of his plan from Stanton.

Waking Stanton well before dawn on this morning of Palm Sunday, the clerk had ordered him to rise without delay. The last leg of their journey, some thirty miles, would be travelled on foot. Blinking awake in the weak candlelight, Stanton could see that the clerk had abandoned his usual black robes and was dressed instead in a rough pilgrim's tunic and carried a staff.

'For the glory of the Martyr,' Barling had said.

That was also the reason he gave for Stanton having to carry the full load of their possessions on his back.

And carried them Stanton had, for the last thirteen hours, through sunny hours that had sweat pour down his spine and sudden showers that soaked him through and chilled him. He rubbed his shoulders. It would be a week before the skin healed, chafed as it was from the rough twine that served as handles. Sore as he was, he was in far better shape than Barling. Here the short, slight clerk came, hobbling back out from the door of Saint Dunstan's church.

Barling had announced when they were five miles from Canterbury that he intended to complete them barefoot. He wouldn't hear a word said about it.

Stanton had watched and winced as Barling's feet, soft and pale as egg white, had squelched in the mud on the road. Had stepped on sharp stones and thorns. Had stubbed against rocks. Had stepped in piles of steaming horse muck. Had had people's booted feet and shoes stand on them in the thick, swaying crowds of chanting pilgrims waving their greenery aloft.

Those small feet were white no more, but in a state of bloodied filth.

When Stanton had seen Canterbury's high city walls and the chapel-topped Westgate ahead, the stone lit by the late afternoon sun, he could feel nothing except relief on behalf of his friend. But no. The silly turnip had announced that he had to call in at the church of Saint Dunstan, just as King Henry had when he had made his public pilgrimage here.

Stanton hadn't responded. The King. The man who had been responsible for the death of the woman Stanton loved. God rot him. Barling could go on his own in there.

'Barling, I think it might be a good idea to put your boots back on,' he said, as the clerk made his way to him.

'Then you think wrong, Stanton.' Barling leaned heavily on his staff, the better to keep weight off his feet, his face etched with exhaustion and pain. 'I am making a pilgrimage. Pilgrimage involves sacrifice.'

As far as Stanton could make out from a group of bearded men that romped past, pilgrimage involved a song about a cock that had no feathers.

Despite the clerk's weariness, they got a glare from Barling's pale eyes. 'Come, Stanton, we are almost there.'

'We are,' said Stanton. 'And just as well. I can't carry you on my back. Though of course, you'd say I was already a donkey, wouldn't you?' It was a poor jest, but he wanted to lift Barling's mood, even as his own was lifting at the prospect of Canterbury's many attractions.

It was as if Barling hadn't heard. He set off, one resolute foot in front of another. Or maybe he had heard and didn't care.

Either way, he was closed off to Stanton.

Tight as the sea-mushrooms on the rocks.

Chapter Three

'We're here, Barling.' The blue-eyed young Stanton gave Aelred Barling one of his widest grins. 'You did it.'

'That was precisely my plan, Stanton.' Barling would not give voice to his joy at their arrival. He had feared on numerous occasions on the road that he would faint from exhaustion and pain. But he had succeeded. He was finally at Canterbury's great cathedral.

It rose before him: huge, graceful, impossible in its scale and glory. The scars it bore from the great fire showed the extent of the appalling damage. The enormous frames of wooden scaffolding that covered a large proportion of it were a sobering reminder of how close it must have come to destruction.

But the wood was keeping the structure intact, much as the staff he held kept him from falling and had done so often on his barefoot journey. He clutched it more firmly, the better to keep the weight from his agonised feet. The better also to contain the tide of emotion that, to his quiet horror, threatened to break from him. He swallowed hard and silently berated himself for such nonsense. Public displays of emotion came from weakness or self-indulgence.

Fortunately, Stanton did not appear to notice. He was busy hauling the bundle of their belongings from his back to throw it on the ground next to them as they waited for entrance to the cathedral.

'Don't worry, I'll push it along for a bit,' Stanton said by way of explanation. 'My shoulders are done.' He pushed his thick, unruly blond hair from his sweat-coated brow.

Barling had little care for what Stanton did with their possessions. In truth, he would not care if they threw them away.

He had made it here, and he gave thanks. After the horrors of Fairmore Abbey, the holy house in Yorkshire where he and Stanton had fought evil beyond measure. After his confession to a priest immediately upon his return to Westminster for his old, old sin: the sin of loving another man.

The priest listened with close and prayerful attention to Barling's full and complete admission.

When Barling finished, he asked, 'You say you had previously confessed this gravest of sins?'

'I did, sir priest. My original confessor was most concerned for my eternal fate.'

'I am in absolute agreement with his judgement,' said the priest.

'I carried out my full penance of fifteen years,' said Barling. 'Alone.' And heartbroken. He pushed the painful memories away. 'It ended late last year.'

'Then I believe I understand what has happened.' The priest gave a sage nod. 'God, in His ultimate and unknowable mercy, spared you from death. But in that sparing, He wants to remind you afresh of the mortal peril in which your sin placed your soul. You must cleanse yourself of it completely. To that end, you must make a Lenten penitential pilgrimage to the tomb of Saint Thomas Becket.'

Barling lowered his head for his blessing. 'I will do so with all praise for the Almighty's mercy, sir priest.'

'Mark this well, Barling.' The priest leaned forward to emphasise his point. 'You must forget any demands of this life. The fate of your eternal soul should be your one and only concern. Nothing, absolutely nothing, else should take precedence.'

Now the Martyr's tomb lay almost within Barling's reach.

It was so near, he knew it was. He had read the extensive writings of the monks of Canterbury. Had even drawn out his own plan of the cathedral, imagining his steps towards the tomb. Towards complete forgiveness. Salvation.

He'd pictured it so many times, as he sat at his writing desk or lay in his narrow bed at night, waiting for sleep that would not come as he relived the horrors of Fairmore that would storm unbidden into his mind. He was helpless against their onslaught. Thoughts of Canterbury became his single meagre defence.

The approach to the cathedral's doors would be a smooth, wide avenue, devoid of obstacle. He would enter a church filled with light and quiet and grace and would walk to the crypt, spent from his long hours on the road. He would sink to his knees in reverence before the tomb, praising the Martyr and begging for his intercession. Would lose himself in confessional prayer to God. Forgiveness would wash over him like cold, cleansing water.

His hands tightened on his staff. His imagination had made a fool of him.

Canterbury's main streets, lined with tall, thatched half-wood, half-stone buildings, had none of the width of London's thoroughfares, yet they seemed to hold twice as many people. And what people. Rude. Jostling. No courtesy given to him, though his tonsure marked him as one who should have been given respectful space. The last steps of the journey had been through alleyways so narrow and packed he had hardly been able to breathe, let alone see ahead.

His spirits had risen when he and Stanton had finally passed through the gate into the cathedral grounds, only for his hope to fall again. The cathedral door, a hundred yards or so ahead, might as well be back in Westminster.

A lengthy queue of pilgrims waited for entry even at this late hour of the afternoon, the line snaking back upon itself such were the numbers and because of the requirement to leave the large graveyard clear. The long, long straggle held every type of humanity. The hale. The blind. The deaf. The lame. The crippled. The mad. All intent on getting their time at the tomb.

The movement forward was the slowest of occasional steps, making it easy work for Stanton to shove their bundle along in front of them with one boot.

Not that Stanton ever sought out hard work. If a challenging task presented itself, the man would find the least difficult means to complete it. He was happy for luck to guide him, not be weighed down with morals. While the happenings at Fairmore continued to cast the darkest shadow over Barling, they had not dimmed Stanton's sunny nature in the least.

Barling would not dwell on that. To be envious of Stanton's artlessness was as productive as envy of a skylark's ability to soar. Barling's focus must continue to be that of his own soul.

The queue shuffled forward a couple of paces, then stopped again.

Barling clicked his tongue in frustration. The lack of progress did not seem to be of the least concern to those present. He could hear multiple prayers. Other people seemed to view it as a time to call and shout and fuss to each other. Several continued to wave their evergreens in the air, proclaiming the day, though it neared its end.

'Alms for a beggar, sir.' A sharp-faced man appeared at Barling's side, bowl held out in anticipation.

He shook his head as the man moved on to the next pilgrim, and the next, in a steady rhythm. 'Alms for a beggar, sir. Alms for a beggar, good mistress.'

'He's a very well-fed-looking beggar, isn't he?' said Stanton.

Barling did not reply.

The man in front of Stanton laughed. 'That he is. Good boots and all.'

15

Stanton needed no further encouragement. He and the man struck up an easy conversation, much to Barling's irritation. It was always the way with his young assistant. He thrived on yarns and yammer with any and everybody, man or woman. Especially women, and young ones in particular.

The man embarked on a dull ramble about his own tedious journey to Canterbury, which Stanton seemed to find of great interest.

On and on. 'Course, I'd heard about the forest of Blean,' said the man. 'Knew we had to get through in daytime. Knew that, so I did. I'd worked it out.'

Worse, the man's even duller wife joined in. 'Can't go round it, can you?'

'All them robbers, out and about,' said the man. 'But guess what happened?'

'You ended up there at night?' said Stanton.

'That we did,' said the man. 'Imagine us, trying to run through, for miles. In the dark, losing our way. Back, forth, round about.'

'Then round again,' said the woman. 'We was in such a fluster.'

'Especially when I fell over a tree root – right on me face. Imagine!'

All three laughed heartily.

'Thought he'd been struck, I did,' she said. 'Such a muddle.'

More laughter.

Barling did not join in, occupied as he was in offering up a silent prayer to Saint Monica for patience.

He would need it to be granted soon, for the shrill notes of pipes and the bang of a drum launched a fresh assault on his ears. A group of musicians had struck up some way down the queue, a minstrel singing a song about a maiden in love. Voices raised to join him, and people clapped along, including Stanton and the couple in front.

'This is intolerable,' said Barling.

'It's good to pass the time waiting,' said Stanton.

Barling sniffed. 'They will want money, mark my words.'

Stanton shrugged and clapped on.

'Hey!' a yell came from up ahead.

'Oh, what is it now?' said Barling. 'A tumbler?'

Stanton stepped out to have a look. 'Some sort of commotion.'

Barling leaned out too. 'It is the beggar.'

The man was running back down the line of singing, clapping people towards them.

'Stop him!' An old man appeared behind him. 'He's got my purse!' His thin call echoed above the noise.

Shouts replaced song, and a few hands grabbed without success at the beggar. Three men started to give chase, but he was too quick.

Not as quick as Stanton.

He picked up their bundle and flung it right at the feet of the beggar.

The thief went over it and onto the ground in a heavy sprawl, to loud cheers.

The men in pursuit grabbed him and hauled him to his feet to yet greater uproar, ripping the stolen purse from his hand. A knot of cathedral servants converged on him to drag him off for his punishment.

Those around gave Stanton praise and handshakes, which appeared to please him greatly. The offers of ale at the city's alehouses made him beam even more.

Barling's irritation rose. Stanton might have carried out a quick-witted act. But that was not their purpose here. Neither was the talk of liquid reward for him.

'As God sees me, that was good work.' Stanton's new friend thumped him on the arm.

'So brave!' trilled his wife.

Stanton finally turned to Barling, wearing a broad grin. 'Not bad, eh?'

'You have done what was necessary in the circumstances,' said Barling.

Stanton's grin faded.

Barling went on. 'Can you please retrieve our belongings before somebody decides to rob us instead?'

Stanton did as instructed.

As he returned to the queue, a black-robed cathedral monk came striding along, shouting out two words that Barling had never expected to hear.

He wondered if he trusted his own ears. 'Is that man calling my name?' he asked Stanton.

'Sounds like it.' Stanton's expression mirrored Barling's own surprise at being sought out by name.

Barling raised his voice. 'Yes, brother. That is I.'

Stanton blew a sharp whistle with two fingers.

Barling winced. Most unnecessary, as ever.

The monk came hurrying over. 'My prior, Benedict of Christ Church, bids you welcome on this holy day.'

'I am most honoured by his welcome.' Barling indeed was. He had read the great writings of Benedict in preparation for his pilgrimage. He could not imagine why the prior's welcome would be conveyed to him. Nor could he imagine why it would be delivered here, in sight of so many gawpers.

'Prior Benedict also respectfully requests your presence,' said the monk.

'Again, I would be honoured,' said Barling. 'The prior will, I am sure, understand that I will first be paying my respects at the tomb of—'

'At once, sir,' said the monk. 'The prior made that absolutely clear in his instructions to me.'

So his entry to the tomb was to be snatched from him, just as it was within his reach. But Barling recognised the order conveyed from one in power. He had followed enough of them over the years. Fighting down his bitter disappointment, he gestured to Stanton. 'Pick up our belongings. We have to make haste.'

Stanton set about strapping the bundle to his back as the monk addressed Barling with a frown.

'Prior Benedict asked for you, sir. Nobody else.'

'Don't worry about me, Barling,' said Stanton. 'You go where you're needed. I'll find a way to pass the time in this godly place.' The younger man showed not a shred of dishonesty in either face or voice. 'Maybe even say a few extra prayers.'

The monk nodded in solemn approval at Stanton's virtuous reply.

Barling itched to admonish his assistant for his cheek. The monk was not to know that Stanton was as likely to go to pray as a fish was to play the harp. But Barling had no appetite for any further public uproar. 'We will both be accompanying you, brother.' He used his oft-practised tone of full authority, making sure that Stanton caught his warning glare. 'As the King's clerk, that is my request. I trust I will not have to tell your prior that you denied it?'

The monk backed down, as Barling knew he would. 'No, sir. Not at all. If you will follow me?'

Barling stepped from the queue to follow the monk, his heart as sore as his feet.

As he did so, he gave a last regretful look back up at the cathedral.

Soon. He would be in there soon.

He had to be. His soul depended on it.

Chapter Four

Stanton matched Barling's slow pace as the monk led their way away from the waiting pilgrims and around the outside of the cathedral.

'Watch your step, sir,' said the monk, and not for the first time.

Though the man was clearly on edge, tasked as he was with getting Barling to the prior as soon as he could, his warnings made sense. The level paving of the path next to the graveyard had given way to a stony, rutted cartway that cut through the grounds from a separate entrance to the one used by the pilgrims. The cartway served a large fenced-off and gated area that hugged the cathedral wall.

'I have my staff,' replied Barling. 'As I did five minutes ago.'

Testy as ever. Stanton paid little mind to that. In truth, guilt nipped at him. He shouldn't have been so quick to try to escape from Barling. The clerk looked near collapse after the journey. And they still would have to get to the inn that Barling had secured for them. Whatever the prior wanted, Stanton hoped it wouldn't take long. He needed drink and rest as well.

They passed through a gated archway and into another graveyard, this one with bigger plots and with carved headstones of the best quality. Stanton recognised it immediately as a monks' cemetery. A shiver passed through him. The memories of last winter wouldn't easily fade. At least he and Barling were back on a good, smooth stone path and the clerk's pace increased.

This place was very different to the crowded pilgrim area they'd left behind. Nothing disturbed the monks' eternal rest save for the birdsong in the stands of shrubs and tall trees that grew along the length of the boundary wall. In the far corner and away from the graves, was a large brick-edged fishpond, its surface broken by the odd ripple and bubble.

As their party rounded the eastern end of the cathedral, the monk addressed Barling.

'You have not long to go now, sir. The prior's chambers are over there.' He pointed ahead to a separate stone building, of good size and with a tiled roof. A high-walled garden was attached to the side. The prior of Christ Church liked his comfort, no doubt about that.

'That is welcome news, brother,' said Barling. 'Perhaps you will advise the prior of my dishevelled appearance? I would not like him to think that the King's clerk has unclean habits.'

'Of course, sir.' The monk hurried ahead.

'Stanton.' Barling stopped him with a tug on his sleeve. 'My boots. Quickly.'

Stanton hauled the bundle off his back. 'Are you sure?' He rummaged through to find them. 'They'll hurt to put on. Your feet need washing and bandaging first.'

'I am not leaving a trail of filth and injury across the floor of the great prior of Christ Church.' Barling clicked his fingers. 'Hurry up, man.' He took his boots from Stanton, who re-secured the bundle.

Grasping for Stanton's arm again, Barling shoved his feet into his boots, biting his lip with the effort.

Stanton could only imagine how much the swollen, broken skin stung. 'This summons from the prior better be important, Barling.'

'That is not for our judgement. Proceed.' Barling made his way to the arched doorway, leaning on Stanton to quicken his pace.

They entered a spacious anteroom, where the monk ushered them through another set of double doors into the large solar, which was lit with many beeswax candles and thick logs burning in the wide fireplace.

It could not be more different to the plainness of the Cistercian house of Fairmore. Deep-seated chairs of carved, polished wood were padded with thick, richly coloured embroidered cushions, and heavy tapestries lined the painted walls. A dark blue wine jug of finest pottery sat on the table along with matching goblets.

'My lord prior,' said the monk. 'The King's man, Aelred Barling.' He left, closing the solar door behind them.

'The blessings of the day to you, Aelred Barling.' At the far side of the room, the black-robed prior stood before a tall, open window that let in the last of the evening light. He would be early in his fourth decade, his tonsured hair still a dull mid-brown. Slightly built and with narrow shoulders, he didn't make for a commanding presence. His jutting top front teeth didn't help, either, giving his voice a nasal whine.

'And to you, Prior Benedict.' Barling inclined his head in a respectful bow. 'I know your brother will have advised of my appearance, but please accept my apologies in person.'

'Yes. Well. One must make do with whatever we are presented with.' The prior's unimpressed gaze went to Stanton. 'The brother informed me that this man's presence is necessary.' Back to Barling. 'Is it?'

'Hugo Stanton is my assistant, Prior.'

Stanton bowed, not daring to say a word. The prior's unhappy mood would appear to trump Barling's.

Barling continued. 'May I say what an honour it is to meet you in person, Prior. I have long been a scholar of your works and have—'

A door opened to the right.

Stanton understood why Barling had been struck dumb when he saw who entered.

The clerk went into the deepest bow, clutching at his staff for support. Stanton matched him, though he feared the heavy bundle on his back might topple him.

He didn't care. Better to fall flat onto his face than not show proper respect to Richard, Archbishop of Canterbury.

'My lord,' said Barling.

'Rise, Aelred Barling,' said the Archbishop. 'You too, man. Benedict, close those shutters.' He pointed at the prior with a rolled letter that he held in one hand. 'We cannot run the risk of being overheard.'

Benedict did as ordered, with Richard taking a seat in the chair nearest the fire.

Stanton had glimpsed the Archbishop occasionally at the court, always at a distance. Up close, Stanton could see that he wore his advancing years well, his gaze still sharp and keen.

The Archbishop addressed Barling. 'It gladdens my soul to see a man who has endured the privations of pilgrimage.'

Barling inclined his head. 'That is most gracious of you to say so, my lord.'

Stanton kept his face safely blank as the prior sat next to the Archbishop. *Not going to offer the worn-out clerk a seat, though, are you?*

'I am sure you will be wondering why you have been summoned, Barling,' said Richard. 'I will explain all. But first, you know of the fire that almost destroyed our great cathedral?'

A meeting with the prior. The Archbishop too. To talk about a fire long put out. Stanton had many questions. But it would not be his place to ask them. Or to make the slightest sound.

'I certainly do, my lord,' said Barling. 'A most calamitous event. I have heard much of it. Read about it too. Yet, my lord, nothing could have prepared me for seeing the damage first-hand.'

'It is a terrible sight,' said the Archbishop, as Benedict nodded sombrely in agreement. 'However, we are blessed that God spared the tomb of Saint Thomas, and that has been our sign to rebuild the cathedral to give greater glory to the Martyr. Prior Benedict is overseeing the work. We have employed one of Europe's greatest architects and masons, William of Sens. While it is no exaggeration to say that his plans have been touched by divinity, the cost has been . . . substantial and is likely to become even more so. Nevertheless, we go on, and have been going on, as God has ordained.' He paused and looked at Benedict. 'But.'

'But we have encountered a problem in this endeavour that nobody could have foreseen,' said the prior.

Stanton froze at his next words, the last words he expected to hear.

'One of the stonemasons,' said the prior, 'a man who has been rebuilding Canterbury Cathedral, has been murdered.'

Chapter Five

A murder. Another murder. That was why he had been summoned here. Dear God. Not again.

Barling did not, of course, dare to put his thoughts into words. Instead, he crossed himself in respect. 'May God have mercy on his soul.' He meant that in all sincerity, appalled at his selfish reaction upon hearing of a man's violent death.

The Archbishop also made the sign of the cross along with Stanton.

'The dead stonemason was a man by the name of Peter Flocke,' said Benedict. 'A man nearing his third decade and in full health and strength. His body was found eight nights ago, in the yard of the stonemasons' lodge, which is next to the south wall of the cathedral. You will have passed the yard as the brother led you through the grounds.'

Barling had but a dim recollection of it, such had been his pain, but he nodded in acknowledgement.

'I was summoned when the discovery was made,' continued the prior. 'He was stabbed many, many times.' He shuddered. 'His blood was splashed all over much of the carved stone that was ready to be put in place.'

'A cut-purse, perhaps?' asked Barling, desperate to provide an answer that would release him from this. 'One set upon an old man in broad daylight not an hour ago, in full sight of the crowds assembled to enter the cathedral. Who knows what boldness evil-doers would dare to show under cover of darkness?'

'Flocke's purse remained closed on his belt, with coins still inside it, so it is unlikely that this was a simple robbery.' Benedict exchanged a glance with the Archbishop, who nodded at him to continue. 'For,' said Benedict, 'the killer not only slew Flocke in such a horrendous manner but mutilated the body as well.'

'Mutilated?' Barling's stomach constricted. He and Stanton had seen the horror of butchered bodies at Fairmore this past winter. At the village of Claresham last summer. Yet he had to ask. It was expected of him, he could see that. 'In what manner?'

'His face.' Benedict's voice wavered. 'He had a symbol cut deep into his forehead.'

Barling suppressed his exclamation of disgust. At the edge of his vision, Stanton's visage twisted in a grimace of revulsion. 'I am sorry to have to press you, Prior. But I need to have as much detail as possible. When you say a symbol, could you describe it?'

The Archbishop answered, his voice sombre. 'It is unfortunately very simple to describe, Barling. It was the holy Cross of Christ.'

Barling stared at him, any reply robbed by shock.

The Archbishop spoke instead. 'I can see you are stunned by such sacrilege. As were, and are, we. Murder is already a profanation of the body, taking what God alone can give. But for the killer to misuse the symbol of Christ's Cross in the act of mortal sin?' He shook his head in disbelief.

Barling found his voice. 'It speaks of the most unholy wickedness, my lord.'

'It is indeed almost beyond comprehension, Barling,' said Benedict. 'Had I not seen it with my own eyes, I would have had trouble believing it. That was also the reaction of the man who found the body.'

Again, Barling asked the appropriate question. 'Who might that be, Prior?'

'Another of the masons employed in working on the cathedral, a man by the name of Adam Drake.'

'Those who find a body are sometimes those who have caused it to be there in the first place, Prior,' said Barling. 'More often than one would think.' Again, a suggestion made out of desperation, but one at least backed up by Stanton's confirming nod.

'I can assure you that I had thought of such an obvious solution, Barling.' Benedict gave him an unimpressed look. 'I do not believe for a second that Drake carried out the heinous act. The man was a blubbering mess about it all.'

Barling inclined his head. 'Forgive my choice of words, Prior. I meant no criticism.'

'It was the right question to ask, Barling,' said the Archbishop. 'But as Prior Benedict has said, it has been answered. Yet we have no answer that could explain this, despite enquiries by Benedict which have been as extensive as they have been discreet.'

'As you will appreciate, we have not, despite our best efforts, been able to contain word of this awful event,' said Benedict. 'Gossip and conjecture are rife amongst the builders and even some of the cathedral monks, creating a great deal of unease as well as delay to the work.' He drew a hand across his forehead. 'There is also sinful, loose talk of the cathedral being cursed. First the fire. And now this.'

'Loose talk travels far and fast at a time of fear, Prior,' said Barling. 'It matters not whether it is true. However, if I may be so bold: perhaps your enquiries need to be more public, not less?'

'How do you mean, Barling?' said Archbishop Richard with a frown.

'I mean, my lord, that this is a city upon which thousands of strangers converge. An official announcement would serve two purposes. It would help people to be on their guard but could also be of assistance in finding the killer.'

'An announcement?' Benedict looked aghast. 'Are you suggesting that I take up a place at the Bull Stake? Shout to the passers-by that they are either murderers or run the risk of being murdered?' His voice rose. 'Can you imagine the offence? The panic?'

'Prior.' The Archbishop held a hand up to silence him. 'Enough. Barling, you have to understand that the strangers of which you speak are devout pilgrims. To disrupt their pilgrimage when the great feast of Easter is but a week away is completely unconscionable. I will hear no more of it.'

Barling bowed. 'Forgive me, my lord.'

'That such a murder took place is serious enough,' said the Archbishop. 'But now we have a greater urgency to solve it. Count Philip of Flanders has given word that he is going to make a Lenten pilgrimage here, to the tomb of the Martyr.' He lowered his voice to the most hushed of tones. 'The pressing urgency is that King Henry has got wind of the count's visit. The King will not be outdone in his public devotion to the Martyr. He has sent word that he will be arriving in four days' time, on Maundy Thursday.' The Archbishop's face lost all colour. He looked over his shoulder, as if in fear Henry might have suddenly slipped into the room and was listening.

A fear that Barling knew was not without foundation: his lord King was more than capable of carrying out such unorthodox action.

Richard's voice dropped further. 'If the King were to hear of this appalling incident, of any suggestion of a curse on this cathedral, and the fact that the culprit has not been found, it would have the most serious of consequences for me.'

'As it would for the cathedral monks.' Benedict's pallor matched the Archbishop's. 'We cannot allow this matter to impact on his Grace in any way.'

'For we all know what happens to the Archbishop of Canterbury when he angers his Grace.' Richard swallowed hard.

The whole world knew it. Archbishop Thomas Becket had been cut down on the altar in the nearby cathedral almost seven years ago, brutally murdered by a group of knights acting on the King's rash words. Barling admired and respected his lord Henry with every bone in his body, but even he had wondered about such an appalling deed. It had taken the great man that Henry was to admit his sin and acknowledge that it had been terrible, so terrible he had done public penance on the streets of Canterbury and returned regularly to the Martyr's tomb to express his enduring regret and sorrow. 'We do, my lord Archbishop,' was all Barling said.

'I have privately sought advice from the King's justice, Ranulf de Glanville, about how to manage this crisis,' said Archbishop Richard. 'I could hardly believe his reply.' He held up the letter. 'That one of his clerks, Aelred Barling, is a man without equal for this sensitive task.'

Barling wished he could take pride in his lord de Glanville's high opinion of him. But his only response was dread.

The Archbishop went on. 'That you, Aelred Barling, are the man to solve this murder. That, in a coincidence that is nothing short of miraculous, you were already on your way here on pilgrimage. The Martyr has led you to us, so solve it you must. Must.' He pointed the letter at Barling in the same way he had instructed Benedict to close the shutters. 'And with all possible haste. Do I make myself clear?'

'Of course, my lord,' said Barling. 'I am honoured to do your bidding and to serve you as my lord de Glanville has instructed.' *But devastated that I must.* He tried and failed to catch Stanton's eye. 'As are we both, my lord.'

The Archbishop did not even glance Stanton's way. 'Good.' He lowered the letter. 'I am sure I do not need to explain, but I am, for the most part, staying out of the investigation. The responsibility will be Prior Benedict's.' Benedict's sullen expression told Barling what the prior felt about that decision. 'He will be the man to whom you report and who will give you all the assistance you require.'

Barling was unsurprised by Richard's distancing of himself. His reputation was well known: the Archbishop was very much King Henry's man, appointed by him for compromise and cooperation. He would not attach himself to anything that would upset his comfortable relationship.

Not that Barling would dare to utter any of those thoughts aloud. 'Thank you, my lord,' he said.

'Furthermore,' said the Archbishop, 'the master mason, William of Sens, is to be untroubled by this matter. He is a man whose genius is matched by his reputation. The work to rebuild Canterbury ultimately rests on his shoulders, and that is burden enough.'

Though disagreeing with the Archbishop was not to be recommended, Barling drew breath to ask the necessary question.

Richard's raised hand stopped him. 'I know what you are about to say: that as William is responsible for the work, he should still be consulted. Rest assured that Benedict has informed him.'

'Indeed I did,' said Benedict. 'Barling, William was laid low with a badly pulled back two days before the murder and did not get back on his feet until three days after. My infirmary brothers were with him throughout, as he required assistance with every task and function. He is improving but remains impaired.'

'Such circumstances mean I am completely satisfied William the master mason had nothing whatsoever to do with this,' said the Archbishop.

'Of course, my lord,' said Barling.

'We will start tomorrow morning at daybreak, Barling,' said Benedict. 'If you come back here, I can share my ideas with you.'

Barling did not need ideas. With so little time available, he needed to impose order on this task. 'May I request a different action, Prior

- that our first task is to view the site of where Peter Flocke's body was found?'

'A sound suggestion,' said the Archbishop.

The prior did not appear best pleased, but he could hardly contradict the Archbishop. 'Either way, Barling, you should avoid the main gate as the crowds will delay you unnecessarily. I will come to your inn to escort you in through another entrance. Where are you staying?'

'The house of a man called Osbert Derfield.'

'I know it well; he is a good, reliable tenant. Make sure you are ready.'

'I will, Prior.'

'Now leave us,' said the Archbishop. 'I have many pressing matters to discuss with the prior concerning our royal visitors.'

Barling bowed as low as he was able with the support of his staff, while Stanton put out a welcome hand to steady him. 'Good evening to you, Prior, my lord Archbishop.'

'Remember, Barling: four days.' The Archbishop waved them away.

Barling fought his desire to turn and flee from the room, no matter how sore his feet, flee from what he could tell would be required of him.

But his duty weighed as heavy on him as their bundle of belongings would on Stanton's back. Peter Flocke's appalling murder was now his responsibility. He had no choice but to do what he was ordered. His opportunity for penance had been taken from him, and he feared for his soul.

But his soul must wait.

Barling had no other choice.

Chapter Six

'Let me know if you need any more, sir.' Osbert Derfield, the plump keeper of their inn, handed a heavy pail of steaming water to Stanton, along with a set of fresh linen cloths.

'My thanks, fellow.' Stanton took them from him, his chafed shoulders in a new protest at the weight of the bucket.

'Pleased to serve you, sir.' He peered past Stanton into Barling's room, where the clerk sat on the edge of the bed, eyes closed, groaning softly. 'Is your companion all right, sir?'

'Too many miles in his limbs, that's all,' said Stanton. 'Mine aren't much better.' The last leg of the journey, half-carrying Barling as well as the bundle on his back to the inn through the darkening, busy streets should have done for him. But the anger coursing through his veins at what he'd just witnessed in the prior's solar, anger that he hid from the clerk, gave him strength. A man had been horribly murdered, and all concern was for how the volatile King might react.

'Like so many that travel here, from all over and for every reason,' said the innkeeper. 'You're sure I cannot help?'

'We are only in need of privacy.' This from Barling.

'Thank you again, Derfield,' said Stanton.

'Anything at all, sir. Just ask.' The innkeeper gave a final peek at Barling and withdrew.

Barling opened his eyes. 'Nosiness is a common talent amongst innkeepers. It would appear this man Derfield is no different. Make sure he has departed. It is imperative that we are not overheard.'

Stanton put the pail and cloths down. He stepped out to check the corridor that led to the staircase. The sound of Derfield's feet on the creaking wooden stairs died away. 'He's gone.' He picked up the pail again with a wince and shut the door behind him. 'To his credit, he keeps a clean house.'

Stanton had already checked, and his small room next door was identical to Barling's: on the top floor, with sloping ceilings that held the roof beams. The bed against one wall, a wooden chest against another, along with a table and stool and a washstand, all in good repair. A horn lamp, free from soot, that gave a fair glow. The straw mattress and its wool covers smelled of dried lavender, and he couldn't see any new flea marks on the whitewashed walls. If all had gone to plan and they hadn't had the shocking summons from the prior, he'd have slept like a dog in the sun, no question. Not any more. What he and Barling had been charged with had destroyed his peace of mind.

'I would never have selected a dirty inn, Stanton,' said Barling. 'Come away from the door. We have a great deal to urgently discuss.'

'We do.' Stanton crossed to Barling's bed, where he put the pail down on a floor free of dust and dirt. 'First things first.'

'I beg your pardon?'

'Those boots have got to come off.' Stanton hunkered down in front of him, his own leg muscles protesting.

'Later. Our priority is to speak about the task which we have been given.'

'Barling, if you can't walk tomorrow morning, you can't do anything. The longer you leave them, the worse it'll be.' He took one boot in both his hands. 'It's coming off on my count of three.'

'Later will suffice, do you hear me?'

'One. Two.' Off it came.

Barling shrieked. 'You said thr—'

And the other one.

The clerk shrieked again. 'Unhand me!'

'Saints alive.' Stanton stood up and placed the boots to one side. 'You'll have Derfield back up here.'

'And whose fault would that be?' Barling glared at him as he fetched the wide wash bowl and put it before the clerk.

'I'm not the one making noise.' Stanton poured water into the bowl. 'Let your feet soak for a bit. It'll help to soften the skin. Then you can get the stones out easier.'

'Since when did you become a surgeon, Stanton?'

'I'm good at fixing sore feet. Sore buttocks from the saddle too. That's about it.'

Barling lifted one foot and placed it in the water. 'By the blood of the Virgin.' Then the other, teeth clenched, clutching at the woollen coverlet with both fists. 'Oh, my.'

'They'll start to ease soon.' Stanton dipped one of the cloths in the bucket and scrubbed at the dirt on his own face and the back of his neck.

'That every problem were so easily solved.' Barling sniffed.

Stanton knew that was the clerk's version of sincere thanks. He cleaned off his hands as Barling went on.

'The real challenge before us is the solving of the murder of this stonemason, Peter Flocke. A murder that involved the profane use of the symbol of the holy Cross.' He shuddered. 'And, if that were not enough, to solve it in four days. In truth, something I never imagined we'd have to deal with on our pilgrimage.' Barling stared at his own feet in the bowl, his expression grim.

'We'll do it, Barling.' Stanton dropped the used cloth back into the pail. 'Like we've solved others before, eh?' He went over to the bundle of their belongings that he'd dumped in the corner and set to undoing the knots. Maybe this unexpected turn of events would be a chance for the clerk to open up to him, the only good thing about it.

No such luck.

'Our task is not to look at the past, Stanton. As our lord de Glanville has instructed, our task is to serve the Archbishop of Canterbury in finding this killer before the arrival of the King. We cannot risk the wrath of his Grace being aroused.'

The King. Again. Stanton's ire tightened his chest. He couldn't risk the clerk noticing. He tried to change the subject. 'Maybe there's something in that talk of a curse that the prior mentioned.'

Barling clicked his tongue in impatience. 'Stanton, you must learn to curb your erratic approach.'

'It was only a—'

'You should have enough experience by now not to jump ahead with ideas of what might have happened.'

'An idea, Barling.' Still riled, Stanton muttered to himself. 'I do have good ones, as you well know.'

'Stanton, we do not have the luxury of time. As I have tried to impress on you, we have but four days to find the killer. Scattered ideas do not make for successful enquiry. An investigation should be conducted with method and order. Line, by line, by line.' The clerk was at his lecturing worst, pointing a finger at him. 'Do I make myself clear?'

By all that was holy, Barling was treating him like a witless page, not the man who'd saved his life. 'Unless the killer has a very different story. Then it's not much help to you, is it?'

The clerk physically flinched at Stanton's sharp remark.

Those had been words too far. 'I'm sorry, Barling,' he said quickly. 'That was uncalled for.'

To his relief, Barling collected himself. 'Emotion never serves any purpose in these matters.'

'In truth, the Lenten fast would test anyone's mood.' Stanton tried to suck his teeth, but he had no spittle left. 'My belly's empty, and I'll wager yours is too.' He took out Barling's folded black robes and other clothing from the bundle and placed them on the bed. 'I'll fetch us something to eat and drink, shall I?'

'I have eaten my one meal today. I will not eat tonight.'

'You can have your collation.'

'All I require are my tablet and stylus. Bring them to me, then push that table in front of me. That way I can start work while my feet soak.'

Stanton did so, despairing at the clerk's stubbornness.

'Examining the site of the body of Peter Flocke is merely the first step.' Barling tested the sharpness of his stylus with a fingertip. 'Prior Benedict will be with us, and that gives us the opportunity to glean from him what he has compiled thus far. I have also decided that viewing where the man Flocke worked is essential. The rest, I can decide on in a logical fashion.'

Stanton noticed the clerk's use of 'I' rather than 'we', but he let it pass. He didn't enjoy strife at the best of times, and he and Barling had had far more harsh words this evening than he would have liked.

'I'll leave you to it, then, and say good night, Barling.'

The clerk nodded, his features once again in the preoccupied mask Stanton had come to recognise so well.

Stanton gathered up what remained of the bundle and left. He flung it into his room, where it landed on the floor, spilling most of the contents. Never mind. He wasn't going to waste another minute by picking them up. If he didn't get something in his belly soon, he'd pass out. He closed the door and headed down the steep, creaky stairs, two at a time.

With a quick wave to Derfield, who lurked before a hearth in a back room, he went out the main door into the street.

The cathedral bells were sounding for Compline, but the streets were still thronged.

He couldn't help a twinge of regret for the merrymaking he'd looked forward to but was not to be. It didn't matter. What mattered was working with Barling to solve the murder of that unfortunate stonemason as quickly as possible. Then Stanton could leave Canterbury, putting many miles between him and the city. He would never be able to abide the rejoicing at Henry's arrival, the praising of the man's piety. Not when his Rosamund, his love, lay cold in her grave because of the King.

A pastry seller stood on a corner, doing a brisk trade as folk made the most of the last of Palm Sunday. He hurried over, as the woman was down to the last one.

'Any chance I could have that excellent-looking crust, goodwife?' He gave her his best smile, his stomach growling at the smell of warm, yeasty dough.

He got the usual blush in return. 'A pleasure, sir.'

They exchanged coin and pastry and he took a deep bite of his prize as he walked off, the sweetness of the apple it contained flooding onto his tongue. How Barling could choose to sit in his room, scratching away at his tablet, over devouring good food, Stanton would never know. He took another huge mouthful, feeling a bit better.

Somebody collided hard with his aching back, sending him lurching to one side. The remains of his pastry flew from his grasp and splattered into the street muck.

'A plague on it.' He turned to tell off whoever had done it.

A wild-eyed man in a threadbare pilgrim's tunic stared back at him, his hair and long beard clogged with greasy dirt and all of him covered in layers of filth. 'Praise the Martyr,' said the stranger. 'Praise him!'

'I was praising my pastry,' said Stanton. 'Now look at it, fellow.'

The man banged the battered, badge-covered staff he held in his left hand on the ground in front of Stanton. 'Open your heart to the Lord our God. Before death comes for thee.' He thrust his right hand in Stanton's face.

Stanton recoiled. The man's hand curled over in a twisted claw, his stained fingers and long, dirty fingernails tangled worse than a bundle of tree roots.

A group of laughing, jostling men of Stanton's age pushed past, sending the man bumping into him.

'Be watchful, be watchful.' The stranger stank worse than the spoil underfoot.

Stanton stepped back. 'On your way, fellow.'

The man staggered away again, into the path of a burly carter. 'Thou livest and are dead!' he wailed at the carter.

He got a string of curses for his trouble.

Stanton shook his head as he watched the man stagger on, shouting and gesturing all the while.

Time for that ale. God's eyes, he needed it.

And once he'd finished it, he'd have another. And another.

It would be the only way he'd sleep tonight.

God rot the King.

Chapter Seven

Pilgrim Robert Norwood pushed himself away from the blue-eyed young man, staggering into the crowd amid a chorus of oaths and shoves.

'Saint Thomas be praised,' he called. 'Your hand kept me from falling, from hurt. Saint Thomas be praised, be praised!'

He carried on through the streets, lauding the Martyr at the top of his voice, hoarse from his many days here, where he had been calling out his worship for the saint. Despite the crowds still abroad, people moved away from him as best they could.

Dirt from the many hundreds of miles he had walked plastered his threadbare short woollen tunic. His bare legs wore braies of grime. His feet bore as much spoil as any boot, their hardened, toughened state a living leather. His filthy hair and straggled beard had bothered him in the first months on the road. After almost three years, they troubled him no more.

Nothing mattered now, only his soul. His soul that bore the stain of the worst sin: the sin of killing another.

The sin of murder.

His sin coursed through him with every beat of his heart.

Bone on stone. Blood on stone.

The torments of hell were almost upon him. Satan awaited him; the chains of darkness ready in his hands to trap Norwood for all eternity. The bottomless pit. The second death of fire. Agony that would endure for all time.

Norwood knew that was his fate.

Yet he had one chance – one last, slim chance – to be saved.

He shoved through a knot of chattering young men and women, who dawdled along.

Their protest surrounded him.

'Begone, fellow.' One of the men whipped a hand at his shoulder.

'By Saint Peter of Rome.' A woman put a finger and thumb to her nose.

'Off with you.' Another man lifted an elbow, the jab landing on Norwood's ribs.

The pain sparked through him, but he didn't fall. He carried a far greater agony within him, one that was consuming him by the day.

Bone on stone. Blood on stone.

Norwood raised his voice again. 'Saint Thomas resides in the light of God!'

The tomb, the tomb of the Martyr. He had to get back there again.

His very life depended on it.

Chapter Eight

Monday

'The masons' gate is down this next lane.' Prior Benedict led the way with Barling and Stanton in his wake, Barling glad of his usual robes and cloak. The pilgrim's tunic he had worn yesterday would have given little protection from the morn's chill.

Although the day was breaking clear and bright, the wind had shifted and gained in strength as well as cold. It whistled down the street, funnelled by the high buildings set close on either side.

He gave thanks too for the warmth and comfort of his soft hose and booted feet. Another barefoot day would have been the end of him. He gave further thanks for the restorative sleep he had had last night. Given the shock of being burdened with another murder to solve and his devastation at having his penance interrupted, he had expected not to close an eye. But as soon as he had finished picking the last of the stones from his feet, exhaustion had claimed him. He had slumped onto his bed and not moved until the innkeeper woke him as arranged.

Barling had not relied on Stanton to wake them, as he knew Stanton's aversion to rising before noon if at all possible and he could not risk any delay to this investigation.

To his surprise, Stanton had been awake and ready without the need for a call.

His surprise ended there. Barling could smell stale ale from his assistant as Stanton walked along in silence beside him, with Stanton's face paler than the inside of an oyster shell. Barling had not had the opportunity to say anything to him. He would find one later, no question.

People busied the streets, a small fraction of the crowds Barling had encountered here thus far. Bakers carried baskets of freshly baked bread. Carters sat atop their loaded wagons, guiding their horses with care on the cobbles. A boy pushed a barrow of vegetables. A young woman bore pails of smelly salted fish on her shoulders.

Shopkeepers opened up their shutters, setting their goods out in enticing displays. Their wares were the usual one might expect, such as shoes and pots and cloth and baskets. But this being Canterbury, the shops that sold items for pilgrims equalled them in number. Barling could not take in the full array of lead badges, carved candles, votive offerings and crosses and brightly painted images of the Martyr on offer. Even at this early hour, pilgrims were already out buying them.

And while the streets might be quieter at present, before many left their beds, the air echoed with noise. Not the soothing sound of church bells or birdsong, but the steady bang and rap and rasp of hammers, picks and saws. Back at work after a day of rest on Palm Sunday, the builders filled the scaffolding on the cathedral high up above.

As if reading his thoughts, Prior Benedict said, 'I know it is still in the distant future, but I long for the day when that hideous cacophony ceases.'

'I can imagine how it must grate, Prior.'

'It is impossible to describe how wearing it is.' The prior's lips puckered in displeasure over his protuberant teeth. 'Impossible to escape from as well. I can hear it from my chambers as clearly as if they hammered on my wall, even with all the doors and windows shut.'

'Intolerable.'

Barling caught Stanton in a stifled belch, which he changed into a cough under Barling's glare.

They turned a corner, and the masons' gate came into view, a loaded cart making its way out. The prior led them through and along the rutted track that cut across the cathedral grounds.

Barling dimly recollected it from the previous evening as the rough roadway that had caused him extra torment. Another gate stood open directly ahead and he could see the stonemasons' lodge. Piles of cut stone filled the yard, along with buckets, wheelbarrows and carts that were fitted with pulleys and what he guessed were all manner of lifting devices.

The lodge's ample size reflected the scale of the work being done on the cathedral. While it consisted of a single storey, it covered the ground of at least two good-sized houses and had a sturdy roof of tile. A covered area extended off to one side, constructed of solid wooden uprights and open to the elements. Beneath it, four men worked at individual blocks of the same cream-coloured stone of the cathedral, the sound of each of their tools in a different rhythm. Dust powdered their clothing and clouded the air around them like fine smoke. One man glanced up, the others keeping their heads down over their work.

As they walked into the yard, the prior halted Barling and Stanton. 'Wait here. I have to check with the master mason if it is safe to proceed.' He went to the door of the lodge and called inside. 'Green?'

Barling addressed Stanton in a fierce whisper that the busy workmen would not hear. 'I can see by the state of you that you are not at your best. But I care not how ale-plagued you are. Pay attention to everything at every moment. Do you hear me?'

'Yes, Barling. Sorry, Barling.'

Another man emerged from the lodge with the prior, his thick leather apron hung with an array of chisels and other pointed metal implements. He held a sharp-angled metal square in one hand. He would be in the middle of his fourth decade, with a ruddied face coarsened from years working outside. Though he'd lost most of his hair on the top of his head, he still kept the remainder, leaving it in thin, rank strands that reached almost to his shoulders. Frowning brows above his close-set eyes told of his displeasure at being summoned.

'Green,' said Benedict. 'This is the King's man, Aelred Barling, and his assistant, Hugo Stanton.'

'Sirs.' The man gave a stiff bow.

'Lambert Green is the master mason at the cathedral,' said Benedict.

'Second master mason, aren't I, Prior?'

'Yes. Of course. I forget that so often. It is because you are always in charge.'

'That's right, Prior.' Green smiled, a smile devoid of warmth, his teeth gapped in hideous rot. 'Somebody has to get their hands dirty every day, don't they?'

'All for the glory of our new cathedral,' said Benedict. 'These men are blessed to be in such holy service, Barling.'

A mute hiccup jolted Stanton.

Barling prayed the prior had not noticed. 'As we are, Prior. Is it possible for us to move on to our task?'

'Certainly.' While Benedict lowered his voice, Barling doubted if the men working the stone nearby could hear a word over the sound of their tools. 'Green, I need to take the King's men to the spot where Peter Flocke was found.'

'Go ahead, Prior,' said Green. 'I'll make sure none of this lot bother you. They won't be taking a break for a good while; they've only just started.' Another grin. 'Takes young men a few hours to get warmed up after a good day like Palm Sunday, doesn't it?' His beady eyes rested on Stanton for a second.

'Come, it's over here.' Benedict made his way to a corner of the yard where an assortment of cut stone sat piled under another covered area.

'Pay good attention,' mouthed Barling at Stanton, who nodded.

'It was here, right here.' Benedict halted and pointed to a patch of ground in front of the storage area – pebble strewn, dusty and harmless to the eye. No sign that anything untoward had occurred, except for the tremor in Benedict's hand. 'This is where the body of Peter Flocke was found.'

'I do not wish to cause you distress, Prior,' said Barling. 'But can you tell us everything you can remember?'

The tremor strengthened, and Benedict folded his hands into the concealing sleeves of his habit. 'I gave you the full account in my solar yesterday evening.'

Barling contained a frustrated sigh. This was of little, if any, use.

'If you'll excuse me for interrupting, Barling, and if you'll excuse me too, Prior.' Stanton wore his most appealing expression, one which could, on occasion, achieve remarkable success in getting reluctant people to talk. 'It's one thing for us to hear things. It's another for us to see them. When we see things first-hand, we often find the answers. If you could go over your excellent account again, it might make all the difference. Then you would've been the one to have solved all this, if you see what I mean.'

To Barling's relief, his assistant's flattery worked.

'Very well,' said Benedict. 'Flocke was lying on the ground. He had been stabbed many times.'

'How many and where?' asked Barling.

'By all the saints, does it matter?' said Benedict.

'Yes, it does.' Barling could feel his ire rising at the monk's hesitancy in progressing. Worse, the Archbishop had said that Benedict had made extensive enquiries about this murder, which had given Barling some comfort. But the true picture of Benedict's competence that was emerging would comfort no one.

'You see, Prior,' said Stanton. 'When we examine a body, we can get all this information ourselves. Right now, you are our eyes, eyes that are needed to bring the killer to justice.'

'If I must. Eight times, as it turned out. I could not tell that when I first saw him.' Benedict gulped. 'There was so much blood. Flocke had been stabbed twice in the chest, three times in the stomach. Once in the throat. Once across the palm of his hand. Once on his forehead.'

'A terrible end, indeed.' Barling crossed himself.

'Does that not make nine, Prior?' asked Stanton.

'What do you mean?' said Benedict.

'You said last night that the symbol of the Cross was cut into Flocke's forehead. To make it requires two actions.' Stanton squatted down and demonstrated by drawing a cross in the dust with his finger. 'Not one.' He looked up at the prior. 'Isn't it?'

'What are you saying, man?' said Benedict. 'I am well known for making sure I have all relevant information when making judgements. It is in my nature.'

Barling had to smooth the waters quickly. The prior was so easily upset. 'Such as your great work in recording the miracles here in Canterbury, Prior. Accounts which I have read with the greatest of interest and devotion.'

His blandishments had the desired effect.

'Yes. Well.' Benedict shrugged. 'I suppose it is correct to say that the profane wound should be described as two cuts and not one.'

Stanton stood up again, dusting off his hands.

'What of the man who made this terrible discovery, Prior?' said Barling.

'As I said to you last evening, it was Flocke's fellow mason, Adam Drake,' said the prior. 'As I also said, he was in a frightful state.'

'A blubbering mess is how you described him, is that correct?' said Barling.

'Yes. I used those words in the presence of our lord Archbishop. The truth was that Drake was hardly in possession of his wits with terror.' Benedict's mouth turned down. 'Terror that had him covered in his own vomit.'

'Most unpleasant,' said Barling, a little disappointed. A man or woman could produce tears and wails that were utter falsehood. Drake's reaction sounded genuine. 'Were there signs of other spoil on him?'

'What do you mean?' said the prior.

'Blood, for example?' said Barling.

'I did not examine the man in great detail,' said the prior. 'He reeked horribly. But, no: there was no blood visible on him.'

'I see.' Barling prepared to move on, but Stanton stopped him with another question for the prior.

'Could I please ask you something else, Prior?' he said. 'What of the stone next to Peter Flocke's body?'

Barling did not at first understand to what Stanton referred. The prior did not appear to, either.

He could not risk the monk getting heated again at any perceived criticism. 'Perhaps you could remind me, Stanton?'

'You told us yesterday, Prior,' said Stanton, 'that Peter Flocke's blood was splashed over much of the stone that was carved and ready to be put in place.'

Well noted, Stanton. Barling recalled it now, but such had been his fatigue, he would have forgotten. Stanton had an uncommon ability to remember the smallest details.

His assistant carried on. 'But this stone looks completely clean. And it can't have been washed off by the rain, as it's under cover. Is this the same stone?'

'No,' said the prior. 'I ordered Lambert Green to destroy it. I could not have had the cathedral built from stone that was stained with the blood of a dead man. The seat of Canterbury has seen enough blood spilled.'

Stanton gave a silent nod.

Barling had not been optimistic about determining a solution from examining this spot, and he had been correct in his judgement. Viewing a body was one thing: depending on another's view was quite another.

Yet he must have order, just as he must press on to the next item on his list.

He had inspected the location of the death of Peter Flocke.

Now he would look at the murdered man's life.

Chapter Nine

Stanton wished his head and guts would stop protesting so much. His own fault, he knew, from the amount he'd drunk last night. Yes, he'd done it to help him sleep. But he'd enjoyed every mouthful. Canterbury brewed great ale, no question. And ale found its way far quicker to his head when his belly was an empty sack from fasting. But he might as well have been kicked by the horses they'd passed on the streets on the way here.

Keeping his mind on the job in hand was about as easy as grabbing an eel in a muddy river, and not helped one bit by the prior and his sighs and trembles. The man had asked for their help; it shouldn't be such a struggle to get him to cooperate. Stanton could tell that Barling just about held on to his temper at the prior's dithering. He hoped the clerk's mood would hold. Stanton couldn't cope with both clerk and monk in a pother at the same time. At least not until his head stopped banging.

'I too wish that the shedding of the blood of Saint Thomas had been the last,' the clerk replied to Benedict. 'It pains the heart that it was not the case. Nevertheless, we must press on to discover the truth of what happened to Peter Flocke.'

Unseen by the prior, who was staring again at the patch of ground, Barling shot Stanton a despairing glance.

'Speaking of Peter Flocke,' said Stanton, 'did he always work at the lodge, Prior, like those men are doing?'

Benedict tore his gaze away from the ground. 'Like all the masons, he went to labour wherever he was instructed to. That could be in this lodge and yard, or in the cathedral.' He gestured at the towering structure that loomed over them.

'Then you will show us. Thank you, Prior.' Barling's tone didn't allow for argument as he set off for the lodge.

To Stanton's relief, Benedict followed without comment, and he, Stanton, kept a respectful couple of steps back.

Lambert Green stood, arms folded, in the large doorway of the lodge. 'Are you and your visitors done, Prior?'

Damn it. Green must've been watching them the whole time, and Stanton hadn't noticed. Ale-head or no ale-head, he needed to pay better attention.

'No, there are a couple of things outstanding,' said Benedict. 'They will not take long.'

'We wish to see all the places where Peter Flocke worked,' said Barling. 'All of them.'

'You're standing in one of them. Sir.' Green swept one arm to take in the entire yard. Polite enough words, but delivered with barely hidden rudeness.

'He also worked in the lodge.' Benedict looked as pleased as a dog with a duck to know something useful.

Trouble was, even a dog or a duck would probably know that a mason worked in the masons' lodge.

'Then it is imperative that we look inside, man. Without further delay.' Barling would only be up to about the height of Green's shoulder, but his tone of authority more than made up for it.

Green moved to one side. 'Step this way, Prior, sirs. I'll come with you. Happy to help in any way I can.' He jabbed a finger at his stone carvers. 'This isn't an excuse for you to slack off, you hear? I won't be gone long.'

The men didn't look up, their 'Yes, master' a cowed, murmured chorus.

'Thank you, Green.' Benedict entered with Barling and the mason, Stanton behind.

Thick stone dust coated every object and surface in the large space. A long, wide table that held pipe rolls and other documents, along with several metal instruments for measuring, including the metal square that Green had been holding when they first arrived. Half-burned candles. A set of four stools arranged around the table. Chests of various sizes.

The dust hung in the air too, drying out Stanton's mouth and eyes and tickling the inside of his nose. Barling and the prior coughed.

'Some of us have been toiling inside this place for the entire winter,' said Green. 'Only started in the yard last month. Good to be out in the air.'

'I can imagine.' Barling coughed again. 'You say Peter Flocke worked in this room?'

'From time to time, when I had to show him a new design.' Green pointed to one of three other doors that opened off the room in which they stood. 'Mostly in there.'

'I would like to see it,' said Barling.

Green walked over and opened up the door. 'See whatever you like. Don't touch anything. Sirs.'

Stanton followed Barling and the prior in.

A large room, larger and dustier than the one they had stepped from, it contained more stone of the same creamy colour and type as that in the yard, stone that had been carved into shapes of every kind and size. Spirals on a section of a pillar. Smooth curves, set with the smoothest of grooves. Diamonds on a set of four larger panels. Bigger pieces sat on the floor, with smaller ones arranged on wide wooden shelves.

'We did this during the months of ice and snow,' said Green. 'Can't carve outside then. Sir.'

'Did Flocke work alone in here?' asked Barling.

'Maybe,' said Green. 'Though not regular. I had twenty masons on site over the winter, double that for the spring and summer.'

Barling frowned. 'Forty men live in this space?'

Green laughed. 'No, sir.'

'The masons do not live in the lodge.' This from Benedict, the man pleased to give another fact that he knew.

'We carve here,' said Green. 'Keep our tools here. Eat if we need to. Take our sleep at midday.' He gestured for them to come back out.

'So where do the masons live?' asked Barling.

'Wherever will take them. They can be a rowdy bunch.' Green scowled. 'The cheap inns, mostly.'

Barling looked at him askance. 'They have no homes?'

'Not in Canterbury they don't,' said Green. 'They've come from all over to work on the cathedral. It's good money.'

'Which inn did Flocke live at?' said Stanton. 'I've visited, um, a couple,' he said in response to a quizzical look from the prior and a fierce one from Barling.

Green shrugged. 'Think it's somewhere out beyond Northgate. You'll have to ask his wife.'

'His wife?' Barling's attention mercifully switched back to Green. 'I thought you said that he did not have a home.'

'Yes, that's right. Sir. Flocke shared a room with his wife, Katerine. She also works for me. She's a mason's servant. Mixes mortar and the like.'

'Katerine Flocke must have been very grief-stricken that night,' said Barling to the prior. 'And she must continue to be so.'

'I believe she was most upset,' said Benedict. 'I am correct in that, am I not, Green?'

'Indeed you are, Prior. She was distraught when she saw the body. I've kept her on, though. Wouldn't see her wanting.'

The murdered man had a wife. Stanton definitely had questions about that. He opened his mouth to ask them but caught Barling's silent warning. *Not for now.*

'A most charitable gesture,' said Benedict.

'Thank you, Prior,' said Green. 'Sirs, if you follow me, you can see the rest of the lodge.'

It was laid out as he'd described. An assortment of axes, hatchets, chisels, mallets, saws and shovels filled the third, smaller room. The fourth had sacks filled with straw strewn on the ground along with a few rough blankets. Half-barrels served as seats and tables, with a pair of forgotten dice on one. A ladder rested against one wall.

'There's a loft on top,' said Green. 'It's not big, but some of the lads go up for a sleep when it's too crowded.' His rotting grin again. 'They think I'll forget about them. No such luck. They wake up quick when I tell them I'll kick them down the ladder.'

Barling and the prior nodded in approval.

Stanton didn't. He often favoured a sleep after his dinner, if one was going. Besides, the man made his flesh creep. More than that, Lambert Green had access to a whole room full of tools without anybody seeing. Tools that could easily rend a man's flesh.

The prior was blabbing praise about the odious fellow as he led the group back outside.

'You see, Barling,' said Benedict, 'Green is tireless in keeping this endeavour going, in making sure that every minute, every second, is used in the holy purpose of rebuilding this sacred place.'

'Truly, God's work.' Barling nodded again.

'Work that I have to get back to, Prior,' said Green.

'Of course,' said Benedict. 'The day can have no greater purpose.'

Stanton wished he could have a minute alone with Barling. Green didn't want them around, no question. He was using the prior to make that happen. But he needn't have worried. The clerk wasn't going to be put off.

'Except,' said Barling, 'we do have a greater purpose, and that is to see every location at which Flocke worked. That includes the cathedral itself.' He pointed up. 'Does it not, Green?'

'Course it does. Sir.' Green's brows drew together. 'But that's not possible. I can't have folk wandering about, not with the state that the building's in. It's dangerous.'

'Extremely dangerous,' said Benedict. 'Why, Green has to accompany me everywhere when I go to check on progress. To make sure I remain safe. Don't you, Green?'

The look that Green gave the prior could crack one of the stones in the yard.

'Then it is possible.' Barling gave one of his tight little smiles. 'I am glad to hear it, as I am glad to hear that you will be keeping us safe from harm, Green. Now, shall we proceed?'

Chapter Ten

'I have to confess that I cannot comprehend the sight of my own eyes.' Barling had to raise his voice so Prior Benedict would hear him over the din of tools, of hammers and chisels and saws. 'The fire was the cause of this destruction?'

'Yes, all of it,' said Benedict. 'We are standing at what would have once been the south-east corner of the monks' choir.'

'God alive.' This, from a gaping Stanton next to him.

They stood with Green on what had once been a smooth stone church floor, but one which was now cracked and strewn with cut stone, rubble and dust and discoloured by burn marks. The space would be many yards long – fifty, perhaps as much as sixty – and was the height of more than ten men. Wooden scaffolding covered every square inch of the interior walls and reached right up to where a solid stone roof should have been, not wooden planks pierced in places by thin shafts of sunlight. Judging by the dirty puddles on the floor, rainwater found its way in by the same route. Yet more scaffolding surrounded huge, scorched pillars with stout uprights and thick planks. A system of platforms and ladders allowed men just like Peter Flocke to climb along, up and down, with buckets and tools in their hands or sacks on their shoulders.

'I am truly shocked,' said Barling. 'You can see little evidence this was or has ever been part of a house of God.'

'I wish I could say that the shock wears off,' said the prior. 'But in truth—'

'Watch out!'

Stanton wrenched at Barling's arm, pulling him a half-step to one side.

A blur shot past his vision, the object landing with a shattering crash on the floor next to him.

A large stone block, dust rising like smoke from the impact.

'Hell's teeth,' gasped Stanton.

'What on earth?' said the prior, pale.

'Oi!' Green glared aloft. 'Oi! Stop what you're doing! Stop!'

The builders' noise stuttered to a halt.

'Are you all right, Barling?' said Stanton, even whiter than the prior.

'I am fine, Stanton.' Barling's heart jumped in fright but he kept his features composed. 'Thanks to your quick reaction. You can let go of me.'

Green was still shouting. 'Who did that? Who bloody did that?'

'Don't know, master.' The voice of an unseen man floated down, contrite. 'Sorry, master.'

Another, respectful. 'Reckon it was just one of the loose ones. We've had lots of 'em.'

'Oh, you reckon, do you?' Green roared back. 'Well, reckon this, all of you: you'll have a penny off your wages for today for carelessness. Back to work! Now!'

The noise struck up again in an instant.

With a final oath directed at his workers, Green addressed Barling with a fresh scowl. 'Sir. You see what I meant. It's too dangerous for you to be here.'

'Perhaps Green is right, Barling,' said the prior.

'I will not be deterred by a simple accident, Green.' Barling kept his voice steady, though he fought to do so. 'And nor will Stanton.' He directed his last words at his assistant, daring him to contradict him.

'That we won't,' said Stanton.

'Now, Green,' said Barling. 'Can you show us what Peter Flocke was working on in the days before his murder?'

'Sir.' Green looked displeased. 'I can tell you. Not sure if I can show you.'

'I am afraid that your description will not suffice,' said Barling. 'Stanton and I want to see the work for ourselves. It is essential that we do so.'

'That pillar.' Green pointed upward. 'Right at the top, it is.'

Barling's gaze followed to where the mason indicated. His heart had no chance of slowing as he took in the pillar's soaring height. He had trouble enough climbing atop a saddle on a quiet horse.

Stanton gave a low whistle.

'If you must insist, Barling,' said the prior, 'we can take the transept stairwell most of the way. That should bring you close enough.'

'I do insist.' Barling refused to let his fear show. 'That is an excellent suggestion.' He had his duty to perform.

'It's still not safe,' said Green. 'You'll need ropes and—'

'Then you will fetch them, please, Green,' snapped Benedict. 'In the meantime, we can start on the stairs. There are many to climb, and the stairwell poses no risk to us. Come, both of you.'

He guided Barling and Stanton along the length of the choir then turned right into the transept, where a set of enclosed stone steps led upwards.

'They are only the width of one man,' said Benedict. 'We shall have to ascend in single file.' He matched his words with his actions, setting off on his climb.

Stanton held back, voice low so the prior would not overhear. 'Are you sure you want to go up, Barling? You can stay down here and take the time to steady yourself. That stone nearly hit you. I can take a look on my own.'

'I am perfectly fine to ascend.' Barling advanced on the stairwell as he spoke. He could not pause for a moment, lest his courage fail him.

He ignored Stanton's mutter of discontent.

As they climbed the steep spiral steps, the air grew dusty and stale. The twisting of the stairwell soon had him dizzy, and he put a palm to the cold, damp wall to steady himself.

'Sure you're all right?' This from Stanton behind him.

'Yes.' He could not manage any other words, as the climb robbed his breath.

'Take care, you're almost at the top,' came Benedict's muffled call.

'You heard that, Stanton?' Barling could hardly get the words out as he glanced around to check.

'Don't worry about me.' Stanton looked and sounded as if he strolled on a street. A flat street.

Barling faced ahead once again. He reached the top step, where the black-robed prior stood watch.

'Take care,' the prior said again.

Barling stepped out next to him onto a wide stone ledge which was edged with a knee-high wall constructed of planks of wood. He could see down. Right down, down to the floor of the choir below. The height of almost ten men, he'd thought while below. Now that he'd reached it, it felt a hundred times that. Worse, it span before his sight, like it was drawing him in. And down.

'Look at that.' Stanton walked out after him and went straight to the edge.

'Stanton, don't be foolish.' Barling kept his back tight against the wall behind him as if he were glued to it.

His assistant took no notice of his warning. 'We're high as the birds up here.' He leaned right over the side to look down.

'We are.' Still tight to the wall. If Barling moved from its solidity, he would fall over.

'You can really see the reach of it. The fire must've been huge to do this much damage.' Stanton shook his head in wonder as he spoke to the prior. 'Just huge.'

Barling itched to rebuke him for his unseemly excitement. The young were always so entranced with terrible occurrences that they had never had to live through. But his spinning head had robbed him of speech. Fortunately, the prior did not appear offended.

'It was, indeed.' While not as bold as Stanton, the prior stood firm without requiring a stone upright to clutch on to. 'It started in the roof.'

Stanton tipped his head back, mouth agape. 'Up there?'

Barling risked a glance aloft. When he'd been on the floor of the choir, the roof planks had seemed halfway to heaven. Now he could easily count each one and the gaps between many. Dizzy, he looked down again.

'No,' said the prior to Stanton. 'The old roof. What you can see now is a temporary cover to shield the choir while the work is carried out.' He made a noise of disgust. 'The poorest one. Green tells me much of it is rotten already and we are having to replace it. The old roof was of the finest oak beams, covered with lead. They had been in place for over four decades without any sign of decay. But they were drier than kindling. Sparks from house fires in the street nearby got in through the lead and lit the beams. By the time anybody knew, the whole roof was aflame, and the blaze was out of control.'

'The whole roof?' Stanton was looking at the prior, hanging on his every word.

'Yes, the whole roof. We did not know the full extent of it. My monks and I assembled as quickly as we could, as did the townspeople of virtue. We had buckets full of water. We had hatchets in our hands. We ran up these very stairs, ready to fight the fire.'

Shame prickled Barling's cheeks. He had struggled to ascend with cautious steps, let alone run with heavy buckets, run towards terrifying peril.

The prior continued. 'That was when we realised how bad it was. Even halfway up the stairs, the smoke was thick and black. But we pressed on. Then we got to this point, and the smoke almost overcame us. The flames, roaring right above us.' He shook his head. 'It was hopeless. We had to flee, flee for our lives.'

'A blessing that God saved you.' Barling forced the words out.

'You could say that,' said the prior. 'But it does, in truth, feel more like a punishment.'

'I am not sure I follow you,' said Barling.

'My deliverance from the staircase meant that I saw with my own eyes the horror of the destruction of the Glorious Choir of Anselm,' replied the prior. 'A choir built by a saint, adorned by others over the years.' His face lit at the memory. 'Gold, silver, the brightest marble, the most brilliant glass, the brightest paintings on its high vaults: all decorated its magnificence.' Darkened again. 'As I and others fled for the safety of the nave, the burning roof of the choir gave way. Collapsed onto the wooden seats below, the seats where I had sat and worshipped for a quarter of a century. The wood of those seats fed the fire's unstoppable appetite, causing it to rise up a full fifteen cubits, consuming everything it could and injuring even the hardest stone.' He wiped a sheen of sweat from his brow, as if the heat of the spent flames burned anew.

'To have seen such a sight.' Stanton puffed out a breath of wonderment.

'Who's going to look at the pillar?'

The loud voice had Barling start and clutch harder at the stone behind him.

Green, emerging from the stairwell.

'What ails you?' The second master mason looked from one face to another. 'You look like you've seen demons.'

'I was relating the account of the great fire to the King's men,' said the prior.

'Very bad fortune for Canterbury,' said Green. 'And many would say that bad fortune spreads worse than a disease.'

'Green.' Benedict raised a hand. 'That is enough.'

Green shrugged and held up a coil of rope. 'Again, who's going to look at the pillar Flocke was working on?'

'Me.' This, most definite, from Stanton.

Barling had to allow it. He could not budge from this spot if he tried.

Green knotted a loop of the rope around Stanton's waist, brought a length to his own, and did the same, then finally tied the end around one of the scaffolding uprights. 'Come with me.'

'Be careful, Stanton.' Barling wished he did not have the tone of an anxious mother.

Green's smirk told him he did.

Stanton just gave him a wave.

Barling watched as Green led his assistant over to where the stone ledge gave way to the wooden planks that formed a platform next to the pillar, jutting far out into the heights of the choir. Planks that bounced under their boots as they walked on them. That creaked.

Barling swallowed hard. He feared he might faint as he watched. 'I can see, Prior, even at this distance that Flocke was skilled,' he said to try to keep his panic from overwhelming him.

No reply. He turned to look at Benedict.

The prior was staring at Green and Stanton, a hard, distant look on his face. 'No matter how they try, they will never succeed. Nothing could replace the old choir, Barling. Nothing.'

Stanton still conversed with Green, the mason pointing to different areas of the pillar.

Another loud creak came as they shifted position.

Barling could not hear a word they said, could not hear because his pulse pounded in his ears with the terror that any second now, the rickety platform would give way and send Stanton and the man with him plummeting to the stone floor below, smashing into it as hard as the block of falling masonry.

Chapter Eleven

Stanton stepped from the staircase onto the floor of the transept and waited for Barling to catch him up. He didn't know what could be keeping the clerk. From the shuffling noises coming from the stairwell, it was quite possible that Barling had resorted to coming down the steps on his backside.

The prior and Green were already down.

Green gave a swift bow to Benedict. 'I'll be getting back, Prior, I have a lot of work to do.'

'Certainly,' said Benedict. 'I do not wish to keep you from it any longer.'

As Green headed off, a breathless Barling finally came out of the stairwell.

'Oh, and thanks for the rope, Green,' called Stanton.

Green didn't answer, as he'd paused to speak to another black-robed monk who'd appeared further down the south aisle. The monk had a writing satchel slung across one shoulder and carried a rolled-up letter in one hand. Green pointed back at where Stanton and the others stood.

'Prior Benedict, may I have a word?' The red-haired monk came hurrying up as Green went on his way. He'd only be around ten years older than Stanton and much more powerfully built. His fine features and strong jaw made him a handsome fellow, looks that were a bit spoiled by a softness to his face that told of years of good living in the cloister.

'Not now, William,' said Benedict. 'I am otherwise engaged.'

'My sincere apologies for my interruption, Prior.' The monk's voice had a different accent to that of the prior.

Stanton recognised it as being from the island of Ireland, a place known for its holy men. He'd met several in his days as a monastic post rider.

'But,' continued William, 'an urgent matter relating to the tomb of the Martyr has arisen.'

'Urgent?'

'I am afraid so, Prior,' said the monk. 'One which is most sensitive. I have to speak to you in private.'

'Barling, Brother William is the monk who records the miracles at the tomb,' said Benedict. 'William, these are the King's men whom, as I announced at chapter, are assisting us in our hour of need. The King's clerk, Aelred Barling, and his assistant, Hugo Stanton.'

'You are most welcome to our holy church.' William gave a smooth bow.

Stanton noticed the man's hazel eyes sweep over them both as he straightened.

'I thank you for your gracious welcome,' said Barling. 'I have read your accounts, as I have those of Prior Benedict, of the miracles with great admiration and interest.'

'Thank you, sir.' The monk bowed again.

'Barling,' said the prior, 'if you will excuse me.'

'Of course.' Barling gestured for Stanton to move with him from the earshot of the two monks.

The prior took the letter and unrolled it. Both men hunched over it, William pointing to different lines as he spoke in quiet tones to his superior.

Barling clicked his tongue. 'An unfortunate interruption,' he said to Stanton, equally quietly. 'But nothing could be more important than the miracles of the saint.'

'Doubt Peter Flocke would agree.'

'Stanton, that is close to blasphemy.'

'Sorry.' Stanton looked at him. 'Are you sure you're all right? After that stone falling, I mean.'

'I will confess that I was quite shaken,' said Barling. 'But I will not let it delay our work.'

'Which might have been the reason for it happening?'

'It might. But we carry on.' He cleared his throat. 'That I can do so is down to your quick reaction.'

'Is that a thank you, Barling?'

'It will suffice.' The clerk sniffed. 'To more important matters: did you glean anything from viewing Flocke's work at the pillar?'

Stanton couldn't resist. 'You mean like you've no head for heights?'

'Anyone with an ounce of sense would pay a height like that the very greatest of respect. What is more—'

'I wasn't being serious. But no, I didn't find out anything other than Flocke seems to have done outstanding work. The curve on the pillar was smooth, just like most could do with a good blade on soft wood. Don't know how you do that with an axe on stone.'

'It is interesting that Benedict does not appear to fully appreciate Flocke's skills. In fact, the prior does not appear to appreciate any of the work on the choir.'

'How do you mean?'

'When you were with Green, at the pillar, I experienced a brief episode with Benedict that was quite odd. He said that the work would never replace any of the old choir, that the work would not succeed in doing so.'

'Nothing especially odd about that,' said Stanton. 'The old choir's gone forever. The fire saw to that.'

'What caught my interest was not so much the words he used,' said Barling. 'More the way he said them. He had the strangest look on his face. A type of hardness, if you will. Hardness that I have not witnessed in him thus far.'

'I'd agree with you that's odd, then. From what I've seen of him, he's the complete opposite of hard. Everything about Flocke's murder seems to make him nervous. He didn't want to talk about the body. We really had to push him.'

'I would describe it more as working around him,' replied Barling. 'But the result is the same: we have made scant progress. It is to our disadvantage that we did not see Flocke's body first-hand. Any information we have is from Benedict.'

'He did say that Flocke had a stab wound on the palm of his hand. That could mean that he tried to defend himself.'

'That is entirely possible,' said Barling. 'Yet we cannot know that for definite, not without sight of the body. Furthermore, there is still the issue of the carving of the Cross. Most important, but again we have not witnessed it ourselves.'

'We definitely need to speak to the mason, Adam Drake.'

'Drake, the man who was sick when he found the body?' Barling frowned. 'A natural reaction to such a heinous discovery, so it does not sound like he was the culprit.'

'Maybe. We want our own opinion of him, Barling. Not Benedict's.'

'I agree, and he may well have vital information. We require Lambert Green to direct us to him. We also require Green's assistance in getting to speak to Flocke's wife. Her name escapes me.'

'Katerine,' said Stanton. 'And speaking of Green, he seems a nasty piece of work. His workers are afraid of him.'

'That is necessary rather than nasty,' said Barling. 'A master should keep his workers in line. They think they know everything, which can lead to all sorts of trouble.'

Stanton ignored the pointed remark. 'I think he's a liar.'

'Oh?' Barling's thin brows went up. 'What has brought you to such a thought?'

'Something he said about the stone carved by Peter Flocke. I want to go back and check.'

'Then let us do so, but without the prior,' said the clerk. 'One thing that is now quite apparent is that Prior Benedict is hopelessly out of his depth in conducting this investigation. Despite the assurances from Archbishop Richard that the man conducted extensive enquires, I can see little evidence of it. Yes, I have seen what I want to see in terms of where Peter Flocke lived and died. But seeing it with Benedict, a useful individual for getting us access here, is a hindrance when asking questions. With him accompanying us, I fear that we might not get all the truth.'

'Agreed.'

'Then we return with all haste to Lambert Green. We can—'

'Barling.' The prior, who still held the letter, walked over with William. 'I am afraid that I have to cut short my time with you. Something has come up that requires my attention. My apologies, but it simply cannot wait.'

'While it is a shame to lose your company, Prior, I completely understand.' Barling's polite response didn't let on that the clerk wanted to be free of the man.

As did Stanton. Now they could go and talk to Green again.

But they couldn't.

'William has agreed to show you the Martyrdom, Barling,' said the prior. 'Flocke repaired a step nearby.'

'Not merely agreed. It would be an honour, sir,' said William, with another smooth bow.

To his credit, Barling didn't let this change throw him. 'That would be most welcome, brother. I look forward to doing so.' He looked at Stanton. 'Go and see to the tasks I charged you with earlier. Make haste, you understand?'

Stanton made his reply and bow suitably humble. 'Yes, Barling.' As he did, he caught Barling's murmur, which was for his ears alone: 'Meet me back at the inn when you are finished.'

At least one of them could go back to Green. That it would be Stanton alone might be no bad thing.

Chapter Twelve

Standing outside in the huge queue of noisy pilgrims for the cathedral yesterday, Barling had wanted to shout in frustration at how slowly it moved forward. With Brother William at his side, he was able to move at will.

Cathedral monks herded the chattering, praying, singing, shuffling lines of people within the building.

He and William passed them with swift steps, heading across the west transept of the cathedral and towards the Martyrdom.

'I hope, Barling,' said the monk, 'that you have been told that Peter Flocke did much more skilled work than repairing steps.'

'I have had a variety of reports, thank you, brother. You knew Flocke well?'

'Hardly at all, I'm afraid. But I knew his work. His carvings were remarkable. I used several of his designs as inspiration for my illuminated manuscripts. I like to think I have talent with a pen, but he had an exquisite eye.' He crossed himself. 'A terrible end and one made horrifyingly worse by the sacrilege of the killer.'

They were approaching the Martyrdom, and Barling's mouth dried. Yes, his stated purpose was to view the work of Peter Flocke. But he could not help the fast beat of his heart; faster than when he had been at the top of the choir, faster even than when the falling block of stone had so narrowly missed him. For he was about to see the place, the exact spot, where Saint Thomas had been struck down by a group of murderous knights.

William stopped at the top of a flight of stone stairs that led down to the Martyrdom. 'The repair that Flocke did to the step is here,' he said softly.

Barling doubted if anybody would hear him even if he spoke in his usual tone.

Pilgrims lined one side, held in place by black-robed monks and cathedral servants, though nothing could contain their clamour.

Barling forced himself to look down at the step under his feet, every inch of him aching to lay eyes on the sacred place that was the Martyrdom. 'The step repair looks very sound.' A section about the size of a man's hand was a slightly different colour. Other than that, it was as smooth as the rest of the surface.

'It is. And it is vital that it is.'

Barling looked up at William. 'Meaning?'

William inclined his head at the line of pilgrims nearby. 'People fall down these steps all the time. They forget to look where they're going, for any number of reasons: lameness, blindness. Rapture. Falls cause enormous delays. A broken step would send yet more bodies tumbling.'

'I can imagine.' The press of people would be hard to escape.

'So while Peter Flocke's work here in this spot was modest, I give thanks for it every day. Shall we return to—'

'May I see the Martyrdom?' The question burst from Barling.

'Of course.' William's look of surprise was quickly replaced by one of smooth politeness. 'Come this way.'

They descended the steps, William moving the monks to one side with the lightest of taps to their shoulders.

The majority of those filling the space held candles and carved votive offerings in their hands, doing their best to lay them before the altar.

Equally determined and in a constant chorus, the monks forbade them from stopping or from laying the offerings down.

'No, not here, not now.'

'Please hold on to your offerings.'

'You can place these on the tomb. Not here.'

William brought Barling through the crowd to a clear space on the stone pavement before the ornately carved altar of the Sword's Point. To *the* clear space. The exact spot where the sword of a knight had cut off the crown of the Martyr's head, the tip of the sword breaking off on the stone, such was the force of the fatal blow.

Barling could swear he heard the echo of the brutal shouts. The horrifying sounds of the fatal assault on the Martyr's body. The calls of courage from the dying Thomas. He took a long, deep breath. 'I am overcome.'

William looked at him. 'As countless others are. As am I, no matter how often I am present.'

'I have never seen it before this moment.'

William nodded as if Barling had answered a question. 'Then I am honoured to be the first to show it to you. It is an extraordinary place, filled with holiness.' He lowered his voice to a whisper. 'I always feel we are in the presence of Saint Thomas himself. For within the altar, in a crystal reliquary, sits a piece of the Martyr's brain. Along with the point of the sword of the evildoer.'

'Then we are, in truth, in the presence of the Martyr.' Barling made the sign of the cross.

William did the same, before asking, 'May I be so bold: if you had not seen the Martyrdom, does that mean you have not seen the tomb?'

'Regrettably, I have not,' said Barling. 'I was waiting yesterday when Prior Benedict called upon me.'

'Then let your reward for coming to our aid be to see it now,' said William.

'Brother, that would give me the greatest joy.' Barling's heart panged as he said the next words, for say them he must. 'But I am afraid I have to decline your offer. I can see that the mass of people waiting to visit it is enormous. It would take too long to get through, even with your help.'

'But I have another way of showing it, Barling.' The monk smiled. 'From above.'

Above? Barling's stomach dropped. Not again.

'This way.' William held out a hand to usher him forward.

Barling need not have worried.

William brought him back up out of the Martyrdom, then through a series of locked doors and mercifully short flights of steps and corridors, all deserted. 'You walk in the footsteps of the monks now, Barling.'

Then Barling could hear a familiar noise. 'That sounds like the pilgrims again?'

'It is.' William opened up another door, and the noise hit louder than ever, along with a wave of sweet incense in the air.

In the room before them, another monk stood watching from a stone arched window.

'You can leave, brother,' said William. 'I'll call you back when it is necessary for you to resume keeping watch.'

The man left.

William went to the window, Barling with him.

'Behold, the tomb,' said William.

Barling put a hand to the sill as he caught his breath in wonder. They overlooked the huge crypt beneath the cathedral.

The room he and William stood in was about ceiling-height, but the roof of the crypt was many times lower than that of the choir above. A multitude of candles pierced the dark, the rows of carved pillars and arches casting shadows over the moving hordes of pilgrims.

And in the midst, in a pool of the brightest light, the tomb of the Martyr, protected by a circle of black-robed monks who controlled the flow of people approaching and departing.

'The walls of the tomb are formed of stone,' said William. 'Those window-like openings you see in the sides are to allow the faithful to kiss the sarcophagus inside. The top stone is of the best marble in order to protect the sacred bones of Saint Thomas. And although the tomb is secure and made of the toughest of stone, we guard it every minute of every day.'

'Against those who would try to steal the bones of Saint Thomas?'

'Yes, and those who would try to chip pieces from the tomb with knives, chisels.' He sighed. 'It is more common than you would think.'

As pilgrims filed in to kiss the tomb, to call out in reverence and for help, they placed carved votive offerings and coins onto the lid. The guardian monks collected the piles of objects as quickly as they were laid down, scooping the coins into waiting baskets. They placed the carvings onto iron racks with sloping supports in order to display each one. The quantity of carvings meant that they quickly overlaid the others beneath.

'So many,' said Barling.

'It is always extra busy around great feast days,' said William. 'With Easter being the greatest of all, the additional souls number in the thousands. A true blessing is the associated increase in generosity. The coins we collect are helping us to build the magnificent new choir.'

'You do not mourn the old choir, brother?' Barling kept his gaze fixed on the view beneath the window, the better that his question appear unimportant.

'The fire was a terrible shock,' said William. 'But I see, as do most of my fellow monks, the choir's destruction as a sign from God, that we raise a new one to even greater glory.'

A very different view, then, to that of Prior Benedict, but Barling did not comment.

More hands continued to place more carvings and offerings on the tomb as he watched, with the monks continuing to remove them.

Barling shook his head in wonderment. 'I am reminded of people battling to contain a flooding river. If anybody ceases, all will be lost.'

'Eloquently put, Barling,' said William. 'I can tell you are a man of letters, as am I. But I look on it like miners digging for gold amongst mounds of earth and rock. Each of those wax carvings you see, be it of a leg or an arm or a head, could be a plain lump of earth, a plea to the Martyr for a cure, for a miracle that is not yet answered.' He snorted. 'Or one that has been delayed by foolishness.'

'Delayed?' Just as he, Barling, was from doing his penance. He looked at William in alarm. 'I do not quite understand, brother.'

'I am referring to those foolish people who put their trust in physicians to cure them. Useless, every one of them. Filling people's bodies with potions and medicines and their heads with false hope.' He held up a finger. 'There is but one medicine that people need: true faith in Saint Thomas. It is only a shame that it takes some a long time to come to their senses.' He dropped his hand and shook his head. 'Physicians. Parasites, more like.'

'But the Martyr cannot cure all the sick.' Though Barling despised himself for thinking the thought, he could not help it: how could Saint Thomas ever hear his own pleas amongst such a multitude of requests?

'No,' said William. 'But once in a while, just like the gold miner, a gleaming nugget is found amongst the common stones: the Martyr grants a miracle. Sight is restored. A cripple walks. The devil leaves a body.' He patted the satchel he wore slung across his body. 'I will be summoned, and the miracle will be recorded.'

'I cannot imagine the grace of such a moment.'

'It is remarkable,' said William. 'But even if such a proclamation is made, the miracle must be thoroughly investigated. Unfortunately, not every account stands up to scrutiny. But for those that do, I write a full account in laudation of the Martyr. The number we are notified about by letter now far exceeds those here at the tomb. Again, I investigate them all.' He spread his hands wide and smiled. 'Yet greater glory for the Martyr.'

The mention of letters prompted Barling's memory of seeing both William and the prior poring over a letter in the choir earlier on. 'Given the numbers you must receive, I presume you share the load with Prior Benedict?'

William's smile remained but left his eyes. 'Why do you ask?'

'Only because I have read his holy accounts of the sacred miracles as well as yours.'

'Prior Benedict performed the task for the first two years after the murder of Saint Thomas.' The smile dropped. 'He was not prior then, but a humble monk like me. You mentioned battling a flood, words which struck me to my heart. For Benedict was overcome by the flood of miracles. He simply could not cope with the number, nor the relentlessness of the reporting.'

'I am sorry to hear that,' said Barling. And he was, for he knew first-hand, as he knew here at Canterbury, the disquiet in the soul that an overwhelming task could bring. But he was equally disquieted to hear of yet another example of where Benedict was not up to a task with which he had been charged.

'It was a difficult time,' said William. 'But Saint Thomas saved us.'

'Oh?'

'The saint appeared to me in visions. "Choose what thou wilt," he said to me and told me to follow the truth of the miracles and not the order.' William's smile was back. 'Thanks to the intervention of the saint, I was able to take the burden from my brother Benedict. I have done so ever since.'

'A great undertaking, indeed, brother.'

William patted his satchel once more. 'All for the glory of Saint Thomas.'

Barling smiled in return. The monk worked for the glorification of the Martyr, no doubt.

But as far as Barling could surmise, William was far more interested in his own personal glory.

As qualities in holy men went, pride could be dangerous.

And in some instances, as Barling knew only too well, it could even be lethal.

Chapter Thirteen

The yard of the stonemasons' lodge was deserted as Stanton walked back through it. Now that the masons with their noisy tools weren't here, it struck him what a quiet place it was compared to the bustle of the streets and cathedral outside. It had been a clever place to kill a man, especially at night, when there was no chance of anybody happening to look down from the cathedral scaffolding and see what was going on. The door of the lodge stood open, which told him somebody must be around.

He rapped on the frame with his knuckles. 'Green?'

Nothing.

'Lambert Green, are you in there?' He knocked again.

Still nothing.

'Green?' He stepped inside at the same second as Green emerged from the open door to the carving room, holding a heavy mallet and a wide-tipped chisel in his thickly gloved hands.

'You're back.' Surprised. 'Sirs.' And not at all pleased.

'No, just me,' said Stanton. 'I have a few more questions for you.'

'About?'

No 'sir' now that Green knew Barling and the prior weren't with him. Never mind. It might make things easier.

'First, about the widow Flocke, Peter's wife, Katerine.'

'What about her?'

'You said that you've kept her on. Which was most charitable, as the prior said.'

'Course I have. Not for charity, neither.' Green's voice dripped heavy with scorn. 'I need every pair of hands I've got.'

'Can you show me where to find her?' said Stanton. 'I want to speak to her about her husband.'

'I'd show you, except it's well over a mile away. She's had to go back to her lodging, said she was feeling very poorly. Women.' Green snorted in disgust. 'Can't never depend on them, can you? Like I told you, the inn's one of the ones out beyond Northgate, though there's that many there it would take you an age to get the right one. She swore she'd be back in tomorrow morning. What else?'

'What do you mean?'

'You said you had questions. So ask them. I've got work to do.'

'What was Peter Flocke like?'

Green shrugged. 'Flocke was like every other worker that it's my penance to have. They all need watching, all the time, or they'll never do a hand's turn if they can help it. He had a bit more of a mouth on him, but nothing I couldn't handle. Naught special about him. Except for one thing.'

'What was that?'

Green laid down the mallet and chisel on the worktable with a heavy sigh. 'The man had the most gifted pair of hands I've ever seen in a freestone mason. Come in here.' He beckoned with a gloved hand for Stanton to follow him into the carving room with the worked stone, then to a corner at the very back of the big room.

Stanton hadn't noticed on his first visit in here that another row of shelves rested behind the first. The objects arranged on them had him marvelling. Flowers, leaves, birds, faces. 'They look real, except for the colour.' He peered closer. 'But they're all stone, aren't they?'

'That they are,' said Green. 'As God is my witness, Flocke could carve stone so well, you'd think it was alive. A griffin? You'd swear it was about to fly off. A saint? You'd believe it could shed tears.' He picked up what looked like a section of a wing. 'Look at the detail on that.'

'Don't know how anybody could do that.' Stanton's uncle had carved him a wooden puppet when he'd been a small boy. While he'd been astonished at how Master Milo could move his stick-like arms and legs, his friend's polished face had had blank circles for his eyes and mouth and a peg for a nose. Nothing like Flocke's work. He looked a bit closer, his interest caught by marks half-hidden by Green's large glove. 'What are those?' Maybe Flocke had left a message of some sort. 'They look like letters.'

'They are.' Green turned it over, the better to show Stanton. 'FL. His mason's mark, for Flocke. Shows who did the work.'

Stanton nodded. No luck with a message, then.

Green put the section of wing back with care and brought Stanton outside the lodge again, talking as he did so. 'On a building of this size, I could ill afford to lose any worker. But losing one of Flocke's talents? I'm going to have a devil of a struggle to replace him.'

Stanton nodded. 'Didn't need to replace that, though, did you?' He pointed over at the cut stone under the cover, next to the spot where Flocke's body had been found.

Green's look darkened. 'What do you mean?'

'I asked Prior Benedict earlier if that was the same stone under that cover, the stone that had been stained with Flocke's blood. He said it wasn't, that he'd ordered you to destroy it.'

'And I did.' Green's large, gloved right hand moved to a hammer that hung from his belt.

Stanton readied himself to run. 'No, you didn't. You lied to the prior.'

Green took a step toward him. 'Say that again.'

79

But doubt had crept into the man's voice. Stanton held his ground. 'You know what I'm talking about. That stone looks as well carved as all of Flocke's work that you've shown me. I'll bet his mason's mark is on it as well.'

Green opened his mouth. Closed it again.

'Listen, Green. I don't care about the stone. That's not what me and Barling are here for. We need to find out who killed Peter Flocke and to do that as fast as we can.'

'Don't you wish I knew that?' Green scowled at him. 'But I don't. Know naught about it. As for the stone, of course I didn't bloody destroy it. Saints alive, man. Hundreds of hours had gone into that stone. For a start, it has to come all the way from Normandy. That's before any mason even touches it. Destroy it?' He sucked his rotting teeth. 'Not on your life. I just told the prior I had. The man was flapping around like a whore's skirts on a holy day.' Green spat on the dusty ground in disgust. 'He wouldn't know the individual masons' work if it fell on him.' His voice lowered to a bitter hiss. 'Which might be no bad thing if it did.'

Stanton moved back a pace. 'Like the block of stone that fell earlier?'

Green's eyes narrowed. 'My way of talking, that's all. But, on my life, that prior is a nuisance. So yes, he thinks I destroyed it. He'll never know the difference, and it calmed him down.'

'Then you're telling me that you'll put stone stained with the blood of a dead man into the walls?'

'Course I will.'

'There's been talk of a curse.'

'There's always tales that spread on a big job like this. Passes the time for some.' Green gave a hollow laugh. 'But I tell you this: if the blood of a stonemason can curse a cathedral, then every single one in God's kingdom is cursed, for every cathedral is built on blood. And not just stonemasons', neither. Carpenters', quarrymen's, plasterers'.

That many perish in creating these houses of God on Earth. It means nothing to the monks nor to regular folk, neither. They keep on building, and no cost is too great. So I washed off Peter Flocke's stone with water and lye and it'll be put where it needs to go.'

'I see,' said Stanton.

'It's part of one of the major arches,' said Green. 'Fully finished and the perfect angle, as only Flocke could do. If I'd got rid of it, it would've set us back weeks. Try explaining that to the prior. Because I bloody couldn't.'

'But you're his second master mason. He was full of praise for you earlier. Surely he'd have listened to your opinion?'

'A waste of breath, talking to that prior. He doesn't understand any of it. What's more, second mason doesn't matter on a job like this one. The man of Sens, William, is the master mason. That's all that counts in the end.' He pointed to the mess of papers on the table. 'There are those who plan and those who do. Trouble is, those who plan usually have their heads in the clouds. If you're lucky.' He sucked his bad teeth. 'They're more likely to be up their own backsides. They want the impossible. As God sees me, I swear the next thing the man from Sens will come up with is that the cathedral should be able to float in thin air. And what will Prior Benedict say? "Yes, that's a wonderful plan, William. Show it to Green. He'll do it. But make sure he does it with the same number of men for the same money and half the time, won't you?"' Another angry suck. 'That's the planners for you. That's on a good day. On a bad day, the thing they draw out on vellum falls down and kills people. I've seen it too many times.' He glared at Stanton. 'Now, is that it? I've told you everything and I'm a busy man.'

'As am I,' said Stanton. 'Busy trying to find out who killed your freestone mason.'

Green snorted. 'That won't bring him back, will it?'

Stanton ignored the remark. 'Adam Drake, the man who found the body.'

'What about him?' said Green.

'Where can I find him?'

'A hundred feet up there.' Green pointed to the roof of the cathedral. 'And he's staying up there until he's finished his work.'

'I need to speak to him.'

'Then you'll find him at the Roulf alehouse after sundown. It's in an alley off Burgate Street. Most of the masons go there.' He gave Stanton a sour look. 'You can do your work in an alehouse. I wish I had it that easy, so I do.' He took his hammer from its belt loop, looking Stanton right in the eye.

Stanton reckoned it was time to go.

Chapter Fourteen

Barling entered his room at the inn to find Stanton already waiting for him.

His assistant sat cross-legged on the broad sill of the low window, with the shutters ajar to catch the best of the bright midday sunshine. The smell of Stanton's dinner of salted herring filled the room, despite the open window. His assistant's cloak lay in a rumpled heap in the middle of the floor.

'I see you are applying yourself to your work.' Barling closed the door behind him.

'I'm not back long, Barling.' Stanton spoke with his mouth full. 'Honest. Lambert Green had a lot to say.' He gestured at the table with the piece of bread he held in his hand. 'That bowl's yours. The innkeeper prepared it for us.'

Barling took a suspicious sniff at the dollops of thick yellow liquid that partially covered the chunks of bony white fish. 'Mustard?'

'Lots of it.' Stanton took another large scoop with his bread. 'Thank the saints.'

'I have never once in my life been thankful for the addition of mustard to anything.' Barling sat down at the table and pushed the bowl to one side with a grimace at the foulness it contained. 'The burning of one's tongue whilst eating is an abomination.' He drew his wax tablet towards him. 'If you will be kind enough to spare me further distraction, we need to share what we have found. I can say with confidence that Brother William too had plenty to say.'

'Did he now?' Stanton's eyebrows went up. 'Then that was a piece of good luck that he appeared when he did.'

'I simply remarked upon the quantity of his contribution, not that it was necessarily of any use.' Barling picked up his stylus to check the point. 'But it might be, which is why we must review it. I pray that what they have told us will shed the light on Flocke's death that we sorely lack. What did Lambert Green say?'

'Well, I was right about the man in lots of ways.' Stanton's mouth was full again. 'Still think he's a nasty piece of work. He believes his workers are all slack and lazy. He drives them really hard and doesn't give them any credit.' Stanton paused to extract a long fishbone from between his teeth, then flung it out the window.

Barling was sorely tempted to comment on the quality of workers but held his tongue.

Eating steadily once more, Stanton proceeded with relating his conversation with the cathedral's second master mason. 'But he was a lot more open about Flocke than he'd been earlier. Green had an extremely high opinion of his work. He showed me more of it, and it's a marvel. It looks real.'

'That is interesting.' Barling made a note. 'Brother William has the same opinion. That was not something we had gleaned from Prior Benedict, not in any way.'

'Speaking of opinions,' said Stanton, 'wait till you hear what Lambert Green thinks of Prior Benedict.'

Barling listened as Stanton gave his usual clear, concise summary. This time, the man's mouth was mercifully empty, although he still seemed to find thorough licking of his fingers necessary. Yet his words were of great interest.

'Goodness,' he said when his assistant had finished. 'Then it would appear that the prior is out of his depth with regard to two areas of his responsibility: the conducting of the investigation into Flocke's murder, and the rebuilding of the choir.'

'I know we only have Green's word for it, but we saw enough times with our own eyes how Benedict had to ask Green about things he should've known himself.'

'We did,' said Barling. 'It is most concerning that although Benedict is the prior, he seems to lack the confidence that the office should bring.' He made a note. 'Brother William, however, is short of neither.' He went through his encounter with William, Stanton listening intently.

To his shame, Barling had to keep much from his assistant. But Stanton could not be told how Barling's fears for his own soul had intruded as he had spoken to William. That was between Barling and God. Anything that was pertinent to the investigation of Flocke's murder, he made sure to relate.

'Doesn't surprise me,' his assistant said when Barling had finished. 'Thought he was very full of himself.' He grinned. 'Visions of the Martyr, eh?'

'I shall ignore that last remark.' Barling looked at the notes he had made so far. 'For I have to decide on our next steps.'

Stanton scrubbed at his stubbled chin and gave a wide yawn.

Barling shot him a warning look. 'I hope you are not thinking of skulking off to your bed.'

'No, I'm not.' He scratched at his chin again. 'The early start this morning's catching up with me, and it's nice to have something in my belly for a change. That's all.'

'And perhaps a shortage of sleep last night? A shortage brought on by an excess of ale?'

'You could say that.'

'I would forbid you from such conduct. But—'

'Now hang on, Barling—'

'But.' Barling held up a hand. 'We will have to go to an alehouse tonight.'

'We?' Stanton's mouth fell open. 'You and me? An alehouse?'

'Yes, we. Do not look so startled. I refer to a particular alehouse, the Roulf alehouse, the one where Green told you that the masons go. There, we will find Adam Drake, the man who found Flocke's body. It is frustrating that we have to wait until Drake has finished work.'

'I'll go by myself, Barling.'

'That will not be necessary. I will accompany you.'

'Barling, don't be offended by what I'm going to say.'

'I hope you are not thinking of rudeness?'

'No, not in the slightest. But listen: it's an alehouse. At night. Full of stonemasons and other builders. You'll stick out like a peacock in a pig shed. I want Drake comfortable, to let his guard down as much as possible. If you're with me . . .' Stanton opened his hands.

Barling would not admit it, but Stanton was right. 'Very well.' Barling busied himself with sharpening his stylus. 'And what of the widow Flocke? She will have been the closest to Peter and may well be aware of somebody who wished to do him harm. But once again, we cannot get her account yet.' He gave a sharp sigh. 'These delays are intolerable. We have little enough time as it is.'

'Have hope, Barling. We could get our answer within hours, when I speak to Adam Drake.' Stanton got down from the windowsill and picked up his cloak.

'Where are you going?'

'To find Flocke's widow, Katerine.' Stanton threw his cloak over his shoulders. 'And before you say it, yes, that'll mean I have to go on a search of the inns.' He tied the fastening in a deft knot. 'For all we know, Katerine could be ill again tomorrow and not come to work. Like you said, Barling, we have little enough time. I have a few hours before I can meet with Drake later,' said Stanton. 'It's at least worth a try.'

Barling had indeed been about to mention Stanton wanting to search inns. 'Then I can only commend your extra diligence.' Despite the visiting of inns, it was a somewhat surprising display of effort for Stanton, if Barling were to be honest. His assistant usually liked to choose the methods of least exertion. 'In the meantime, I shall write the necessary notes. When I have completed them, if I have time, I shall visit the tomb of the Martyr while you are with Drake.' He rolled back his sleeves out of the way. 'Make sure you report back to me, Stanton. No matter what the hour. Is that understood?'

'It is. And don't forget your dinner.' Stanton went to the door and was gone, leaving his empty bowl on the window ledge.

The ensuing silence should have been Barling's usual balm and a solace. But instead it mocked him, allowing his worry of how little he was progressing to torment him. Despite Stanton's reminder to eat, Barling had no appetite, not even if the bowl next to him had contained the best venison. His stomach churned almost as badly as his thoughts. He had seen the tomb today, for which he was profoundly grateful to Brother William. But what if Stanton had not pulled him out of the way of the falling stone? What if he had been killed in the choir, dead before he could make his penance? His could have been a terrible fate.

Barling shook his head, berating himself for such selfish thoughts. He had to concentrate. He must. *A man of letters* was how William had acknowledged him earlier. His writing must be his saviour, as it so often was. He squared his tablet before him and began to write.

Peter Flocke. The dead man. A skilled mason. A savage murder. The mutilation of his flesh. The holy Cross. Sacrilege. He underlined the word three times. *Leaves a widow, Katerine – not yet seen.*

Lambert Green. Second master mason. Master to Flocke. Acknowledged Flocke's great skill. Master to Katerine Flocke and Adam Drake. Disobeys the orders of Prior Benedict.

Adam Drake. Mason. Found the body – not yet seen.

Prior Benedict. In charge of the new choir. (Peter Flocke carved stone for it.) A man who mourns the old choir. A man who has been raised to heights beyond his skills. Overwhelmed by tasks. Used to record miracles at tomb.

Brother William. Skilled with pen. Illuminations inspired by the work of Flocke. Records miracles at tomb.

Skilled with pen. The words mocked him.

Barling laid down his own writing implement in defeat. He could see many ways in which these people and the accounts of their lives and work intersected. But no pattern emerging that would show him who the killer was. He looked at his notes again. There must be something. *Not yet seen.* Perhaps a faint hope from those three words. As Stanton had said, Adam Drake or Katerine Flocke may well hold the key. Their accounts would enable him, Barling, to solve the murder. All would be well for the visit of his lord King. But if they did not?

His eyes went to a different three words.

Miracles at tomb. His defeat threatened to become despair. He needed his own miracle, for the sake of his soul.

But until this murder was solved, he could not devote his time to that end.

Chapter Fifteen

'Evening, flower.'

The alewife at the Roulf alehouse greeted Stanton with a broad smile and a gesture to one of the few empty benches in the long, narrow room. 'Take your ease, I won't be a minute.' She put another log onto the warm hearth, which threw out good heat and sweet smoke, welcome after the strong, cold breeze outside.

Stanton slid onto the empty bench with a sigh, grateful to take the weight off his feet after so many hours. Almost empty – he hadn't noticed a wizened, grey-haired man half-slumped in the dark corner. Never mind. The fellow looked quiet enough.

Green had been right. Stanton had had no luck finding Katerine Flocke. The inns along the roads that led from Northgate had been too numerous to count. Some of them had a cheek calling themselves inns, being little more than lean-to hovels or sheds where people slept with a pig or a goat. But in these days before Easter, every single one of them had been crammed with people: hosts, pilgrims, travellers, whores.

Stanton made sure he had his back to the wall, the better to see the whole room. He'd no idea what Adam Drake looked like; the mason could be any of the men sitting here. Men of all ages, stone dust coating their clothes and boots, all of them with big cups of ale. In groups. Alone. Arguing. Laughing. Gesturing.

Barrels lined the far end of the room, over which hung rows of candles, carved wax votive offerings and pilgrim badges. A man sat on a high stool next to them, hunched over a rough table as he made yet another batch to sell. Behind him, the warm, yeasty smell of brewing ale wafted through a half-open door.

'What can I get you, sir?' The alewife was at his bench. 'A badge or a candle?' Though she'd be about the same age as Stanton's mam, her large dark eyes and clear skin gave her a life and appeal much younger than her years.

'The ale looks good for now.' He gave her his best smile.

But instead of a blush, he got a wink. 'Like everything here, sir.'

'Ida,' called the man on the stool. 'Behave yourself.'

She laughed. 'My husband never allows me any fun.'

'Too right.' The man gave a gap-toothed grin in response, then returned to his work.

'Won't be a minute.' Ida hurried over to the barrels, smacking with a shriek the hand of a drunk man who tried to pinch her leg. 'Get off, you lusty swine.' She poured the drink, then scooped out a small bread bun from a basket that rested on a wide shelf.

Stanton's mouth would have watered at the sight had he any spittle left after his distant dinner of salt fish and mustard.

'There you go, sir.' Ida put his ale and bread down in front of him and straightened her coif, which had half-slid from her sweat-dampened dark hair.

He took a deep, deep drink. 'Even better than I'd hoped.' He raised the cup to her.

She put her hands on her ample hips, her eyebrows arched. 'Always an honour to serve one of the King's men. There's free ale here for you for life if you catch Peter Flocke's killer.'

'How did you know who I am?'

'News travels very fast here, sir. I heard all about it when the lads from the cathedral were in at dinner time. And I don't mean the monks. We don't get them in here. Well, except for the ones with an unholy thirst.'

Stanton smiled in spite of himself. 'Then, as you know the cathedral lads, can you tell me which one is Adam Drake?'

'Don't think he's here.' Ida scanned the room. 'No, he's not.'

Damn it all. 'I was expecting him to be here. Lambert Green said—'

'Lambert Green is a lying devil.'

The loud, slurred voice startled Stanton. It came from the man along the bench from him in the corner.

Slumped no longer, the man sat up straight and pointed an unsteady finger attached to a stained, bandaged palm. Stanton winced at the scars that covered the man's face, the skin pink and smooth and pulled. 'A lying, bloody devil. D'you hear me?' He narrowed hooded eyes at Stanton. 'Who're you, boy?'

Ida rolled her eyes. 'I'm sorry, sir.' She pulled the table out enough to make a gap, while summoning her husband. 'John.'

John got down from his stool and made his way over, to a chorus of hoots, whistles and laughter from the whole room. Though not much taller than his wife, his powerful shoulders wouldn't have been out of place on a bull.

Stanton grabbed his drink.

'You don't have to move, sir,' she said. 'We'll get rid of him.'

'I'm fine where I am,' said Stanton. 'Just don't want any spilled, that's all.'

John squeezed past his wife. 'Come on, Martin.' He grabbed hold of the drunk. 'Time to go.'

'No, it's not. Let go of me, John Roulf.'

John ignored him and lifted him easily from the seat, pulling him out, to further hilarity.

'Yes, it is, Martin.' Ida picked up his cup. 'If you don't get going, you'll be out of work again.'

'Aye, work,' said Martin. 'Stood over that lime pit all night, every night.' He waved his bandaged hands in Ida's face. 'These should be at work carving. Not burned in agony and useless.'

John bundled the still-protesting Martin to the door.

'Let me go back for my bag,' he wailed. 'I need my bag, it's got my burn ointment in! Ida!'

'Oh, for the love of God.' The alewife bent to scrabble around under the table and hauled out a filthy sack, which she threw to John.

'Off with you.' John carried bag and man out to a loud cheer.

The noise subsided, and folk returned to their drinks and chatter as Ida pushed the table straight again.

John was back.

'Is he gone?' said Ida.

'He's on his way.'

Ida blew her husband a loud kiss. 'Sorry about that, sir,' she said to Stanton. 'Martin Eustace isn't a bad soul, is he, John?'

John grunted. 'No, but he's a prize fool. If he'd learned to curb his tongue around Green, he'd still be in good work.' He lumbered over to his stool.

'No need to be sorry on my account, mistress,' said Stanton. 'I feel bad that you had to throw a man out because of me.'

'Oh, don't you worry about that, sir,' said Ida. 'Martin Eustace is forever flapping his lip in here. He really did have to go to work. Tell the truth, it's like dealing with a band of apes in here sometimes.' She wiped her damp forehead with a corner of her apron. 'Let me fetch you another ale, sir. It's the least I can do.'

'I wouldn't say no to that,' he said.

Ida was at his side in moments with another cup and its accompanying bread. 'There you are, sir.' She pointed over to the door. 'And here's Adam Drake now.'

Chapter Sixteen

Bone on stone. Blood on stone.

Before this night was over, pilgrim Robert Norwood would be at the tomb of Saint Thomas once again. He had to be. The pain in his head pounded worse than if a hammer struck his skull.

But the crowds down here in the candlelit crypt of the cathedral were thicker than ever. Among the hundreds of sung and chanted hymns and prayers, he could hear mutters around him of disgust and worse about his filth, his stench. But people continued to press in on him from all sides. They had no choice.

'Praise to Saint Thomas, praise him!' He tried to shove his way forward with his deformed right hand.

A chorus of disapproval met him.

'Go easy, fellow.' A fat scribe, bright red in the face.

'Watch what you're doing, fool.' A toothless old woman clutched carved votive offerings of feet in her wizened hands. 'My joints are terrible.'

'Saints above, fellow.' A young man and his wife, the silent woman cradling a floppy, sightless baby against her chest.

One of the guardian monks stepped forward to address Norwood. 'Enough of that, do you hear me? Otherwise, you'll be removed.'

'I need the tomb.' Norwood could hardly form the words over the throbbing pain in his skull. 'Need it now.'

'We all need it,' said the old woman. 'What makes you so special?'

'You'll get your turn,' said the monk to Norwood. 'If you conduct yourself properly. Otherwise, you're out.' The monk jerked his thumb. 'Understand?'

Norwood nodded. He couldn't explain even if he were allowed, such was the thudding of his head.

The baby gave a listless cry, and its mother soothed it with kisses and gentle murmurs.

A different pain gripped Norwood, an old, old one. One that took hold of his heart.

His first wife, Ursula. A good wife. Clean. Kept a tidy home. Shared his bed, though no child ever came. Not for years and years. Then God had smiled: a baby in Ursula's belly. The baby that died in her as she died too, trying to birth it.

The same bed, cold and empty, for five lonely harvests. Until the night Paulina, his Paulina, the thatcher's pretty daughter, his new young wife, lay in it with him. He told her he had no lust for her, that he was a godly man. That his lying with her, her body stiff and silent beneath his, was for them to be blessed with child. No such blessing came. Instead, a sickness, with Paulina pale and quiet and listless all the time. He prayed to the Virgin that she might be well, that she would smile at him. That when he climbed onto her at night, her arms would close over his back and not stay by her sides.

Sweat trickled from Norwood's temples as he gritted his teeth against the fresh torment in his skull. To scream out now would see him removed from the crypt by the monk. He could not allow that to happen.

Then the summer came, almost three years ago, and with it, a miracle. Paulina blossomed too. Colour returned to her cheeks. She smiled, she laughed. She worked hard in the busy fields to help, worked even later than him. Worked later and later.

One night, so late that the full, golden moon rose over the warm fields and there was no sign of her in the last of the stragglers coming home from their labour.

Norwood went to find her, worried that she had fallen asleep from her many hours' toil.

It took a while, but find her, he did. Found her not sleeping.

Found her in the long grass of a meadow beneath the broad, arched back and thrusting hips of young Matthew Levick, a labourer in much demand for his strong arms and his skill with an axe. Paulina's soft mewling and Levick's loud gasps masked Norwood's approach.

Paulina saw Norwood first, her eyes widening in shock, her noise cutting off in a filthy oath that warned Levick.

Levick was on his feet in an instant, pulling his braies to cover himself up.

Norwood could not remember the words he used. He could only remember standing there, fists balled, fury pounding within him, from him, in a torrent that filled the soft night air.

If Paulina had been sorry, if she'd been ashamed, if his anger had cowed her, then he could have dragged her home with a morsel of his pride intact.

But Paulina gave him no apology. Nothing. Just got to her feet, in no hurry to close her rumpled clothing. He glimpsed one breast, one perfect, white breast, flushed through with pink from Levick's broad hands and mouth.

The same mouth that twitched in a knowing grin. 'I'll bid you good evening, Mistress Norwood,' he said to Paulina as he stepped past Norwood to leave.

It was too much.

Norwood swung his right fist, smashed it into that smirking, handsome mouth, those lips that had tasted his wife.

To his shock, Levick fell like a tree. Straight down. Flat on his back.

Paulina shrieked and ran to his aid. Hunkered down to administer to him.

Norwood stood there, fear coursing in him along with his anger, trembling hard.

Levick stood a head taller than him. His answering punch, when it came – and he knew it would – would send Norwood halfway across the field. He probably should run, but he couldn't. Not while Paulina was still with her lover, her sole concern for him and not for her cuckolded husband. Were he, the wronged party, to run, his humiliation would be complete. He couldn't stomach it.

Her hands cradled Levick's face. 'Matthew, wake up, wake up. Look at me.'

Levick still hadn't moved.

Her voice climbed. 'Matthew. Please. Matthew.' More urgent.

Then screaming. 'Matthew, Matthew, Matthew.' Screaming that carried across the whole field.

And then Norwood saw it.

Bone on stone. Blood on stone.

The dark stain that oozed from the back of Levick's head onto the grass. And onto the sharp-edged rock half-buried in the soil.

Matthew Levick was dead. Because Norwood had killed him.

The pilgrims that crowded around him here in the crypt did not know that they pushed up against a killer, against the walking embodiment of sin.

Norwood faced his lord's judgement. No case to answer in the circumstances. *But you, Robert Norwood, would be better reserving your fists for your disgracefully wayward wife.*

Norwood kept his fists to himself. They would have been useless to stop Paulina's grief. Her mourning for another man cut him as keenly as if she had used a blade. And while the lord of the estate had ordered no earthly punishment, he commanded that Norwood make his full confession. Norwood did so, telling the priest of his sinful anger. Of his sinful actions.

The priest emphasised the gravity of what Norwood had done. *You have taken a life. Your soul is in mortal danger and must be cleansed. Therefore, your penance must be severe.*

Norwood must never eat meat again. Fast every day. Say the Lord's Prayer a hundred times a day. And he must don the pilgrim's tunic and walk barefoot to the shrines of the saints for three years, never spending more than two weeks in any one place. The same priest also heard Paulina's confession of adultery. She too had to fast and pray and enter a local nunnery to work as a servant. Once Norwood completed his penance, she would be returned to him.

He could have despaired. But he did not. The years would pass. Paulina was still his. He had that secret consolation. He could laugh at his own foolishness.

Better that than weep, which he often did these days. Which he did now, his tears flowing as he could see the tomb of the Martyr come into view. The tomb, his one remaining hope.

For no matter what words he'd used to the priest about forgiveness for Levick's death, he had not been sorry. Not truly sorry. Because had Levick lived, Norwood would have lost Paulina. He'd seen for himself the pleasure on her face at the man's body in hers. The briefest second, but seared into his memory like a brand on the flesh of cattle. She would have sought Levick out, again and again. Now she could not. Could never.

But there were no secrets from God. God could see what was in Norwood's heart, in his soul, in a way that the priest had not. God could see that the sin of Levick's death still festered there. And now it was consuming him.

Two months ago, he'd been as he ever was, walking his penance from shrine to shrine, each step he took a step closer to his return to Paulina. And then had come the pains in his head. Bad on some days, worse on others. Then the morning he woke in horror to find his right hand curled in on itself. Useless, immovable, no matter what he did to straighten it. If he returned to the village like this, the priest would be able to tell immediately that Norwood had not been granted forgiveness by God. He would be sent away again, he was sure of that. More miles, more years, without Paulina.

God's wisdom knew no bounds. He was showing Norwood, a humble sinner, that he must truly repent. Norwood did, he told God he did, prayed and begged for forgiveness and mercy. But God had not yet granted that. Norwood's hand got tighter and tighter while the pains in his head reached new, sharper heights with each day that passed.

Days that had brought his faltering steps to Canterbury, where the skull of Saint Thomas Becket had been smashed open on the cathedral floor. *Bone on stone.*

Canterbury, where the lifeblood of Saint Thomas had been splashed across the altar, granting miracles to so many. *Blood on stone.*

The pain in Norwood's skull pounded, pounded. He was sure it was about to break. He bit his lip to stop his scream of agony.

Only blood, the Martyr's blood, could save him now.

Chapter Seventeen

'Get us an ale quick, will you, Ida?'

The man who marched in would be about Stanton's age and height but was at least three times his size in girth. He came over to the alewife, still talking although he was very out of breath.

'Green made us do extra time, so he did, because of the time we lost while the King's men were there and—' He caught sight of Stanton and stopped dead. 'Oh, my days.' He looked at Ida with panic in his wide face.

'This is Adam Drake, sir,' she said.

'Have a seat, Drake,' said Stanton.

The mason plonked himself down as if struck by a piece of wood.

'You'll have an ale?'

'Me?' Drake's unruly brown eyebrows almost disappeared into his equally thick, dusty, messy hair.

'Ida, please may I have an ale for my friend here?'

'Am I in trouble, sir?' asked Drake.

That depends. 'No, not at all,' said Stanton. 'I know you've heard that my master, Aelred Barling, and I are looking into the murder of Peter Flocke on behalf of the prior.'

The alewife placed a cup of ale and a bread bun before Drake, and he grabbed for the drink. 'Yes, that's right, sir.' He took a huge gulp, ale trickling down his two chins. It seemed to steady him. A bit.

'Because you were the one who found the body,' said Stanton, 'I wanted to check a few things with you, the things you told Prior Benedict.'

Another gulp, and Drake wiped his mouth with his dirty sleeve. 'I didn't tell the prior much, to be fair. He didn't really ask me a lot.'

Of course he didn't. 'Not to worry,' said Stanton. 'We can go back over it all.' He picked up his own bread bun. Nice and hard and perfect for dipping in his ale.

'It was the worst thing I've ever seen, I can tell you that.'

'It sounds horrible.' Stanton chewed on his tasty mouthful. 'The prior said you'd been sick at the sight.' No harm in testing out the monk's story.

'I did and all. Couldn't help it. It was either that or piss myself, I can tell you.' Drake's wide cheeks reddened. 'Did a bit of that as well. I were that scared. Thought every shadow was a devil with a knife, coming for me.'

'I can understand that reaction, my friend. No shame in it. In fact, I've done it myself a few times.'

'Really?' Drake's mouth fell open.

'God's truth.' Stanton signalled to Ida to bring another couple of ales. Drake was beginning to relax, which Stanton wanted him to do. Nervous people talked a lot but often said very little.

Ida put the ales and bread down, and Stanton raised his cup to Drake. 'Your health.'

'And yours, sir.'

'So what happened on that night, the night you found Flocke's body?'

'Well, I'd finished work and gone for a few ales, same as tonight. Every night, actually, even Sunday. You can't get rid of the stone dust. Gives you an awful thirst at the best of times, twice as bad as any Lenten thirst.'

'That would plague any man.' Stanton nodded in sympathy.

'But when I went to pay Ida, I realised that I didn't have my purse with me. I'd taken it off for my midday sleep, after my dinner, like, and forgot to put it on again. I went back to the lodge to get it. I didn't want somebody to find it and take it.'

'Wouldn't the lodge be locked up at that time of night?'

'It should be. But we often have to work late, especially if Master Green says we're behind. And I thought if it was locked, then at least nobody could steal it. If it was there. If you see what I mean, sir.'

'All open, then? The gate as well?'

'The masons' gate is never locked,' said Drake. 'Master Green insists on it. It used to be, but a marble delivery came late one night and the carter couldn't get in. He went to find out if he could get entry but somebody stole a whole lot of the marble while he was gone. The master was angry as a demon. It's not been locked since.'

'So you went in,' said Stanton. 'And that was when you found Peter Flocke's body?'

'Yes. In the yard.' Drake swallowed hard at the memory. 'By the stone.' Swallowed again. 'It was bad.'

'Even worse to find a friend in that terrible state.'

Drake picked up his cup and examined the inside. 'I wouldn't say he was a friend. I knew him, and we worked together. Played dice with him at dinner time sometimes.' He took a long draught. 'Always beat me. Clever, he was. With a high opinion of himself to match.'

'Did you dislike him?'

'No.' Drake almost dropped the cup. 'I mean, we might have had words from time to time, like what happens with any of the lads. Nothing more.' He clutched the cup tight in his hand. 'Nothing, sir.'

Faith, the calm was gone, that was for sure. Stanton called for another drink. Drake was going to need one, for he had to ask about the body again.

'So you found Flocke dead, with a number of wounds.'

'Yes.' Another gulp of ale.

'Can you describe them?'

'There was lots. Lot of blood and all. But they were different.'

'How do you mean?'

'Well, the cross on his forehead was. The other wounds, from what I could see were not good cuts.'

'Good cuts?'

'I'm only a roughmason,' said Drake. 'But I still have to know what a good, clean cut is. Flocke's wounds weren't that.' He looked around and lowered his voice, as if the killer might be listening. 'They were slashes, like somebody had really gone at him but there was no pattern or anything. His forehead?' Drake blew out his wide cheeks. 'It was a definite mark. The killer had made sure of that. It was the Cross of Christ. No doubt about it.'

Stanton nodded. 'That was how the prior described it. Horrible. Green said that Flocke's wife was distraught when she saw it. I can only imagine what it must've been like for her.'

'Awful. Poor Katerine was beside herself.' Drake's fleshy face drooped. 'She was a good wife to Flocke. A good worker too. Flocke was lucky to have her.' He gave a wistful sigh. 'So lucky.'

'Are you married?' said Stanton.

'Me?' said Drake. 'No.' He flushed. 'Never know what to say to women. And you have to say something to get them to marry you, don't you?'

Stanton could remember plenty of times when he'd been with women and it had all worked out extremely well without either of them saying very much at all. But he didn't want to rub Drake's nose in it. 'True words, my friend.'

Another chorus of whistles and cheers and laughter broke out.

Stanton looked up to see an ancient man wander past towards the front door, naked on his lower half, muttering to himself.

'Ida!' called a man from another table. 'You have a new customer.'

'Don't think he's happy!' shouted another.

Ida came through from the room at the rear, wiping her hands on her apron, John behind her with a long stirring spoon.

'As if I haven't enough to do.' She hurried up to the man and took him gently by the arm. 'Come on, flower. Back upstairs.'

John came over as well. 'Can you manage, Ida?'

'I'll be fine. You just watch things down here.' She led the man to another door in the far corner to more cheers. 'And you lot can close your mouths.'

'Sorry about that, sir,' said John to Stanton.

'No need.' Stanton offered up a brief prayer of thanks that he'd persuaded Barling not to come here tonight. 'We all have families.'

'He's not family, sir. He's a pilgrim. We take them in.'

Stanton nodded. 'The man I'm travelling with and I were taken in as pilgrims.' He grinned. 'Not places as lively as this, mind. But you offer great charity.'

John gave a rueful grin in response. 'Not much of a choice about charity, I'm afraid, sir. In Canterbury, the monks of Christ Church priory will only rent you a home if you take in pilgrims. We do what we can.'

A man called for ale from John, and he hurried off.

Drake drained his cup. 'Are we done for tonight, sir?' He looked hopeful.

Stanton was about to confirm that they were. But Ida's mention of the word 'mouth' brought to mind something Green had said to him about Flocke. *He had a bit more of a mouth on him, but nothing I couldn't handle.* 'A couple more things, won't take long. Did Flocke and Green ever argue?'

Drake fiddled with his cup, wouldn't meet Stanton's eye. 'I suppose you could call them arguments. It was more about the work.'

'In what way?'

'Flocke had his own ideas about how the choir should be designed. All of it. Green hated that, told him to stay in his place, do

103

what he was told. So they'd row about it, and Flocke would threaten to walk off the job. He was the only one who dared to talk back to Green. I wouldn't, that's for sure. Mind you, I'm only a roughmason. We're two a penny, Green says. Nearly as common as carpenters. But Flocke was the best freestone mason I've ever seen. Think that was the only reason Green didn't sack him. Anybody else would have been out on their ear.'

'Was there any other strife between them?'

'You could say that.'

'Such as?'

'Y'see, a freestone mason like Flocke, he's supposed to make sure he puts the right marks on the stone he's finished.'

'I saw that. FL, for Flocke.'

'No,' said Drake. 'That's only his mason's mark, so folk know who did it. Believe me, Peter Flocke would never have forgotten to do that. He wanted the whole world to know who he was. The mark that Flocke left off was the placement mark. That's the one that shows exactly where the piece is supposed to go. It matches up with Master Green's plan. Flocke would sometimes leave that mark off, and it used to make Green so angry.'

'Maybe he forgot?'

'Not Peter Flocke. I think he was getting his revenge on Green for Green refusing to listen to his grand ideas. He used to laugh a lot about the master having to climb up and down ladders to ask for his help in placing a stone.'

'Would Lambert Green have got so angry about that, that he would have killed Flocke?' Stanton could've kicked himself. The direct question pushed the nervous Drake too far.

'Sir.' All the colour left Drake's wide face. 'Sir, you shouldn't ask me something like that, not about Master Green. I don't know, and I don't want to guess. It's not my place to guess anything, not like that.' He stood and opened his purse with trembling hands, slapping coins down on the table. 'That will pay my way for tonight. Good night to you, sir.'

With that, he was gone and out the door, moving with surprising speed for a man of his bulk.

'Another ale, sir?' asked Ida.

'No, thanks, I'm done for tonight.' Stanton got to his feet, and the room tipped, and he cursed to himself.

He'd enjoyed every mouthful he'd had. But it'd made him careless in his questioning.

And he still had to report back to Barling.

Chapter Eighteen

Stanton made his way up the stairs of the inn he shared with Barling, each step a loud creak under his unsteady boots.

'Shh,' he said to himself.

God's eyes, but John and Ida Roulf brewed a strong ale. Like the best of strong ales, it had tasted smooth and lent itself to many cups.

In truth, he'd lost count of how many he'd downed with the nervous Drake. He'd had all his attention on the questions he'd needed to ask and the man's answers in turn.

Drake hadn't appeared much affected. But he'd be used to the Roulfs' brew. And he was three times the weight of Stanton.

He stumbled on a stair and fell on one knee with a stifled oath.

The other thing about the best of strong ales was they had a way of creeping up on a fellow and making his legs not work.

A fierce whisper hissed from the top of the stairs. 'Stanton, is that you?'

'Coming, Barling.' He managed to get upright and climbed on.

The clerk was waiting for him. Another whisper. 'I was beginning to fear that you had fallen asleep in the alehouse.'

'No, I'm here.' It came out louder than he expected.

'By Saint Peter of Rome, keep your voice down, Stanton. I can see that you are here. What is more, I can see the disgraceful condition of you. My room. Now.'

Stanton followed the clerk in and went to sit down on the bed.

'Remain standing,' said Barling. 'I do not want you bringing the filth of an alehouse onto my blankets.' The clerk did not sit, either.

'It wasn't filthy. Or not very. And they sell badges. Bought you one.' He fished under his cloak for it and held it out. 'Look.'

Barling didn't. 'I can see my utter lack of judgement in not accompanying you tonight. I should never have listened to your claims that you could be trusted to search inns alone.'

'I didn't drink in the inns. I drank in the alehouse.'

'Clearly.' Barling glared at him. 'Did you find Katerine Flocke?'

'No.' Stanton put the badge on the table, wishing he could stop swaying. 'But I got to talk to Adam Drake at len . . . at len . . . for ages.'

'I pray that such a protracted dialogue was fruitful. Not that it was simply two fools looking at the bottom of their ale cups all night.' The clerk's nostrils pinched, a reliable sign that he was losing his temper. 'Wasting valuable time instead of solving a murder.'

'No, Barling. No, no.' Stanton went to shake his head, but thought better of it. 'I drank with Drake to calm him down. Get on his side. He was jittery from the minute he arrived.'

'Did you obtain information of value from him?'

'Think so. But I don't know what any of it means yet.'

'Go on. That is, if you can remember.'

'Ale doesn't always rob you of memory, Barling.'

'Ale does not rob me of anything because I do not let it pass my lips.'

Stanton waved a hand. 'You know what I mean.' He listed what he had found out. Drake's return for his purse. The body. The symbol of the Cross. The savagery of the attack. Drake's views on Katerine Flocke. Peter Flocke's skills. Bad blood between Green and Flocke. 'And then it all went wrong at the end.'

'How do you mean?'

'I asked Drake if Flocke would have made Green angry enough to kill him.'

Barling clicked his tongue. 'A clumsy question.'

'I know, Barling. It was too much for him. He turned tail and ran, wouldn't say another word.'

'Ale might not have robbed you of your memory, but it has certainly impaired your judgement. In addition, you have had your mind made up about Green from the beginning and your certainty led you to make an imprudent error.' The clerk pointed a finger at him. 'My initial conclusion was correct. I should never have permitted you to go without me.'

'Wait.'

'Wait? For what?'

'Your finger. It reminded me. There was another man at the alehouse who had had a run-in with Green. Green had sacked him.'

'He told you this?'

'Some of it, yes. He was very drunk.'

'I am astounded to hear so.'

'But the folk who run the alehouse backed it up. They said the man had spoken back to Green, so he'd sacked him. He works as a lime burner now.'

'And did this man know Peter Flocke?'

'I assume so.'

'Assume?' Barling glared at him. 'That will not help us to solve anything. But we will have to speak to him at some point, in case he knows something of use. What is the man's name?'

Oh, hell. He was going to have to say the name Eustace. 'Martin.' He sucked hard to clear his mouth of ale-spittle. 'Eusis.'

'Am I supposed to be hearing the name Eustace?'

'The very one.'

Barling rolled his eyes. 'Is there anything else that is going to suddenly occur to you?'

'No. Think that's it.'

'Then you need to go and sleep off that ale, if that is even possible. I want to go and see Katerine Flocke first thing tomorrow morning.'

'I'll go.' Stanton paused. 'Did you have a nice time at the tomb?'

It was like something snapped in Barling. 'A nice time? I did not go to the tomb of the Martyr for a nice time.' The clerk's pale cheeks had two spots of high colour. 'A ridiculous question. I went there to pray. What is more, I was thwarted in that virtuous pursuit, despite having spent an unacceptable length of time in an unruly queue to get there.'

'How?'

'If you must know, I was kneeling near the tomb in the crypt, praying in perfect contemplation. When a pilgrim, a dishevelled man who could not have been in control of his senses, started shouting at the top of his voice about the Martyr saving him. He launched himself at the sacred tomb and tried to bite off a corner of it. It is made of solid marble, yet he chewed at it like a dog with a bone.'

Stanton felt a twitch of a smile. But he kept his face still as Barling ranted on.

'The guardian monks had to drag him off, but he resisted them with all force. Shouting, struggling, wailing about the Martyr. It took them a considerable while to eject him from the crypt as it was so crowded. By the time they had, my contemplation was ruined. Ruined! I departed not long after.' Barling looked at him accusingly. 'I have been awaiting your return ever since.'

'It's not that late, Barling.'

'The hour is extremely late, by any sensible person's standard. Thanks to your dallying in the wretched alehouse, I can only now start writing my notes on what you have learned. I shall be awake half the night.'

'Sorry, Barling.' His conscience nipped at him for taking so long and for having had such an enjoyable evening in the midst of a murder enquiry.

Barling flung out an arm. 'Leave.'

'Sorry, Barling. Night, Barling.'

The slam of Barling's door at his back was the only response.

Stanton made for the door of his own room. He fumbled it open, kicked it shut behind him and collapsed on his back onto his bed, arms above his head.

He waited to slide into ale-cushioned oblivion as he had done the previous night.

Trouble was, he hadn't had cross words with Barling then. Guilt panged through him again that he'd not thought about the hour.

He could picture the clerk sitting at his table, writing, writing, long into the night, completely alone.

Stanton sighed. He wasn't a lot better. His drinking companion had been a witness in a murder enquiry. He'd come to bed on his own. He sighed again.

He wondered what Rosamund would make of him now. No longer Hugo Stanton the messenger, the young man who rode a fast horse and who she could sneak to her chamber whenever she dared. She hadn't cared how long they might have, would snatch the briefest few minutes hidden behind the folds of a wall tapestry if she had to.

But that Hugo Stanton was gone.

He had no way of knowing what she would make of the Hugo Stanton who examined dead bodies. Who spent hour upon hour asking questions. Who chased down murderers. Who brought men and women to justice.

Who had a fussy clerk for a companion. The idea of Rosamund with Aelred Barling made him smile. She would use every single one of her charms on him, because that's what she used to do to every man she met. She would have no idea why they didn't work on Barling.

But in truth, Stanton couldn't picture them together, in the same way that he was finding it harder and harder to imagine being by her side. He'd gone through a whole year without her.

He could never be with her again, could never go back. He knew that.

Knowing it didn't take away how much he missed her. Her bright hazel eyes and thick, curled ropes of golden hair that he could tangle his fingers into. Soft, beautiful flesh. Murmuring giggles in his ear, on his neck, his mouth. Lips hungry for every inch of his body.

All he could do was try to dream about her, one of the few ways he could soothe his hurting heart.

But to dream, he'd have to sleep.

And so he did.

Chapter Nineteen

Tuesday

If the first night's Canterbury ale had felt to Stanton as if it had kicked him in the head like a horse, John and Ida Roulf's brew had him trampled by a runaway steed and run over by the cart it pulled. Also, the sun had decided to come up extra early this morning. He was sure of it. The birds should've been abed for at least another two hours, as should he. He should be rolled in the inn's warm blankets, his bones cushioned by the soft straw mattress, not travelling through the streets with Barling, who strode along with unseemly haste.

'I hear no mirth this morn, Stanton. Is something amiss?'

'No.' It wasn't a lie, because it wasn't that something was amiss. Everything was. Head. Guts. Legs. Not that he'd admit it. The clerk was gloating enough as it was.

'Good,' said Barling. 'Because I need your full attention when we get to speak to Katerine Flocke. I also do not want you asking ill-judged questions like you said you did of Adam Drake last night. Think about every word before you open your mouth. I will not have things disrupted by your rashness. Is that clear?'

'Yes, Barling.' Hell's teeth, Stanton preferred the clerk's gloating to this pecking. At least it was quieter.

'Morning, sir!'

Stanton looked around at the source of the call, careful not to move his head too quickly.

Down an alley to his right, alewife Ida Roulf stood outside her alehouse. She gave Stanton a brief wave and smile, and he returned it. Her husband John was with her, deep in conversation with a priest who held a wheeled barrow on which a bundled figure lay. Ida had hold of the ancient man who'd wandered from the inn's stairwell last night, who, fortunately, appeared to have all his clothes on. Stanton was in no fit state to deal with Barling faced with unexpected nudity.

'Permit me to guess.' Barling sniffed. 'Those are the persons who were your hosts for last night?'

'Yes, that's them. John made that badge I gave you.' Stanton waited for Barling's thanks. He didn't get it.

'I cannot believe that they are at work so early,' said Barling.

'I thought you approved of folk who worked hard?'

'I do.' Another sniff. 'I merely assumed that they would have little need to work for some time, given how much they will have earned from your copious imbibing.'

Oh, no. Barling was trying to jest. 'That's a good one.' He gave a small laugh to encourage him, one that ended in coughing.

'What is?'

Then it wasn't a jest. Thank goodness. 'Nothing. But as regards the Roulfs, they are at work. That very old man is a pilgrim.'

'The man the priest is leaving with?'

Stanton wished Barling wouldn't stare so openly at folk. There were ways of looking without being so obvious.

The priest was indeed walking off with the ancient man, and John was wheeling the barrow with its occupant inside.

'That's right. They take pilgrims in for charity.'

'Unexpected virtue.' Barling nodded in approval.

'Not really. The monks insist on it as part of the rental agreement for the houses in Canterbury.'

'Another source of income for the rebuilding of the choir, no doubt.' Barling frowned. 'The Archbishop did admit to the costs being substantial but gave no details.'

'That's true,' said Stanton. 'And Green has spoken to me of the pressure on him over cost.'

'I wonder if—'

'Excuse me, sirs.' A small-boned young woman stepped into their path. 'If I may be so bold.'

Stanton guessed her to be about his age. Neatly dressed in a dark yellow wool cloak and dress, with a snow-white linen hood drawn tight over dark blonde hair, she didn't look like a beggar. He still put his hand to his purse.

Barling didn't. 'No, you may not. Stand aside, girl. We are on the King's business.'

She blanched but didn't move. 'That is what I hoped, sirs.' No smile lit her serious face or deep blue eyes.

'Talking in riddles is simply adding to your rudeness and to our lateness.'

'It will take but a moment, sirs.'

'Be gone with you.' Barling went to step around her but she put a hand on his arm.

'Please, I desperately need your help.'

Barling halted, and she let go of him.

Stanton guessed, correctly, that the clerk stopping was in shock that someone, a young woman, no less, would ignore his direct instruction.

'Have you gone quite mad, girl? That you would dare to—'

Stanton interrupted. She intrigued him. 'We can give you a moment.'

'Stanton.' The clerk's warning was clear.

'Go on.' He gave the girl an encouraging smile but got no response.

114

Instead, she took him at his word, speaking as quickly as she could. 'My name is Elena Whitehand, sirs. I am from the village of Harden in Kent. My younger sister, Sybil, is missing.'

'This is intolerable.'

She ignored Barling. 'She came here on pilgrimage with a group that my family does not know well. The group returned home without Sybil, and my father has sent me to come and bring her back. I have been here for some days and can find no trace of her. I am staying at Saint Cuthbert's inn. If you hear of anything, can you please send word?'

'Have you finished, girl?' Barling glared at her.

'Yes, sir.'

'Then I have this response for you. If you think that your daring to delay us was somehow proper, if you think that your presumptuous request had even the most slender hope of being granted, you are either not in possession of your wits or you come from the roughest stock. As your dress would suggest it is not the latter, then it must be the former. I will waste no more time on your ravings. Come, Stanton.' The clerk marched off.

Stanton stayed back. This poor girl, Elena, didn't deserve the full force of Barling's wrath. 'Please don't be upset, he doesn't mean to be so rude.'

'I am not, and he does.' Her hands were balled fists as her deep blue eyes followed Barling. 'But thank you, sir.' She returned her gaze to Stanton. Not a hint of tears.

'Stanton!'

He had no choice but to respond to Barling's testy call. 'I'm sorry.'

He quickly caught the clerk up. 'You could've been a bit gentler with her, Barling. And we might have been able to help.'

'Why am I not surprised?' said Barling.

'I don't know what you mean.'

115

'There is but one thing that is more effective at stopping you in your tracks than a cup of ale, and that is an attractive young woman.'

Fair enough. But Stanton didn't dare say it.

Barling went on. 'Neither of which is going to solve the murder of Peter Flocke, which must be the sole matter that concerns us. Now to his widow, for she is the only woman that it is necessary for us to find.' He gave Stanton a warning look. 'The only one.'

Chapter Twenty

'Yes, Katerine Flock is here this morn. Sirs.'

Barling let out a relieved breath at Lambert Green's surly greeting from the door of the lodge as he and Stanton walked into the masons' yard. The last thing he had wanted to do was scour numerous unsavoury inns and alehouses with Stanton in a further time-wasting endeavour to track this woman down.

'You can use the resting room. Sirs. I'll go and fetch her.'

'Thank you, Green.' Barling went in as Green directed, Stanton with him. 'Now, remember, Stanton: we have to obtain every possible detail from this woman. We have been waiting long enough.'

'I know.'

Green appeared at the door. 'In you go, Katerine.' He ushered in a short, stocky, dark-eyed young woman, who looked at Barling with the wariness of a stray dog.

'You don't need me, sir?' said Green.

'No, thank you,' said Barling.

'I'll make sure you're not disturbed, then. Sir.' Green closed the door.

'Katerine, perhaps you would like to sit?' Barling indicated one of the crude barrel stools.

'I don't know, sir. Should I, sir?' Still wary.

Barling turned to Stanton in a wordless plea for assistance. Stanton's skills with the common man – or, in this instance, woman – were going to be required.

Katerine Flocke was certainly common. She had a pleasant-enough, rounded face, but one coated with builders' dust and dirt, as were her coarse woollen skirts and thick apron. Her head covering was no neat coif but a tightly tied hood of the same rough, dull cloth of her dress.

Stanton reacted to the request. 'I think we should all sit. Good to talk in comfort, eh?' He matched his words with his actions, and Barling and Katerine followed.

'That's better, isn't it?' Stanton smiled as if he'd had a chorus of agreement.

'Thank you, sir.' Katerine clasped her raw, filthy hands together on her lap, her fingernails broken and split.

'Katerine, my name is Hugo Stanton.' Stanton leaned forward to rest his elbows on his knees, as if talking by a fireside. 'This is Aelred Barling. We are the King's men. Prior Benedict has asked us to carry out an important task, which is to look into the murder of your husband, Peter.'

She bit her lip. 'Thank you, sir.'

'Your gratitude is not necessary, Katerine,' said Barling, equally keen to put the wretched woman at her ease. 'For it is our solemn duty, which we are pleased to discharge.'

Katerine looked blankly at him.

Barling nodded for Stanton to continue.

'We are so sorry that you have lost Peter,' said Stanton. 'And we know that it is especially hard for you to have to talk about what happened. But you may be able to help us find the killer.'

'Me, sir?' A look of horror came over her face. 'But I don't know who killed him. Who said that?'

'Nobody has said it, Katerine,' said Stanton. 'All you have to do is answer the questions that we ask you. That's all.'

She nodded.

'Can you tell us where you were on the night that he died?' said Stanton.

'I was in bed. It was late, when it happened, and I was already in bed. I always sleep as long as I can on a Sunday. I'm that tired from my work.'

'What work is that?'

'I'm a mason's servant, sir. I mix the mortar for them, do some plaster work as well. I have to fetch things, carry things. I do that for lots of the masons. But I mostly worked with Peter. He was a very good mason. Good at lots of things, really. Picked things up quick. He could always find work in all sorts of places. We moved around quite a bit before we came to Canterbury. I don't know what I'll do now.' She scrubbed the beginning of tears away, smearing the dirt on her cheeks.

'Yet you still have work here as a servant, do you not?' asked Barling.

'Begging your pardon, sir. I meant I don't know what I'm going to do without my husband.'

'Of course.' Barling refused to meet Stanton's accusing eye at his careless remark.

'But yes, sir, I'm ever so lucky that Master Green is keeping me on. He's been good to me.'

'Katerine,' said Stanton. 'You were saying about the night Peter was killed?'

'Yes, sir. I was in bed, our bed, Peter's and mine, at the inn where we – I – live. I got woken up by a messenger. I went as fast as I could. But there was nothing to be done. His blood...everywhere. And the Cross, on his forehead. Splitting the skin open.' She rubbed at her eyes again. 'Peter was a good man. I still can't believe it. Who would do such an evil thing?'

'That is what we are going to find out, Katerine,' said Stanton.

'I used to worry about him so much, sir. Like when he got sick last winter. But he got better, and now he's dead.'

Barling resisted the urge to tap his foot in impatience. Stanton's questioning was making little progress. He drew breath to intervene, but Stanton continued.

'Sick? How?'

'I don't know, sir. He had a bloody flux that wouldn't go. He got thinner and thinner and could hardly lift a tool. I said all my prayers. Even bought some offerings and went to the Martyr's tomb with them. But he was still very bad. The monks told me I should be patient and trust God. That I should make more offerings, coins as well, as many as I had. But Peter was getting worse and worse. I was so scared that he was dying.'

'But he was granted a miracle?' Barling could not help his eager question, which brought a frown from Stanton.

'No, sir,' she said. 'I was at my wits' end, so I turned to a physician, a good one, Master Gilbert Ordway. That's who made Peter better. It also made Peter angry. Very angry.'

'Why was Peter angry about this physician, if he made him better?' said Stanton.

'It was because it cost a lot of money. Peter earned a lot less in the winter, like us all. I didn't tell Peter, just got the medicine and put it in his food. After a short while, it began to work, and Peter started to get strong again. But he caught me one day, wanted to know what I was doing. I had to tell him, and he got so angry when he heard the price. But he also said that because he was cured and he hadn't needed to take all the medicine, he should get money back from Master Ordway.'

'Did he get it back?' asked Stanton.

'He went to ask for it, sir, but Master Ordway refused. Like I said, Peter was a good man, but he could have a bit of a temper. So there was a big row, and I had to drag Peter away. I think a lot of folk have a temper when it comes to money. My pa was exactly the same.'

'Did Peter ever argue with anybody else?' said Stanton. 'Lambert Green, for instance?'

'Master Green?' Katerine looked appalled. 'Oh, no, sir. Master Green thought Peter's work was the best of all the masons. Peter got impatient with the master sometimes. But that was just his way. He thought everybody could see things as quick as him.'

'Katerine, you've been a big help,' said Stanton.

'Have I, sir?'

'Without a doubt,' said Barling. He met Stanton's eye, and his assistant nodded.

Barling went on. 'One final question: where can we find this physician, Gilbert Ordway?'

Chapter Twenty-One

'We might have had to wait a while to meet Katerine Flocke,' said Stanton to Barling as they made their way along the busy streets to the physician Gilbert Ordway's house, 'but it was definitely worth the delay, wasn't it?'

'It was,' replied Barling. 'Nobody else had mentioned Flocke's troubles with this physician. You did good work in persisting with that matter. Excellent work, in fact. I thought she was merely rambling, as women tend to do.'

Stanton smiled inside. Barling had as much experience with women as a fox had in dancing a carole. Good, though, that the clerk seemed to be cheered by the morning's progress.

Stanton weighed up whether he should bring up another woman, the one who'd stopped them earlier, the young woman who'd called herself Elena Whitehand. Her request had intrigued him. He decided against it. As well as Barling's improved mood, the plague Stanton had suffered from the ale had lifted. Running the risk of spoiling a better day wasn't worth it.

Instead, he said, 'I wasn't expecting that a physician might be the man behind Flocke's death. Their work is to keep people alive, not the opposite.'

Barling clicked his tongue. 'Stanton, I fear you are running away with your thoughts again. Such a conclusion is several jumps ahead.'

'But it's a possibility.'

'Until we meet Ordway and have the chance to speak to him, it is sheer conjecture. We know nothing of the man.'

'True.'

'But what we do know is that Peter Flocke liked an argument. We knew he had strife with Green. Now, it turns out that he argued with this physician as well. We may find from Ordway that there are others.'

'One thing struck me as odd, though,' said Stanton. 'Katerine dismissed the accounts of her husband arguing with Green.'

'I did notice that. I think it shows the value of getting different viewpoints. They matter a great deal.'

'Or somebody's lying through their teeth.'

'That is also a distin—'

'Sirs! Wait, please!'

The call from behind them had an edge to it. An urgency.

Stanton turned as one with Barling.

'Sirs!' An ashen-faced cathedral monk came pushing through the crowd to them, not responding to people's objections. 'Aelred Barling, sir,' panted the monk. 'Prior Benedict requests your urgent presence back at the cathedral.'

'Urgent?' The clerk frowned. 'I am investigating a murder for the prior. What on earth could be more urgent than that?'

'Oh, sir.' The monk shook his head. 'The only thing. There's been another murder.'

The world rocked beneath Stanton's feet for a second. He was sure of it. Maybe he still slept.

Barling's face told him he didn't.

The body had been found near the fishpond in the cathedral grounds. That was all the messenger knew, despite the clerk firing question after question at him as he and Stanton made all haste to answer the summons from Prior Benedict.

The messenger had not told them that Prior Benedict was beside himself. He hadn't needed to.

The prior was waiting for them when they made their way through the monks' graveyard, his frustrated shout directed at the messenger, though Stanton knew it was for him and Barling.

'For heaven's sake, what kept you?'

'My apologies, Prior,' said the messenger. 'I found them as quickly as I could.'

'What's Brother William doing here?' Stanton made sure his questions reached Barling's ears only.

The red-haired monk stood in solemn silence, his joined hands hidden in the sleeves of his black habit.

'I do not know, Stanton. But we will find out.'

'It's happened again, Barling. This way, this way.' Benedict led them around the edge of the pond, William following along, then flung out a trembling hand at a pitiful heap that lay half-hidden in the thick shrubs near the boundary wall. 'Exactly the same. It's here, it's over here.' The prior's eyes were wild.

Brother William, by contrast, appeared in full control of himself. 'I should warn you, Barling, it is the most grisly sight.'

'It has been our misfortune to witness such sights, brother,' said Barling.

'Many of them,' said Stanton. He looked down and uttered a stifled oath.

'May the saints preserve us,' gasped Barling.

'I am sorry,' said William. 'I know my words were inadequate to—'

'No, no,' said Barling. 'My shock is that I know who this is.'

Stanton looked at the clerk in horror. 'So do I,' he whispered.

Chapter Twenty-Two

Katerine Flocke bent to her work in the masons' yard, scrubbing out mixing pails with a stiff horsehair brush and water, her knuckles raw from the wet. She went over and over in her mind what she'd said to the important visitors. She prayed she'd got everything right.

'Katerine.'

She stopped dead at the sound of her name and dropped the brush into the water. She straightened, wiping her hands on her apron, heart hammering.

Lambert Green stood before the open door of the lodge, beckoning to her with one gloved hand.

The group of masons were working under the covered area as usual. None of them so much as glanced up as she passed them to join Green. She was used to that.

'Yes, Master Green?'

'Get back in that room.'

She did so. Did so, for she had no choice. She could still hear the tools of the masons working the stone outside. But they might as well be on a distant shore across the sea. None of them would come to help her. Because she was alone.

Green joined her and closed the door behind him.

Again, there was quiet, like when the King's men had spoken to her. Yet a different quiet. A silence that held menace. A menace she knew. Knew how it would end.

'You did well, Katerine,' he said. 'Saying the right thing.'

'Thank you, Master Green.' Her voice was a whisper. She knew then that he would have been listening in, his thin face pressed against the planks, the better to overhear what was being said. Thank the Virgin she'd not said a word against him. About what he was doing to her.

'Lucky to still have a job as a servant, eh?' His thin lips parted in a knowing smile, showing his rotting teeth.

'I am, Master Green.' Another whisper.

He stepped closer to her, put his hands on her shoulders. 'And how will that luck continue?'

'If I do as you tell me, Master.' If she spoke any louder, she might be sick.

'That's right.' His hands dropped to her breasts, and he squeezed hard.

She stifled a cry at the pain that shot through her flesh, flesh that had become so tender during these past few months.

'Quiet.' His order sent a mist of stinking spittle against her cheek, his hips pushing hard against hers as he backed her into a corner, shoving her against the wall. 'Now do what I want.'

Katerine opened his braies with shaking hands, found his revolting flesh. Every inch of her wanted to dig her nails in, rent him, shove him aside. Run for the outside, the fresh air, the yard, the busy streets. To scream and scream about what he was making her do. For people to make him stop.

But all she could do was as he ordered, make her escape silently in her head, watch that other, dreamlike scene so she could take her mind away from the present.

He finished with an oath, then pushed himself from her.

'Lucky.' He pulled his clothing to and walked off. 'For another day.' He was at the door. Opened it, left it open.

Katerine sank to the floor, rubbing her palms on the dusty planks, then on one of the rough sacks nearby, rubbing and rubbing, ridding her skin of Green's foul spoil. She would not cry. Would not.

She stood up and brought her hands to her stomach, felt its swell. A swell that had been growing for five long months. Was unstoppable.

For the time being, she could conceal it. All her life she'd wished she'd had the slim waist and narrow shoulders of other girls. Not any more. Her plump form and thick skirts and apron could hide her changing body.

She could keep working. Keep getting her meagre wages. Keep a roof over her head. Food in her belly.

But there would come a day when that belly would show. When her baby would be here. A baby she had been desperate for, when Peter was alive. She'd put up with his wandering eye, with his temper. Because that was what a wife had to do. A temper that he would unleash on her, like he did when he found out what she had paid Ordway, the physician.

You stupid mare! Slap. *What were you thinking of?* Slap.

Peter, please. Fending him off. *I was trying to save your life.*

Beggar us, more like. Slap. *Stupid. Stupid. Stupid.*

He'd not been happy, either, when she'd told him she was with child. But there was nothing he could do about it. She had put away her disappointment that he hadn't shared her joy. That was also what a wife had to do.

And now Peter was robbing her of her joy, even in death. For the arrival of her baby, her precious, precious baby, would mean destitution. Starvation.

Peter had done this to her. Left her like this. Left her at the mercy of Green. Out on the streets on that fateful night, as he so often was. Not at home with her. Out, where death could find him.

And find him it did.

She hoped he rotted in hell.

Chapter Twenty-Three

'You know this person, Barling?' asked the prior. 'How on earth is that the case?'

'When I say I know him,' said Barling, 'I know him to see. He is the pilgrim who caused such a commotion at the tomb last night.'

'I recognise him as well,' said Stanton. 'He bumped into me in the street the night of Palm Sunday. He made me drop my pastry.'

Barling looked at his assistant. 'Definitely a memorable occurrence for you, Stanton.'

'No, it was his wildness and his unkemptness. He was talking on and on about death too.'

'As he was in the tomb.'

'I know him better than that, as many of the guardian monks do,' said William. 'His name is Robert Norwood.'

'It matters not,' said Prior Benedict. 'Whether you know him or do not know him, or whether he is a pilgrim or a prince. He is dead.' His voice climbed. 'Murdered in the same manner as Peter Flocke. And I will have to tell the Archbishop, and the Archbishop wanted all this dealt with and—'

'Prior, please.' Barling held up a hand. 'I can understand your distress. But emotion will not bring this man, Norwood, back from the dead. Stanton and I will examine the body, and we will need to do so without hindrance. May I suggest that you, Brother William, take the prior to his chambers, where you can both collect yourselves?'

'May I ask who found the body?' This from Stanton.

Barling berated himself for omitting such a vital question.

'It was me,' said William.

'I therefore respectfully request, brother, that you return alone once you have ensured Prior Benedict's comfort,' said Barling.

The prior started again. 'I can have little comfort when—'

'Prior.' Barling raised a hand once more. 'Every moment we debate unnecessarily is a moment lost to solve this crime.'

Benedict drew breath, presumably to argue anew, but instead gave a long sigh. 'If you insist.'

'Come, Prior,' said William. 'Barling, I will return as soon as I can.'

Barling waited until the monks were out of earshot. 'Stanton, we can proceed. It was out of genuine concern for the prior that I asked for him to go. But I also wanted to afford us as much privacy as possible when examining the body.'

Barling squatted down, Stanton next to him and holding the branches of the bushes back.

Norwood's filthy body, in its stained tunic and with his wild hair and beard, could be a pile of discarded rags, were it not for the horrific bloodstains that covered him.

'The wounds are indeed savage,' said Barling. 'I count five stab wounds to his chest, neck and stomach. Judging by the amount of blood splashed around, any of these would have been fatal. And then there is the cross on his forehead. It is unlike the other wounds.' He fought to keep his composure. 'It is indeed the Cross of Christ.'

'It all looks exactly like how Adam Drake described Flocke's wounds to me,' said Stanton. 'Violent slashes, with no pattern or anything. I agree with you about the Cross. Very neat. The killer's blade was certainly an extremely sharp one.' He grimaced. 'Nothing on his hands, though. At least, from the sound of it, Peter Flocke had tried to fend off the attack. Not this poor fellow.' He shook his head.

Barling willed himself to give the next order, one he loathed to the depths of his soul, and he knew Stanton did too. 'Let us establish what we can discover by touch.' Barling kept his mind on the sensation of what he held and moved in his hands, not on the fact that he held the limbs of a corpse that had once been a living man called Robert Norwood. 'It would seem from the stiffness we can feel that he has been dead for quite a few hours.'

'Agreed,' said Stanton. 'Poor fellow is skin and bone, isn't he?' He grimaced. 'Don't know what made his hand curl up like that.'

'Overall, not a picture of a healthy man,' said Barling. 'In either mind or body.'

'I can come back later if you like.'

Barling turned at the voice to see Brother William standing a short distance away. Barling had not been aware of the monk's return, and from Stanton's displeased expression, he suspected his assistant had not heard him, either.

Barling got to his feet along with Stanton. 'That will not be necessary, brother. We have concluded our examination.'

They went over to the monk.

'It must have been quite a shock for you, brother, finding this unfortunate man's body,' said Barling.

'In truth, I doubted the sight of my own eyes at first,' said William. 'I had been on duty at the tomb as usual and had come outside for a short while to take some air. I like to come to this corner as it is nearby and it is peaceful. And that was where I found the body of the pilgrim Robert Norwood.'

'So that's how you know him?' asked Stanton. 'As a pilgrim?'

'Yes, he has been in Canterbury for a couple of weeks.'

'You were able to pick him out of many thousands of faces?' asked Barling in surprise.

'You already knew him, Barling, did you not?' William gave a small smile.

'As did Stanton. That is a fair point.'

'I mean him no disrespect,' said William, 'but Norwood tended to make people aware of his presence. On top of that, he had been on penance for years. I have no idea from whence he came, as he never said, but he was a regular visitor.'

'Years?' said Barling.

'I am afraid so,' said William. 'While I may be mistaken, I believe this was the third. Naturally, I do not know what sin he had committed, as that is sacrosanct between him and his confessor. But it must have been particularly grave, given his many visits. He had travelled the shrines of England. He told me that once. Several times, in truth. He would pray aloud, begging for forgiveness at the top of his voice. That, and praising the Martyr.' He sighed. 'He was always fervent. But on this visit, he seemed possessed with an extra urgency. Desperate, if you will.'

Barling could not meet the monk's eye. Desperate for forgiveness. He could understand that only too well. Instead, he addressed Stanton. 'I think we are concluded here, unless you have any more questions for Brother William?'

'Just one,' said Stanton. 'Did Norwood ever do any work on the cathedral?'

'Most definitely not,' said William. 'His purpose in life was his pilgrimage.'

'A life so tragically ended.' Barling closed off any further enquiry, though the question had been worth asking. He had considered it and dismissed it as unnecessary.

'A terrible tragedy,' said William. 'We of course have to conduct the funeral rites. Once those are completed, I have arranged for

Norwood's body to be buried in the lay cemetery, for we are not aware of any home to which he can return for burial. I think to lie there would at least have given him some solace.' He gestured to a group of cathedral servants who stood at a distance, ready with a bier, to start coming forward.

'An act of great charity, brother,' said Barling. 'We shall take our leave and allow you to proceed.'

'One thing before you go, Barling,' said William.

'Yes?'

'Prior Benedict was at great pains for me to impress on you that this matter should be resolved as soon as possible. He was equally adamant that it be kept as quiet as possible. He says you will understand why.'

'Of course, brother. Good day to you.'

'Good day.' William commenced his instructions to the servants.

'Keep Norwood's murder quiet?' muttered Stanton to Barling as they headed off across the monks' graveyard. 'Not much chance of that. Look.' He nodded upwards.

Barling looked up.

Several of the builders were watching from the external scaffolding of the cathedral, the height giving them a perfect view of the scene unfolding below.

'I note Katerine Flocke is aloft,' said Barling.

'She is. And the big man next to her? That's Adam Drake.'

'The man who found Flocke's body.'

'The very one,' said Stanton. 'It'll already be all over the masons' lodge and the alehouse, you mark my words.'

'People should attend to their work,' said Barling. 'Distraction is not a virtue.'

To his irritation, Stanton merely shrugged.

Barling went on. 'As we must attend to our work, work which has become more urgent than ever now that there has been another murder.'

'But another murder that makes no sense of any kind. There's nothing to link Peter Flocke and Robert Norwood.'

'Other than them both being slain in exactly the same way?' said Barling.

Stanton looked at him askance. 'You know I didn't mean that. I meant a stonemason who's been working here alongside others. Who's a skilled craftsman. Who has a wife. Compared to a wild pilgrim, alone in the world, who spends his years walking the shrines. Like I say, it makes no sense.'

'It does not make sense, Stanton, because we have not yet found the killer. It will only make sense when we do. Come. We must make all haste.' Barling matched his actions with his words as he set off walking.

Stanton fell into step beside him. 'Where are we going?'

'As I had previously decided,' said Barling, 'we need to make our way to the physician, Gilbert Ordway.'

'But is that still the best move? The picture has changed.'

'That was my plan, Stanton. And we will follow it.' But Barling did not meet Stanton's eye. In truth, he could not tell if it was the right decision. He could only cling to the hope that his initial approach would work.

For the complication of the second murder was putting his own penance further and further out of reach.

And his soul in even greater jeopardy.

Chapter Twenty-Four

Barling stopped by a finely carved gate that was set with an elaborate iron handle and hinges. 'This looks like what Katerine Flocke described, and we have followed her directions, which were surprisingly clear.'

Stanton nodded. 'They were.'

Barling opened the gate into an ample courtyard filled with greenery and early flowers, a merciful respite from the bustle of bodies and voices on the busy streets.

An old woman, enormously fat and dressed in the clothing of a servant, sat on a bench next to the closed door of the house.

'Begging your pardon, sirs, but the physician is busy.' Her words came out on puffs of short breath.

'The physician by the name of Gilbert Ordway?' asked Barling.

'That's him, sir.'

Barling entered the courtyard with Stanton, his assistant pulling the gate closed behind them.

'My name is Aelred Barling, and this is my assistant, Hugo Stanton. We are the King's men, and we have to speak to your master urgently. Fetch him at once.'

The woman rose to her feet to bow, her breathing more laboured from her actions. 'I'm sorry, sirs. But I am not a servant to Master

Ordway. I am Hilde, servant to my mistress, Isabel Tyson. She has come here to seek his services.'

'It is regrettable to hear that your mistress is unwell,' said Barling. 'Do you know how long she is likely to be? It is most important that we see Master Ordway.'

'My lady's not ill,' said Hilde.

'May the saints grant me patience.' Barling marched over and raised a hand to knock on the door. 'Then she will not mind being disturbed.'

'Oh, please don't, sir.'

Barling paused.

The old woman appeared genuinely distressed.

'We don't want to cause trouble for you, goodwife,' said Stanton. 'Our business is urgent.'

'I'm so sorry if I was rude, sir. But it's her daughter what's the patient. Lucia. Not ten years of age till the summer.' Her voice choked on a sob. 'And her father dead just eighteen month ago. Worried to death, I am.'

Barling did not know what he would do if this woman broke down. He looked in despair to Stanton for help.

In a stroke of good fortune, the door was opened by a man of about Barling's age, one who wore the fine robes of a wealthy man. He was in the middle of conversing with somebody else, stopping when his gaze lit on Barling and his assistant.

'May I help you?' His voice had the cultured tones of a man who had spent a large part of his life with the best books. Barling knew it well. His ash-coloured hair and smooth complexion gave him an extra nobility.

'It's the King's men, Master Ordway,' said the old woman. 'They want to see you.'

'Thank you, Hilde,' said Ordway. He stepped out to allow whoever was inside to leave. 'Good lady, if you will forgive me.'

'There is nothing to forgive, Gilbert.' The woman who came out would be Isabel Tyson, mistress to Hilde. She wore clothing even more luxurious than the physician, with a deep red cloak trimmed with the best fur over dark green skirts that made the rustle of heavy silk. She held an equally well-dressed, fragile-looking, pretty child by the hand. Though she shared the same age as Barling and the physician, the woman possessed a haughty, arresting beauty, her face framed in a white, silk coif secured with gold pins.

'Come to Hilde, chick.' The old woman embraced the child.

'The King's men?' Isabel looked Barling up and down, while giving a passing glance at Stanton.

'Good mistress, Master Ordway,' said Barling with a bow to the lady, then gave his and Stanton's introductions. 'I must apologise for our interruption. We seek an audience with Master Ordway on a private matter.'

'Of course.' Isabel gave the physician a charming smile. 'It appears that you are more sought after than ever, Gilbert.'

'Good lady.' He took her hand, which had a gold ring on each finger, and bent to kiss it, a blush warming her cheeks. 'It is an honour to be in your service.' He let go of her to brush a gentle palm across the child's hair. 'I will continue to do all I can for Lucia. I am sure it is only a matter of time before we have success.'

'I will continue to pray that we will.' Now Isabel's eyes glistened with tears. 'Thank you, Gilbert, from the bottom of my heart.'

As the women and child left, Ordway's look darkened. 'Always the most difficult when it's one so young. Especially tragic for a new widow.' He shook his head. 'Tragic.'

'A heavy responsibility indeed,' said Barling, while Stanton gave a sober nod.

'My apologies for my distraction.' Ordway indicated that Barling and Stanton should follow him inside. 'Please.'

Barling took in a large, comfortable room warmed by a large fireplace. The walls were lined with shelves that contained a huge array of stone jars bearing labels with Latin inscriptions and glass flasks of all manner of shapes. Rolls of manuscripts and piles of books were stacked neatly on yet more shelves. A large manuscript lay unfolded on a wide desk, the images drawn upon it showing the pattern of the stars in the heavens, with copious notes written against each one.

Ordway shut the door and looked at Barling. 'I would say, sir, given your pallor and demeanour, that your bloodletting is overdue.'

Stanton made a noise that sounded suspiciously like a suppressed laugh.

Barling stared at the physician. 'I am not ill, Master Ordway.'

'Then does your assistant require treatment? He looks in rude health to me.'

'We have not come to seek your services as a physician,' said Barling. 'We are here to enquire about a freestone mason that you treated last winter.'

'Last winter was extremely busy. Many people fell ill throughout the cold months with a fever and an ague. Dwellers of this city as well as pilgrims. I cannot remember them all. Why?' He frowned in puzzlement.

'This man's name was Peter Flocke,' said Barling. 'His wife said she obtained medicine from you, as he had been suffering from a bloody flux. She says he came here to demand some money back.'

Ordway's expression cleared. 'Then certainly I remember him. I did not treat him here, as his wife has told you. I helped her because she was desperate.'

'Helped?' asked Stanton, much to Barling's annoyance.

'Yes, helped,' said Ordway. 'I cured the fellow. Curing people costs money. As I am sure you will have found with the monks and their requests for offerings.' His lips lifted in a brief smile. 'But unlike the monks, I have many cures at my disposal, and they work.'

Much to Barling's relief, Stanton did not respond.

Ordway went on. 'Despite my having cured him, Flocke arrived here one evening, in a frightful temper. He would not listen to a word I said. He was aggressive and threatening and went away, or rather, was dragged away by his wife, only when I threatened to report him to Master Green.' He shook his head. 'A very rude fellow, indeed. What of him? Has he got the flux again? Though I am at a loss as to why the King's men would be involved in such an undertaking.'

'I am afraid Peter Flocke has been murdered, Master Ordway,' said Barling.

'Murdered, eh?' Ordway appeared unperturbed. 'I cannot say I am surprised. With a temper like his, he was bound to pick the wrong fight eventually.'

'It was no mere street brawl,' said Barling. 'It is an extremely delicate matter, and I need to be assured of your discretion.' He gave Ordway a brief account, including the pressure that the prior was under.

'I see.' Ordway nodded. 'Rest assured, I will not be spreading any word of this.' He gave his brief smile again. 'Physicians are the best keepers of secrets in the world. Now, you are sure I cannot bleed you, Barling? One should not neglect the maintenance of one's health.'

'Not right now,' said Barling. 'You have my thanks for your offer. I know where to find you if it is necessary. Come, Stanton.'

Ordway showed them out, but Stanton stopped before the physician could open the front door.

'Could I ask you about somebody else, Master Ordway?'

'Stanton, no.'

Stanton ignored Barling and carried on. 'A pilgrim called Robert Norwood. Very wild in both dress and behaviour. Did you treat him?'

Barling was silenced by Ordway's unexpected response.

'I have done,' said Ordway. 'He came to me first complaining of terrible pains in his head and a hand which had become twisted. He visited me repeatedly in a short time. I could see how much his condition was worsening and concluded that he did not have long to live. Yet he still held out hope. I tried everything until I refused to treat him any more.'

'Thank you, Master Ordway,' said Barling, with a fierce look at Stanton.

But his assistant had not finished. 'Why did you refuse to carry on?'

'Because Norwood told me that he was also getting treatment from a local herbalist, Margery Clement.' Ordway frowned. 'I cannot have my patients reject my expertise and resort to some withered old woman, with her potions and her poultices and the strange smells that come from her door. I have no trust whatsoever in that ignorant crone and her like. I told Norwood that he should not, either. She is not being so bold as to claim she has cured him, is she?'

'No,' said Barling. 'I am afraid Norwood is dead.'

'Ah.' Ordway gave a knowing smile. 'It is reassuring to see that the skill of the herbalist is as effective as ever.'

'Robert Norwood was murdered in the same way as Peter Flocke,' said Stanton.

Ordway's smile dropped.

'We have taken enough of your valuable time, Master Ordway.' Barling had to finish this encounter. If they did not, he, Barling, would be tempted to wring the headstrong Stanton's neck. 'We wish you good day.'

In truth, that temptation already presented itself.

He could only pray he did not act on it.

140

Chapter Twenty-Five

By all that was holy, Stanton had rarely seen Barling so angry with him. And in fairness, Stanton was almost as equally riled, arguing with the clerk as they threaded their way through the streets that had become even more crammed in the time they'd been with Ordway.

'Barling, we need to go and see the herbalist that Ordway mentioned, the woman called Margery Clement. She treated Robert Norwood.'

'No, we do not.' The clerk side-stepped and shot a vexed look at a passer-by carrying three brimming baskets without looking where she was going. 'We have been told – no, instructed – by the prior to keep this quiet.'

'Saints alive, Barling, you told Ordway all about Flocke!'

Barling was back at his side again. 'Master Gilbert Ordway is a physician. He is used to keeping the most sensitive of secrets. The old woman he spoke of will be far more expert with gossip than she is with her leaves and powders, you can be sure of it.'

'I'm beginning to wonder about your judgement on this case, Barling. Are you all right? After all, the great Ordway, whose opinion you value so highly, said that you looked pale and off.'

'I am perfectly well, Stanton, and less of your cheek. Do you hear me?'

'How many times have you told me that we need to have the complete story in order to find the truth?'

'That is still the case. But we have not had the arrival of his Grace to consider. Loose talk could reach his ears, and the consequences could be dreadful.'

'Two men are dead. Is that not dreadful enough?'

'It is. Of course it is.' Barling balled his small fists. 'But we face two enormous challenges this time, Stanton. Not just to solve the murders. But to contain this matter as far as we can. You must understand, Stanton, that matters of the court are as weighty as the direst of crimes.'

'Believe me, I know,' said Stanton. 'Only too well.'

'Explain yourself.'

Damn it all, he'd said too much. 'It's got nothing to do with you, Barling.'

'I see. When I want you to speak, you will not. But when I require your silence, you blather at will.'

Stanton gave a hoot of laughter that had no mirth. 'I'm glad your opinion of me is at new heights.'

'Opinions mean nothing. Facts are all.' The clerk glared at him. 'What I have to do now is escape the noise and bustle of these streets. I need to think clearly and look at what logical steps we should take, not just run off on a whim. Whims are no help.'

'Whatever you say, Barling.'

'And I then must report back to Prior Benedict. He was most distressed about the discovery of Norwood's body. Hopefully, he will be calmer by now.'

'So that's what you, Aelred Barling, are going to do?'

'Yes.'

'On your own?'

'Yes. It is my strength.'

'Then if that's the case,' said Stanton, 'I'm doing what I do best.'

142

'Which is?'

'I'm going for ale. And lots of it.' Stanton walked off without waiting for a response, refusing to answer Barling's calls.

A plague on the clerk. Let Barling fuss over his tablet and mop the prior's brow.

Stanton didn't care. It took him longer than he'd have liked to get back to the Roulf alehouse, having to force his way through the thick crowds with his pace slow as the worst dawdlers.

He sat down at a bench just inside the door, which was propped open as the day was so fine.

'Afternoon, flower.' Ida already had a cup and bread bun in her hand for him. 'There you go. You look like you need it.'

'I do. Thanks, Ida.'

'Call me when you're ready for another.' She was already off serving the next customer.

Stanton took a long, cold drink. And another. That was better. The knots in his shoulders started to lessen. He'd make it up with Barling later; he always did.

A figure on the crowded street outside caught his attention, a young woman in a snow-white linen hood, making her way along, stopping people to ask them questions.

Elena Whitehand. She was still halting people as she'd done with him and Barling earlier.

She was right outside the door of the inn now, and he could hear her questions, the same ones over and over again.

'Excuse me, I'm looking for my sister. Have you seen her? Her name is Sybil Whitehand. Have you seen her?'

Over and over, with folk laughing, mocking, rude or ignoring her every time.

Not as rude as Barling had been to her, though. He knew how that felt. Stanton dipped his bread in his drink to soften it. He should ask her to come and have an ale with him to say sorry.

He raised his voice. 'Elena!'

She looked his way, her face lighting with hope for a second before she saw who it was that had called her.

He beckoned to her, and she came inside. 'What is it, sir?'

'It's Hugo Stanton, not sir. And you look spent. An ale and a bite would do wonders for you.' He popped his bread in his mouth to prove his point.

'Thank you, Hugo Stanton. But I need to find my sister.'

'Then sit and talk to me. You can have an ale at the same time.'

'I don't want to talk. I want to do.'

'Believe me, talking to me will help. I promise. Have a seat. Please.'

Elena Whitehand was much too modest for his usual tastes. But her serious, dark blue gaze drew him in, in a way he couldn't explain.

It would be no hardship to talk to her for an hour or two. No hardship at all.

And he really did want to help her. If nothing else, it would annoy the daylights out of Barling.

Chapter Twenty-Six

Stanton called for two ales from Ida as Elena sat on the bench opposite him.

'Is your companion with you?' she asked.

'Aelred Barling?' Stanton drained the last of his current drink. 'No. The King's clerk doesn't approve of alehouses. They make him cross.'

'I am not an alehouse,' she said. 'But I also made him cross.'

He smiled at her reply but she didn't. 'Sorry about how he was with you,' said Stanton. 'He's like that with me as well. In fact, he's like that about most things.'

'Any luck, flower?' Ida asked the question of Elena while placing two ales and accompanying bread on the table.

'None, Ida.'

The alewife clicked her tongue.

'Ida knows my story,' said Elena to Stanton.

'Such a shame,' said the alewife. 'Me and John are still keeping an eye out.'

'Ida!'

A shout from a corner that Stanton recognised from last night.

Martin Eustace, the drunken lime burner with the scarred and burned flesh. Barling had said about talking to him at some point.

'A man could die of thirst, y'know,' came a slurred whine.

The alewife rolled her eyes. 'Fat chance of that, Martin.' She left to bring him more ale.

Eustace glared at Stanton. 'What are you staring at, boy?'

Stanton ignored him as was always wise in dealing with the truly ale-soaked. If Barling wanted to get sense out the man, let the clerk try to do it. Instead, he said to Elena, 'Then what is your story?'

'I told you a lot of it in the street this morning. I could tell neither you nor your companion were listening.'

'I was.'

'That wasn't meant as a barb. Most people do not listen. Or if they do, they do not care.'

'Let me see if I have this right,' said Stanton. 'Your sister's name is Sybil, and she's younger than you. Sybil came to Canterbury on pilgrimage with a group of strangers, but she's never come back, although the group did. You're here to get her, but you can't find her. Oh, and you're from the village of Harden in Kent.' He took a mouthful of ale. 'So yes, I listen. And I know the route to Harden from my days as a messenger. It's thirty miles west of here.' He waited for a compliment about his remarkable memory. He didn't get one.

'And what about you?' she asked. 'Why are you here?'

'I thought you wanted help,' said Stanton.

'I do,' she replied. 'But I want to know who I am getting help from. All I know about you, Hugo Stanton, is that you are kinder than your companion.'

Hugo Stanton. He liked the sound of his name in her soft voice. Liked the way her lips took a small sip of her ale before she carried on.

'I have met some people here who have appeared to be kind,' she said. 'It turns out they were not. Funnily enough, they have all been men.'

'Elena, I can only tell you that Barling is indeed a King's clerk and I am his assistant. We came here on pilgrimage, and we are also doing work on behalf of the prior of Christ Church.'

'What sort of work?'

An image of the look on Barling's face if Stanton said anything flashed before him. 'I honestly can't say. But what I can say is that I really want to help you and I bear you no ill.'

'You are asking me to trust you?'

'Yes, and you can.'

'You swear to me?'

'I swear to you.' Stanton took another drink. God's eyes. This woman's standing up to Barling in the street was no accident. She did not back down easily.

She nodded. 'Then help me. I don't know how you can, though. I've tried so many places. Asked so many people.'

'I think you need order in your enquiries.' By all the saints, he sounded like Barling.

'You mean start at one end of the city and work my way to the other, searching every street?' She gave him a withering look. 'I should be thanking the Virgin that I have the King's man to give me such advice, advice which I would never have thought of myself. I have already done that and continue to do it.'

'Then you will have missed something.' Barling again. Saints above, he should get his hair cut in a tonsure and have done with it. 'The only way to—'

He paused as Ida was back at the table with a steaming bowl of vegetable pottage.

'Have you broken your fast yet today?' she asked of Elena.

'No, I have not.' Elena gave the food a wistful look. 'I'm sorry, Ida,' she said, 'but I haven't got any money to pay for that.'

'Don't worry about that, flower.' Ida put the bowl on the table. 'Just make sure you keep your strength up.'

'I'll pay for it, Ida,' said Stanton. 'And one for me as well.'

'Won't be long.' With a quick squeeze of Elena's shoulder, Ida was off again.

'You should eat up.' Stanton's stomach growled as the smell of stewed onion and greens wafted over. He couldn't believe he'd forgotten to feed himself. Now he really was turning into Aelred Barling.

Elena picked up the spoon and took a cautious mouthful. 'Too hot.' She replaced the spoon and looked at Stanton. 'Go on.'

Where was he? Yes. Order. 'How old is Sybil?'

'Nineteen. Why?'

'You've said that Sybil came here alone on pilgrimage, with people she hardly knew. It seems an odd thing to do. She doesn't have a husband?'

'No. Neither of us is married. Father has not made a suitable choice for us yet.' For the first time, Elena looked unsure. 'You have said I can trust you?'

'Again, you can.'

'Sybil did not come to Canterbury by choice. She was ordered here by our parish priest. To make her penance for a sin she had committed.'

'There you go, good sir.' Ida placed Stanton's hot pottage in front of him and was gone before Stanton could thank her.

'Must've been a serious sin, especially for a woman of her age.' Stanton dug his spoon deep into his bowl, the vegetables thick with breadcrumbs. 'I'm surprised.' He took a large mouthful, not caring how hot it was. Ida's food was as good as her ale.

'If you knew my sister, you would not be.' Elena sighed. 'Sybil was born wayward. Even when she was little, she got herself into trouble the whole time. She delighted in doing what she shouldn't. My parents would chastise her hard. But she got away with much more than she should have. Her looks helped.' She tested her own meal once more and nodded to herself. 'She has the sort of beauty that makes people stare. And she knows it. Believe me, if it was Sybil who was stopping folk in the street, people would be happy to stop for her. She has the prettiest face and long, golden hair that she would always wear loose.'

This Sybil reminded him of Rosamund. His poor, dead Rosamund.

'You look sad,' said Elena abruptly.

Stanton did not trust himself to speak at that moment. Instead, he busied himself with his food, waiting for Elena to fill the silence.

She stayed quiet, her gaze fixed on him.

'Your description of your sister reminds me of someone, that's all,' he said. 'Go on.'

'But Sybil would gossip freely and often. For her own amusement, you understand, making up outlandish tales to entertain folk. Her audiences were the young people of our village, especially the boys. They found her coarse talk funny. Some of the girls did too, but many were jealous of her.' She took another mouthful of food.

'It doesn't sound as if she was trying to do any harm,' said Stanton.

'I think she saw the whole thing as a game, one she loved to play in the same way as the boys enjoyed playing with bows and arrows. Sybil's arrows were her clever words, landing on their target with accuracy and piercing it hard. If she'd noticed the sour looks and jealous mutters of the girls, she might have taken more care. But Sybil never takes care.' She ate again.

And neither did Rosamund. 'Some people are like that.'

'But then she went too far. Much too far. There's a woman in our village, Joan is her name, who strives to be held up as the most pious soul in the place. Mother and Father are virtuous, but Joan has always seen herself as halfway to heaven. She invokes saints with every sentence, fasts and prays harder than the priests and nuns. Her husband is a morose man who joins her in her sighing and praying.'

Like Barling's pilgrim hosts. 'Some people are like that as well.' His spoon scraped the bottom of the bowl that was empty too soon.

'The trouble was, Sybil loved to pretend to others that she was Joan. I saw it once. May God forgive me, when I saw Sybil turn her pretty mouth down like she tasted sour milk and roll her eyes up and sigh a gale, I could have been looking at Joan. Even I wanted to laugh, though it wouldn't have been heard in the cackles from those around me.'

Stanton smiled. 'Sounds like she could be merry company.'

'Some people think of her as so.' Elena finished her last spoonful. 'But unfortunately for Sybil, many do not. And on that particular occasion, a girl by the name of Lettie was there. Sybil called Lettie a ball of spite to me more than once, and I had to agree. Lettie always glowered at Sybil as if she wished her struck down. When Sybil started acting out lovemaking between Joan and a monk, Lettie saw her chance. She went straight to the parish priest and accused Sybil of slander, saying that Sybil was accusing the virtuous Joan of adultery with a monk.'

'I'd say your sister was right about that girl, Lettie. That was a very spiteful act.'

'It was,' said Elena. 'And it got Sybil in such dreadful trouble. The priest summoned my parents for censure, and they were so ashamed. For her sin, the priest sentenced Sybil to go to Canterbury three times, visiting the tomb of Saint Thomas in a penitential manner, and offer a candle each time. He ordered her to go without any delay. My parents wanted to take her but could not leave their work, so the priest arranged for her to go with a pilgrimage from another parish.'

'Then this was her first trip to Canterbury? Being sent here with strangers?'

'Yes. And she was furious. She had to wear a rough pilgrim's tunic, which she hated, and a full hood over her hair, which she hated even more.'

'Like yours?'

'Exactly like mine. Our mother sewed them for us, embroidered the name and the symbols of the Martyr on them.'

Stanton leaned forward. 'Let me see.' He'd no interest in the patterns of white thread on white linen. He just wanted to look closer at Elena's dark blue eyes and smooth skin.

Elena drew back. 'You are the first man I have met who is interested in whitework.' She cast him a severe look. 'Our mother made them for us to wear to make sure that we were as modest in our appearance as we could be. And to remind us to be as modest in our behaviour.'

Her meaning was plain.

'I meant no rudeness, Elena.' Stanton went back to his ale. 'Please, go on.'

'When word came that the pilgrimage had returned,' she said, 'Father went to fetch Sybil. But she was not with them. There had been, my father was told, a great deal of strife caused by Sybil amongst the pilgrims on the journey to Canterbury. She had received a lot of attention from the men, which made the women angry, and she complained about the slow pace, as she wanted to do her penance and go home. After a big argument, she had parted company with them on the approach to Canterbury.'

'Surely anything could have happened to her,' said Stanton. 'I spoke to a couple of pilgrims who were scared to death about the number of robbers on the road.'

'But she did make it safely to Canterbury, Hugo. A few of the women on the pilgrimage met her when they were coming from making an offering at the cathedral. She told them that she'd been taken in by a charitable house, where she'd been made welcome, unlike by their bitter faces.'

Stanton frowned. 'A charitable house could be any house in Canterbury.'

She nodded. 'I know. As I say, I've tried them all. A few, like Ida and John's here, have tried to help. Even some of those that had whores staying in them. Others cursed me out or asked for money to answer me or slammed the door in my face. Most simply did not care and had no interest.'

'Then maybe she came to harm on the road home,' said Stanton. 'Especially if she tried to travel back alone.'

'You do think things through, don't you?' Elena gave him an approving nod. 'But I had thought of that. I journeyed here with a quiet, aged priest, so I had plenty of opportunity along the way to ask about her. One innkeeper remembers Sybil from the journey as there was so much strife and noise with that group of pilgrims. He was adamant that Sybil had not come back that way.'

'Then you think she's still here?'

'I do. But it feels as if I am in a cloud of buzzing flies and trying to count them. Every one changes by the minute. New face, after face, after face.'

'That's a very good way of describing it. What else are you going to try?'

A small flush crept into her cheeks. 'There is something that may help that I did not know about until today.' Her definite gaze slid from his.

'Like what?'

'Like somebody who can find lost things.' She still wouldn't meet his eye.

'Such as?'

'A necromancer.'

'A necromancer?' It came out louder than he meant it to.

'Keep your voice down.' She glared at him.

'I'm not sure that's a good idea. At all.' He shook his head. 'How did you come across such a person?'

'He is an exorcist. I encountered him by the cathedral, where he was offering to banish the evil spirits of pilgrims. His name is Nicholas Clement.'

Stanton sat up straight. The second mention of the name Clement in as many hours. 'I know of a herbalist called Margery Clement.'

For the first time, she looked impressed. 'Perhaps you do find things out. Margery is aunt to Nicholas. He practises in secret as a necromancer. He told me so himself. He has the skill to summon demons to find lost things.'

'Elena, that's dangerous. Really dangerous.'

'I know. But I have no choice. I am going to see him tonight.'

'Then at least let me come with you.' He could use it as cover to talk to the herbalist. If Barling was angry, so be it.

And it was an excellent excuse to spend more hours with Elena Whitehand.

Chapter Twenty-Seven

Barling approached the prior's chambers, where he knew Benedict awaited him.

He dreaded having to meet with the anxious prior when he himself was in such turmoil. While the fierce disagreement he had had with Stanton had agitated him beyond measure, it was not the only reason for his profound state of unease.

For Barling could not ignore the appalling sensation that, once again, a murderer was on the loose and he was powerless to stop them, a terrible dream from which he could not awake.

Dear God, he'd missed so much last winter, when he had tried to find the killer at Fairmore Abbey. Missed it and almost lost his life in the process.

Worse, he continued to bear the burden of sin, a burden that he had come here to rid himself of. Was God punishing him by adding to its weight at a time when he feared he might break?

He entered the antechamber, knocked on the door of the prior's solar and entered at his order.

The usually tidy long table was covered with piles of papers and pipe rolls but the prior was not seated before them. Instead, he paced the floor, his sweaty and flustered appearance suggesting that he had been engaged in the activity for some time.

'Prior Benedict,' Barling began.

'Finally, you show yourself.' The prior halted. 'Finally! I am supposed to be conducting an urgent review of the spiralling building costs for the Archbishop. But who could concentrate on records of stone and plaster and wages when there is a killer on the loose? I have been waiting and waiting for you to come and explain to me just what is going on. Your tardiness has put me more behind than ever.'

Barling attempted an apology but the prior spoke over him.

'You, who my lord de Glanville announced as a miracle, are turning into a plague. Things may have been bad before you arrived, but they have become significantly worse. I have been considering in earnest whether to order you from Canterbury and resume these enquiries myself. I might as well, for all the good you are.'

Barling's heart almost stopped in his chest at the prior's words. If he were to be sent away from Canterbury, he would be denied his penance. 'Prior, I offer my abject apologies at not having found the murderer of Peter Flocke. But if you will allow me—'

'Nor the murderer of Robert Norwood.'

'Indeed, Prior. It is the greatest of tragedies and to my sorrow that we have two murders now.' Barling fought for calm in his panic that he might say the wrong thing, use the wrong words. Such an utterance would see him banished from here, no question. If Stanton were here, he would choose the right ones, talk the prior round. Barling had few such skills, and he was alone. All he could do was tell the truth as he saw it. 'Yet, in a strange way' – he swallowed hard – 'that may make it easier to find the killer.'

'Have you gone quite mad, Barling? You are actually saying to my face that two murders are easier to solve than one?'

'Perhaps easier was the wrong word, Prior. But . . . but there will be links between the two.' Barling willed the confidence back into his voice, though it had been many years since he had felt its lack so keenly. 'They have been done by the same hand and in the same brutal manner. Where there are links between murders, there are inevitably links to the murderer. A pattern draws the eye more than a simple line. I will be working every minute of every hour to make sure that those patterns are revealed, I promise you.'

To Barling's perturbation, the prior laughed long, his mirth dry and humourless. 'Oh, the wisdom of de Glanville's man.' He resumed his pacing, back and forth, back and forth. 'Has it ever occurred to you, Barling, that no matter how many hours one applies oneself to something, one may never achieve what one is supposed to? I spend all of my waking hours, and many when I should be sleeping, trying to ensure that our choir is rebuilt.'

Barling dared not interrupt the man's tirade, could only grasp at the slimmest hope that the prior's unhappiness was no longer being directed at him.

'And yet, Barling, from every mouth, every voice, I am told that it is too slow.' He grabbed a note from the table and shook it at Barling. 'Too expensive. Too . . . too everything that is wrong, and everything that is wrong is my fault.' The prior stopped dead and sat down hard on a nearby chair. 'My fault. All of it.' His breath came in loud gulps.

Barling waited a few moments, the better to judge that the torrent of words from the prior had ceased for now. 'I am sure that is what it must feel like, Prior.' He kept his tone as low and respectful as he could. 'When one is in a position of authority, when one has to carry the problems of all and get few, if any, accolades for it. That is why it takes a special sort of man to assume that position.'

'And what if one is not that?' Benedict flung a hand up.

'I beg your pardon, Prior?'

'What if one has to carry the weight of high office knowing that one is not a special sort of man, but rather a compromise?'

'I do not follow you, Prior Benedict.'

'Our last prior was removed two years ago,' said Benedict. 'There were strongly differing opinions about who should replace him. The monks favoured one man; Archbishop Richard favoured another. I was a favourite of nobody so was judged to be suitable. As it turns out, I am a disappointment to everybody. I am acutely aware that it would suit all parties for me to be removed. The failure to solve these murders would provide an ideal and convenient excuse.'

'I am not sure that being a favourite is the only thing that matters. My sincere opinion is that your hard work will provide an excellent reason for you to stay as prior.'

'Hard work?' The prior snorted. 'Hard work can count for nothing, Barling. I was working without cease to report and record all of the miracles after the death of Saint Thomas. Yet that task was taken from me as well.'

Barling nodded. He recalled Brother William's words to him when they toured the tomb: *For Benedict was overcome by the flood of miracles. He simply could not cope with the number, nor the relentlessness of the reporting.*

But Benedict went on. 'Taken from me for no other reason than that another style of reporting of the miracles was preferred.'

Barling's shoulders stiffened. This was a very different version of events. 'Do you mean Brother William's style, by any chance?'

'Yes, I do. I tried to be accurate, Barling. To recount the miracles as best I could. But William? He likes to embellish. To add. To . . .'

'Lie?' asked Barling.

'Yes. No. Not lie. But to add to the truth until, I fear, it becomes meaningless.'

'Yet you said he was judged to be better than you?'

'Yes, he was. And that is the part that I do not understand.' His voice rose. 'It is as if people would prefer to believe in falsehood, in an elaborate embellishment rather than a plain, simple fact.' He gave a long, juddering sigh, his voice dropping. 'They care not who they cast aside in the process.' His gaze hardened.

157

He wore the same distanced expression that Barling had witnessed yesterday when they had been high up in the choir. Most odd, but his words gave Barling his chance. 'Then, Prior, as one who understands the pain of being cast aside when one is striving with every sinew to complete a task, I would humbly implore you: please, do not cast me aside.'

'What?' The prior looked at him as one awoken from sleep.

'I would ask, Prior, with my deepest respect, that you permit me to continue with this enquiry.'

'I don't know, Barling.' The prior chewed on his lip. 'I really don't know.'

Barling did not dare to further interrupt the prior at this most delicate moment. All he could do was offer up one of the most fervent prayers of his life, one that would allow him to remain.

'It pains me to say it,' said Benedict. 'But you will have to continue. The arrival of his Grace is now but two days away.' He gave a weary look at the piles of records on the table. 'And I have this to complete. If I had one spare hour, you would be gone from here. Do you understand?'

'Yes, Prior.' Barling gave a deep bow, though he feared his knees might give way with relief that he was staying. 'I give you my sincere thanks for your putting your trust in me.'

The prior waved him away, and Barling did not pause lest this volatile man change his mind again.

More than ever, Barling needed time with his stylus and his tablet. He needed to think.

Chapter Twenty-Eight

'I am afraid Nicholas is not back yet.'

Stanton could make out little through the crack in the open door, bar the glint of one sharp, grey eye. The voice that addressed him and Elena was that of an elderly woman, whom he assumed to be the herbalist, Margery Clement. She sounded unhappy at the idea of opening her door fully to two unannounced strangers at this hour after sunset.

Stanton didn't blame her. He and Elena had passed through Newingate and down dark, dank alleyways to get here. The bearing of the folk who walked the streets made him be sure to step to one side and keep a close eye on his purse. Beggars had called to him from the shadows with little respect. He'd kept a close eye on Elena too, but she didn't quail at anything, not even at a man who'd decided to empty his bowels on the street in front of them.

'My name is Elena Whitehand, mistress,' she said. 'Nicholas may have mentioned me. He told me I could find him here. He said that he could help me.'

'As I said, he is not back. You will have to try another time. Better still, go and look for him outside the cathedral. He is there every day, from early until late.' She went to close the door, but Elena grabbed the handle to prevent her.

'Mistress Clement,' said Elena, 'your nephew said that he could help me in a particular way. His own skilled way.'

A pause.

'Then you'd better come in.' Margery opened the door wide for them to enter. She was as aged as Stanton had guessed, with a frail frame and snow-white hair under her coif.

'My companion's name is Hugo Stanton,' said Elena. 'He is helping me in the matter I wish to consult Nicholas about.'

Elena reminded him a bit of Barling. She didn't bother with trying to put people at their ease.

'Thank you for inviting us in, Mistress Clement,' said Stanton. 'It's very cold standing out there in the street.' Truth be told, it wasn't much warmer in the small, cramped room, with the poor hearth giving out smoke but little in the way of light or heat.

His gaze swept over the bunches of drying herbs, leaves and foliage that hung from each of the blackened beams. Their scents – sweet, pungent, sharp and strange – filled the smoky air so thickly it was as if he could taste them. Like with Ordway's room, pots and jars lined sets of shelves. But unlike the physician's, the containers were cruder in design and piled one on another in an untidy jumble. They bore no Latin inscriptions, either. Instead, a messy hand had marked them with a number of symbols and words he couldn't make out.

Margery looked askance at Elena. 'Have I seen you before, miss?'

'I came to your door last week. I wanted to ask you about my sister.'

'Ah.' Margery's expression cleared. 'She was missing, am I correct in my memory?'

'You are,' said Elena.

'I thought so,' said Margery. 'But I couldn't be sure. I treat many people, all day, every day. Have done for over forty years. I remember a rash or wound far more easily than I do the appearance of a person.'

'The noblest work.' Stanton had had a rash or two in his time. 'No wonder you need so many herbs. You must have treated most of the souls in Canterbury by now.'

'My work is mostly with the pilgrims, sir.'

'Not the townsfolk?'

Margery hesitated. 'A few.'

'I met a man called Robert Norwood the other day,' said Stanton. Elena frowned at Stanton in confusion, but he carried on. 'Norwood was a pilgrim, wasn't he?'

'Yes, he was, sir,' replied Margery. Uneasy.

'When did you last treat him?'

'How did you know I was treating him, sir?'

'The physician, Gilbert Ordway, told me.'

Margery's eyes narrowed. 'Why was he—'

The door clattered open, and Margery started with a stifled cry.

'Hell's teeth, it's only me, Aunt.' The man who'd entered took in the visitors in a swift glance. Dressed in grubby white robes, Nicholas Clement was fine-boned like his aunt and not much taller. He had her piercing grey eyes as well, and, to Stanton's surprise, given that he was barely into his third decade, the man's hair was almost as white as that of the old woman.

'Elena,' he said. 'You have come as you promised.'

Stanton didn't like the way the man used Elena's name so easily. He also didn't like the smile he gave her.

Nicholas moved his gaze to Stanton. 'And I don't know who you are.'

No 'sir'. Normally, Stanton wouldn't care, but this man had an air about him that rankled.

'My name is Hugo Stanton. I am in Canterbury on the King's errand.' Now he would get a 'sir'. But he didn't.

'So many people come to me,' said Nicholas. 'Even the mightiest. But I must ask you to leave and to come back another time. I have arranged to see Elena this evening.'

'Hugo is with me,' said Elena. 'I asked him to come.'

'You should have checked with me first,' said Nicholas. 'Our business on this occasion is private. We discussed that in detail.'

'I have already told Hugo why I am here,' said Elena.

'Oh, miss,' gasped Margery. 'We do not want any loose talk about what Nicholas does.'

'No, we don't,' said Nicholas. 'I told you what the conditions of my helping you must be.'

'I know how to keep my tongue quiet,' said Stanton. 'And my being here tonight is nothing to do with the King.' He hoped he hid his untruth well enough as Nicholas stared at him.

'Very well,' said Nicholas after a long moment. 'Elena, we can proceed with your conjuration, as agreed. But exactly as we agreed. The art of necromancy requires the total concentration of my mind and soul. There cannot be any interruption, or the demons will be frightened away.'

Elena nodded. 'I do not want to put this off any longer. It is far too important.'

'If you stay, Stanton, you cannot become involved,' said Nicholas. 'No matter what happens. I must have your word on that.'

'I understand, and I promise.' Stanton would honour that. He would not leave Elena alone here for a bag of gold coins.

'Then I would ask you to move to one side. Aunt, the door, please.'

Both did as directed by Nicholas, Margery with unsteady hands and Stanton with a glance to Elena. She did not return it, as all of her attention was on Nicholas.

The necromancer went to a chest, from which he took out a number of objects and placed them on the solitary table.

A long beeswax candle and four short, wide ones. An elaborately carved bowl made of dark wood that had a spoon to match. A small woven bag, with an unfamiliar symbol embroidered on the front. A square of parchment.

And last, an object that caused Stanton's heart to near leave his chest: a long, slim knife with a bone handle, the blade tapering to the finest point.

'Now.' Nicholas picked it up and smiled at Elena. 'I think it's time you found Sybil.'

Chapter Twenty-Nine

Barling needed to think. To write.

He did not believe himself to be in a fit state to do either in any coherent form.

He'd returned to his room at the inn, his whole body weak and shaky. He would be the first to admit that this happened on many fast days. He took particular pride in forgoing food all day if he had the opportunity. But though nothing had passed his lips today, his weakness was not from hunger but from fear.

Fear that Prior Benedict would act on his word and send Barling from Canterbury.

It mattered not that he had escaped the threat, at least for now. When he had been with the prior earlier, he had sincerely believed that the axe was about to fall. It had not, but his body still quaked from his anticipation of the bad news.

The innkeeper Derfield had left a jug of water and a cup on his table.

It would probably be a good idea to drink some. He poured it with unsteady hands and took a long draught. It helped a little.

He must remember too that his fierce argument in the street with Stanton had discomfited him greatly before he'd even gone near the prior.

Emotion, always emotion. His favourite criticism of those who allowed it to cloud their judgement. He took another soothing drink. It would serve him well to follow his own advice. He put the cup down and held out his hands in front of him. Barely a tremor left. Good.

Barling could not permit the prior's panic to seep into his work. He must use his usual order and method. He drew his notes and tablet towards him and selected a fresh stylus.

He reviewed his compilation. What he had written last night had been taken from Stanton's drunken ramblings. Barling tutted to himself, not at the recording, of which he had made a great success, but at his assistant's lax behaviour, behaviour he was no doubt engaging in all over again at that very moment.

Barling set the thought aside. He would not allow fresh irritation at Stanton to get in the way of this vital work. Work which was as much thought as writing.

With a heavy heart, Barling wrote a brand-new entry.

Robert Norwood - pilgrim. Family and home unknown. Murdered in the same manner as Peter Flocke. Sacrilege. Brother William found body near fishpond.

Then he turned to his existing notes, relieved that he had taken the time to update them after Stanton had gone to bed, even if it had cost him his own hours of rest. A record should always be made as soon as possible. Otherwise, important information could be missed.

Peter Flocke. The dead man. A skilled mason. A savage murder. The mutilation of his flesh. The holy Cross. Sacrilege. Leaves a widow, Katerine - not yet seen.

Barling crossed out the last three words. He and Stanton had indeed seen Katerine Flocke this morning. Then he steeled himself to make another alteration. He crossed out the word 'The' and inserted 'First'. *First dead man.*

From Adam Drake: Flocke's body was exactly as Prior Benedict had described. Flocke especially talented. Bad blood between Lambert Green and Peter Flocke.

Barling added the information he had gleaned from Katerine to the notes on Peter Flocke. *Sick last winter. Bloody flux. Wife went to tomb. Then to physician, Gilbert Ordway. Had argument with physician over payment.*

Then he went to the separate entry for Katerine. It was sparse up to now.

From Adam Drake: She was a good wife to Flocke. A good worker too. Flocke was lucky to have her.

His addition was not much. Talking to her supported what Drake had said. Katerine had done all she could when her husband became unwell.

Mason's servant. Ill-educated. Grieves for her husband.

Next to Lambert Green's entry. The very opposite of sparse.

Lambert Green. Second master mason. Master to Flocke. Acknowledged Flocke's great skill. Master to Katerine Flocke and Adam Drake. Disobeys the orders of Prior Benedict. From Adam Drake: Bad blood between Green and Flocke. Sacked Martin Eustace, ex-mason and now lime burner. Eustace bears grudge. Need to question.

Barling extended the notes with Katerine Flocke's view.

Peter Flocke did not argue with Lambert Green.

He underlined the word 'not'. An important difference.

Barling had nothing new to add about Adam Drake.

Adam Drake. Roughmason. Found the body of Peter Flocke – when returning to lodge for purse. Nervous. Scared of Lambert Green.

That concluded the additions for the cathedral builders. Dread fluttered through him. He was not seeing anything of significance. He fought the feeling down. He still had not completed his task. Order, he must have order. Next, he turned to the monks.

Prior Benedict. In charge of the new choir. (Peter Flocke carved stone for it.) A man who mourns the old choir. A man who has been raised to heights beyond his skills. Overwhelmed by tasks. Used to record miracles at tomb.

To this he added: *A compromise appointment. Can never work hard enough. Brother William replaced him in recording miracles at the tomb.*

Now to Brother William.

Brother William. Skilled with pen. Illuminations inspired by the work of Flocke. Records miracles at tomb.

Barling wrote his latest addition.

Brother William found body of Robert Norwood. Knows him from the tomb – 3 yrs. Does not know his sin. Replaced Prior Benedict in recording miracles.

Then he added another new name and entry.

Gilbert Ordway. Physician. Treated Peter Flocke through his wife, Katerine. Peter Flocke angry about cost. Treated Robert Norwood. Refused to carry on after Norwood went to herbalist Margery Clement.

A memory stirred.

Gilbert Ordway's words: *But unlike the monks, I have many cures at my disposal, and they work.*

The complete opposite to what Brother William had said to Barling at the tomb yesterday about physicians. *Useless, every one of them. Filling people's bodies with potions and medicines and their heads with false hope.*

Barling sighed and added a note to both entries to reflect their disparaging of the other's approach.

His updating was done.

He scanned his notes, waiting for a word, a phrase, a connection to jump out at him. The pattern that he had assured the prior would emerge. But he could see nothing. Nothing at all. Many grievances, arguments, bad feelings. Disparagements. He was failing. He could not deny it, not to himself.

His eyes went to the pilgrim badge that Stanton had left on the table. The tomb of Saint Thomas depicted on it seemed to mock him.

Barling's worry sprang to life again. He would never get to make his proper penance there, never find—

And then it hit him. Worry.

Every person on that list who was still alive had worries and fears that they talked about freely. Where things had gone wrong, so badly wrong. Were still going wrong. Except one.

Barling went back through the list.

One who stood out as going from strength to strength without any obstacle whatsoever. And not just without obstacle: by active intervention.

Brother William. The Irish monk had taken over the recording of miracles from Benedict by use of embellishment. He reigned over the tomb. He loved the scale of the new choir, praising it while having no responsibility for the onerous, complex work of ensuring its completion, leaving that squarely in the hands of Prior Benedict. Benedict, a disappointment to everyone, even by his own admission. It was only a matter of time before the prior was replaced. The more things that went wrong, the quicker that would be. Killing a skilled stonemason would aid that. And William had admitted to knowing Flocke's work. The monk knew how good he was, what a loss he would be. As for Robert Norwood, it was painfully obvious from Barling's examination of the man's body that there had been no cure. William valued the cures at the tomb to enhance his own reputation.

A reputation that could see him all the way to the exalted office of prior of Christ Church, Canterbury.

Chapter Thirty

The knife, he had to reach for the knife.

Stanton readied to launch himself at the necromancer. But before he could do so, Nicholas picked up the candle in his other hand. He began to use the blade to carve a row of symbols and markings into the wax.

Stanton heaved a huge sigh of relief, hoping that nobody had noticed his readiness to lunge for Nicholas. They didn't appear to have done so.

Elena had her full attention on Nicholas as he set his aunt a task.

'Light the taper, please.' He replaced the knife on the table. 'And then extinguish all the house lamps.'

Margery worked in silent efficiency, and the room dimmed. Before she put the last of the horn-covered lamps out, Nicholas lit the large, carved candle and placed it in the middle of the floor. He stood over it with his hands extended, uttering words that might have been a prayer, but Stanton did not understand their meaning.

The solitary flame lit the necromancer's face from below, the shadows giving him the look of one of the strange creatures that Stanton had seen on the cathedral carvings.

Nicholas concluded his chant, then went to the table, where he scooped some of the contents of the little sack into the bowl. Against the dark wood of the container, the white crystals of salt showed clearly. He brought the bowl back to the middle of the room and walked around the candle, sprinkling the salt in a large, smooth circle, muttering another string of strange words.

'Aunt, the candles.'

Margery passed the four shorter candles to him, and he lit them one by one, each lighting given its own incantation. He placed them at regular intervals on the circle. He finished, then he stood as before with his arms out, his focus back on the central candle.

Stanton glanced at Elena. Her gaze on the necromancer was rapt.

Nicholas returned to the table and picked up the knife.

Stanton's heart protested once more. He should do something, he should stop this. But if he spoiled Elena's chance to find her sister, she would never speak to him again. All he could do was watch, watch closer than a cat at a mouse hole. If harm was about to come to Elena, he was ready.

Nicholas looked at Elena. 'Come, my child,' he commanded in a voice that was now deeper. Older.

Stanton swallowed hard. *Like somebody else's.*

Elena went over to the necromancer, as ordered.

'Give me your hand,' he said.

Stanton fought the urge to yell and pull her away. Then he saw the look in her eye as she extended her steady hand. Wary. He marvelled at her quiet strength. She would not be surprised by Nicholas: she was ready for any attack.

It did not come. But a horrible suggestion did.

'Elena.' Again, the deep voice that was not Nicholas's. 'I need your blood.'

'No.' Her reply came soft but sure.

'Elena.' More insistent. 'This is not the blood of harm. This is the blood that bonds you to your sister. Your shedding of it will be as easy as the falling of teardrops. Any pain will pass quickly.'

171

'Then do it.' Still no tremor from her in either voice or hand.

Nicholas grasped her palm. Then he raised the knife and pierced the tip of one of her fingers. Hard.

She bit down on her lip yet made no sound.

'That cut will suffice,' said the necromancer. He picked up the square of parchment and held it under her finger, squeezing her flesh so that the blood drip, drip, dripped onto the parchment, staining it in a growing circle.

Nicholas released her and replaced the knife on the table. 'You may step away.' Then he went into the salt circle and held the bloodied parchment over the large candle.

First the parchment blackened, the blood disappearing in the heat, then smouldered, and finally burst into flame.

But Nicholas did not drop it.

Stanton's mouth opened in awe as the necromancer held the burning parchment in his hands as if it were cold. He threw it into the air, and it turned to ashes, the pieces falling to the floor.

'It is done!' Nicholas cried out in his normal voice and staggered back.

Margery rushed to his side to steady him. 'My boy, my boy,' she said. 'Please tell me you are unharmed.'

'I am fine; let go of me.' He pushed her off. 'It is done,' he said, quieter.

Elena looked at him, disquiet in her deep blue eyes. 'Then where is she? Where is Sybil?'

The necromancer pointed to the ashes on the floor. They lay in one definite part of the circle.

'There. The spirits have told me that she is to be found to the west.'

Elena frowned. 'I do not understand. To the west of where?'

'Where is your village?' said Nicholas.

'Harden, in Kent,' she said.

172

'But where is it in relation to Canterbury?' said Nicholas.

West. Stanton thought it even as Elena said the word. 'West. Then she is home?'

'I do not know,' said Nicholas. 'I only know what the spirits tell me.' He wiped the hand across his face. 'They use me as a conduit. That is all.' His arrogance had left him, and he looked utterly spent.

'I see.' Elena opened the purse that hung from her belt and counted out a number of coins, more than Stanton expected. 'That is the price we agreed,' she said.

'It is.' Nicholas took them from her. 'The conjuration tonight was powerful. I think it is worth trying again. We may get further revelations.'

'I want to first act on the information you have given me.' She looked next to Stanton. 'It is time to go.'

'Let me get the door.' Margery went over to unlock it.

'Now that Elena's business is concluded,' said Stanton, 'may I ask you and Nicholas something?'

'Certainly, sir,' Margery said.

Nicholas didn't say anything.

'I wonder if either of you knew a man by the name of Peter Flocke?'

'Is that the stonemason who was murdered?' said Nicholas.

'That is he,' said Stanton. 'How do you know him?'

'I do not,' said Nicholas. 'But I have heard about the murder. There is much gossip about it at the cathedral.'

'I have never met the man, sir,' said Margery.

'Thank you,' said Stanton.

'Are you ready to leave?' said Elena to him, and he nodded.

Margery got the door open, and they went outside.

Stanton took a deep lungful of fresh air. Well, fresh as the alleyway could be, but certainly better than the herbalist's stuffy house.

They had gone fewer than half a dozen yards when Nicholas called Stanton back to the door.

'A moment, if I may,' he said to Stanton. 'I didn't want to say too much in front of Elena. But I think I can help you.'

'Help me? How?'

'I could summon Peter Flocke, the murdered man.'

His words drove the breath from Stanton's body. 'Summon the dead? Have I heard you right?'

'You have. My payment is high as it will put my own body and soul in jeopardy. Summoning the dead is a perilous act.'

'You really can bring somebody back?'

Nicholas nodded. 'For a short while, at least.'

'Anybody? You can bring back anybody?' His voice shook as he asked the next question. 'Man or...or woman?'

'If they are willing to be brought back, yes. The vast majority are.'

The joy that rushed through Stanton threatened to fell him. 'Then I'll come back tomorrow night.'

'Hugo!' called Elena. 'It's getting late. I am leaving, even if you are not.'

'I have to go,' said Stanton to Nicholas. 'I'll see you tomorrow night.'

'Come at sunset,' said Nicholas. 'For this conjuration, you must be completely alone. You cannot bring anybody with you, nor can you tell anybody. Do you understand?'

'I do.'

'Good night, Hugo.' Elena was walking off.

'Tomorrow night,' said Stanton to Nicholas for the last time.

Then he ran off after Elena.

Chapter Thirty-One

'Slow down, Elena.' Stanton caught her up, but she didn't slow her rapid pace. 'Unless you're trying to get rid of me.' He meant it as a jest.

'I would be very happy to be rid of you.'

'What do you mean?'

'Do you think I am slow in my wits?' She stopped dead.

Stanton halted too, bewildered.

'You have been using me for your own ends. Whatever they are, because you won't tell me.'

'No, I can't. But yes, I really want to help you.'

'Funny way of showing it. You did not ask a single question about Sybil. It was all about some sick pilgrim and a dead stonemason.'

'No, honestly. I want to help you because I like you.'

'You like me? Oh, I am honoured.' She gave an exaggerated bow. 'Sir.'

'Look, I will continue to help you. I really will. But I have to be careful. My friend Barling doesn't want us distracted. He's under a lot of pressure.'

'Your friend? He's more like your master, isn't he? All I saw was him giving you orders.'

Stanton opened his mouth to object. But she was right. Barling had once been his closest friend. But in the months since Fairmore, the clerk had moved away. 'He was my friend and that saddens me.' He tried to smile. 'Sorry. I'm not usually this soft.'

Elena shook her head. 'I suspect you are.'

'You don't know me.'

'I do not have to. So much is written on your face, Hugo Stanton. Like tonight, when Nicholas Clement was doing his conjuration. You were impressed with what he did, weren't you?'

'Yes. He gave you important information. That Sybil was at home.'

'He told me she was west. That is not at all the same thing. But I saw you grab on to that word and saw you so pleased to do it.'

Now she was being as hard as Barling could be. 'Maybe I jumped ahead a bit too fast,' he said. 'You might not believe this, but I can keep things hidden when I need to. And I'm sorry if you think I've been using you. It's God's own truth when I say that Barling and I have been given an impossible task, and I'm trying to do what I can.'

'I believe you are like all the others I tried to ask for help who refused me. The only difference is that they were honest with me and you are not.'

'I have been honest,' he said.

'Then what were all those questions about?'

'I can't say.'

'You mean you will not say,' she said. 'That is the true answer. Then answer me this: did any of your questions relate to Sybil?'

He wished to the depths of his boots he could explain more. If he were able to do so, perhaps she would understand. But he couldn't. 'No. They didn't.'

'At least we are clear.' She looked at him with contempt. 'I hope I served my purpose well.' She strode away, and he followed her.

'Elena, let me see you back to your inn. It's very late.'

She wouldn't look at him. 'I have managed by myself over the last couple of weeks. I can continue to do so.'

'I don't want anything to happen to you.' To his surprise, he meant it, no matter how hard on him she was being.

'Goodbye, Hugo Stanton.' She raised a hand, still looking straight ahead as she marched on.

By Saint Peter of Rome, she could be stubborn. Yet he knew he would never forgive himself if any harm befell her tonight. That she was out this late was in part down to him. With a muttered oath to himself, he set off after her, making sure he kept to the shadows so she wouldn't see him. But she strode on without a glance back.

To his relief, she made her way through the streets and alleys without incident, arriving at a cheap but clean-looking inn near Westgate, where the door was answered to allow her inside at her first knock. After a few minutes, her outline appeared at a candle-lit, half-open window, and she pulled it closed for the night. She was safe inside.

All seemed quiet when Stanton got back to his own inn as well.

He made his way up the creaky stairs. He could see light under the door of Barling's room, which meant the clerk was awake. He fully expected an irate Barling to spring out like a spider when a fly's feet meet its web.

But no.

Stanton thought about knocking, to relate the happenings since he'd left Barling earlier, but he dismissed it and went straight into his own room. He didn't want another tongue-lashing tonight. Elena's harsh words had been more than enough. Barling would be livid that he had gone to Margery Clement's house. The clerk would probably set about him with his pilgrim's staff if he knew that Stanton was returning there to seek a necromancer's help in summoning the dead Peter Flocke.

And help in calling back one other.

The joy he'd felt when the realisation had struck him flooded through him again.

Tomorrow night, this time tomorrow.

Just one more day.

Stanton would speak to his Rosamund again.

Chapter Thirty-Two

Elena Whitehand sat on her small, narrow bed, pulling her horn comb through her thick hair with hard, repeated strokes.

It was an action that had served her well for most of her life.

Mother and Father did not approve of anger. Temper. Wrath. All were forbidden, as was disobedience of any kind. If she ever displayed such vices, even in the most minor way, Elena would get the switch across her knuckles, knees and backside when she was little. Across her shoulders when she was older.

It mattered not if she thought she was in the right: Mother and Father were the judges of that and found her wanting every time.

She brought the comb up for another pass. The sharpness of the teeth pricked her scalp as she dug it in, then hauled it down her long strands of hair. She pulled out a few as the comb met tangles, but she did not wince. The controlled pain of her own act was what she sought. It gave substance to the anger that raced through her.

The anger of the humiliated.

She could hear Mother's voice as clearly as if she stood over her.

Stay away from young men, Elena. If you inflame their lust, you will be the greater sinner. Their carnal desires are caused only by an absence of virtue.

But she had never inflamed lust. She had thought for a long time that it was because of her parents' insistence on modesty. On the tight hoods over her hair. On her low voice. On her devotion to duty, no matter how unpleasant the task. One day, a man would come along who saw her true worth. And that man would desire her.

Yet any man who looked at her twice stopped and never looked at her again the second he laid eyes on Sybil.

Elena yanked her comb through her hair once more.

Sybil, with her hair that was a cascade of gold tresses. Sybil, with her laughing eyes and knowing looks. Her lips that always glistened. That promised men everything. A few, a lucky few, got to find out what that was. The others would live in hope, pursuing Sybil as hotly as the village dogs did when a bitch came on heat, while she, Elena, tried to keep her sister from harm, just as she'd had to do from the day Sybil was born.

Tried and failed, because nobody could contain Sybil's wildness.

After it all came out about Sybil's slander, Mother and Father's switch had not only landed on Sybil's body, over and over. Elena had been beaten as badly. And while Sybil had wept bitter tears after her beating, wept more the night she'd received the order to go on pilgrimage, Elena had remained dry-eyed, bringing out her comb as usual to soothe the hurt. Neither had she cried the day Sybil went away to Canterbury.

For so many years, Elena had wanted to go on pilgrimage there. The thought of the journey, of the busy streets, filled her with trepidation. But excitement too. She'd heard from others in their village about the size of the city, the huge cathedral. The wonder of the tomb. The many folk one would meet, from distant lands. Her parents would not countenance it. A local shrine was perfectly sufficient for the good of their souls.

Elena had watched with folded arms as Sybil set off on the journey that she, Elena, had always yearned for. Sybil had waved, tears flowing down her cheeks. Consumed with envy, Elena had not raised a hand as her sister disappeared from view down the village road. Disappeared and had not come back.

It had hardly seemed real when Mother and Father decided that Elena should go and find her.

She was going to Canterbury, one of her greatest wishes.

But going because of Sybil's sin. As ever, she was in Sybil's shadow.

Day after day, hour after hour, of searching for her. Seeking her. People pushing Elena aside, mocking her. Cursing her. Ordering her to be on her way. Impatient, rude, just as the clerk, Barling, had been.

And then her gaze had met that of Hugo Stanton. His blue, blue eyes that could have been the clear sky overhead. His thick blond hair. His encouraging smile for her, Elena, to speak to him. It was like the street had emptied, and he was the only one in it.

Not that she showed any of it. She pulled her comb through her hair again. She could not unmake in a moment what she had made of herself for the last twenty-three years.

When he'd walked away with the clerk, she'd thought he might look back.

What, look at you, Elena? A man like him? Mother again. Even in the middle of a Canterbury street.

Elena had gone on her way, back to her task of her search for Sybil. Dutiful Elena. Dependable Elena.

Yet a magical few hours later, Hugo Stanton had called to her from the Roulf inn. And was concerned about her. Wanted to spend time with her. Wanted to hear her story.

Except it was Sybil's story.

Elena pulled at a new, unyielding tangle, not caring about the clump of hair she pulled out.

When Hugo had leaned across the table to, as he'd said, look at the stitching on her hood, she'd dared to believe that he actually found her desirable. She hadn't wanted to jerk away from him. But she could not do otherwise. Her belief had failed her at that moment. All she could do was gather her resolve. He'd offered to accompany her to the necromancer. Her heart had sung when he'd said he wanted to keep her safe.

Made a fool of you, Elena, didn't he?

No.

Didn't he?

Yes. Yes, he had. She'd listened in mute wretchedness as his questions first to Margery, then to Nicholas Clement had flowed. Hugo Stanton had not cared a jot about her. He'd used her for whatever task he was engaged in. Allowed her coins to pay the necromancer, Nicholas.

Nicholas, the other source of her humiliation tonight. She'd had such high hopes that he might be the one, the one that would find Sybil.

Elena would have done as Mother and Father had ordered. Her work would be completed.

Before she took Sybil home, she would have a day, maybe two, in Canterbury, where, for once in her life, she would be free to do as she pleased. No toiling ceaselessly for Mother and Father. No watching out for and watching over Sybil.

But Nicholas had failed her as well. He'd taken nearly all her money and given her very little in return.

Another man who had let her down. Who'd passed over her without a second glance.

Elena pulled the comb so hard through her hair, it snapped in two.

Chapter Thirty-Three

Wednesday

The dawn filtered its way through the shutters of Barling's room. The morning meant little, as he had barely closed an eye all night.

He had spent hour after hour before his tablet, making notes. Crossing them out. Writing them down again.

No matter what he did, he kept coming back to Brother William.

But how to prove it? How to even suggest a full enquiry into the man, without causing the most enormous outrage and offence?

For William was no lowly choir monk or lay brother. He held the revered office of recorder of the miracles of Saint Thomas Becket at Canterbury Cathedral.

Barling could imagine in the most vivid detail the reaction of the Archbishop if Barling were to present William as the likely guilty party, guilty of sacrilegious murder, to him and Prior Benedict, on the day before King Henry's expected arrival.

He stared in misery at his notes again.

Yet what if his conclusions, no matter how difficult for those in authority to hear, were indeed correct? If he held his tongue through fear of the consequences of speaking out, a profane murderer would continue to walk free.

Barling wished he could have discussed his thoughts with Stanton, argued back and forth in a helpful way and not in a fit of temper.

His heart had leapt when he heard the familiar tread on the stairs late last night. He awaited the knock on the door, the whisper that would wake the dead of 'Barling? Can I come in?' from outside.

But the footsteps had creaked past, and Stanton's door had closed.

Barling had been left alone with his theories, went over and over them as the hours of the night slipped by, allowing him only short periods of fitful dozing.

For time was running out. The next time the daylight lit those shutters, it would be welcoming the King to the city.

A brisk knock came at the door. 'I've had orders to wake you, sir.' Derfield, the innkeeper. 'Sorry it's so early.'

Barling opened the door to find the innkeeper still in his nightshirt. 'I am already awake. What is it?'

'Prior Benedict demands your presence at once, sir. He is waiting for you on the street and says that your assistant must come as well.'

A wave of dread passed through Barling, so strong that he feared his legs would give beneath him. 'The prior? At this hour? Did he say what it was about?'

'No, sir.' Derfield's eyes were rounded. 'But he's very agitated. I can tell you that much, sir.'

'Then go and wake Hugo Stanton, man. Quickly. I need to put my boots on.'

Barling hurried from his room moments later and met a yawning Stanton in the corridor. 'By all the saints, Barling. Does anybody ever sleep in Canterbury?'

'Sleep is of no importance, Stanton. I fear something terrible is amiss. The prior has come for us.'

'The prior?' All sluggishness left his assistant's visage. 'Hell's teeth, Barling. That's not good.'

Barling led the way down the stairs as fast as he dared, Stanton behind him. 'Watch your step.'

They emerged onto the street into the freshness of the dawn air.

Prior Benedict sat in a small cart, along with a cathedral monk in the driver's seat who held two lively horses at a stand.

The prior did not only look agitated. He looked furious, his face flushed in his ire. 'Your pattern has become more elaborate, Barling.'

Barling's stomach dropped.

'What's he talking about?' muttered Stanton.

Although he knew the answer, Barling had to ask the repugnant question. 'Has there been another murder, Prior?'

'There has. In precisely the same manner as the others, according to the message I have received.'

A clipped oath came from Stanton.

'Delay no more,' said the prior. 'Get on board.'

Barling did so in one attempt, thanks to an efficient boost from Stanton, who swung himself up and on with ease.

'Where are we going?' Barling held tight as the cart set off, the horses' hooves a loud clatter on the cobbles.

'To the lime kiln,' said Benedict. 'It's well over a mile away, and I do not want to waste time.'

'The lime kiln?' asked Stanton, frowning.

'Are you deaf, man?' replied the prior. 'I have had word that the victim is a lime burner. A man by the name of Martin Eustace.'

Barling met his assistant's horrified look of recognition.

'What devil's done this, Barling?' said Stanton.

But Barling did not respond.

He had made his decision. He would have to confront Prior Benedict with his suspicion that Brother William was responsible. His duty demanded it.

He could not simply blurt it out, not in this bouncing, noisy cart. He needed to compose himself, make sure he chose every word with care.

Line, by line, by line.

Barling would have to say his piece, no matter how difficult.

No matter what it cost him.

Chapter Thirty-Four

The cart bounced along the rutted road.

Stanton sat in the back with Barling, the clerk hanging on like it was a bucking stallion.

They had exited through Worthgate, and left the walled city behind, their progress impeded by the first early pilgrims coming in on the road. The driver had already reassured Prior Benedict three times that they were almost there.

Barling said nothing, which Stanton understood to mean that he shouldn't say anything, either. He first thought it must be because of the monk who drove the cart. Neither prior nor clerk would want to risk talking in any detail about the latest murder in front of such a fellow.

The latest murder. God's eyes, what a way to think about the fate of poor Martin Eustace. He didn't mean to make light of it, not in any way. The shock he'd felt when he'd heard the news had been profound.

But hearing of Martin Eustace's murder, tragic as it was, should not have reduced Barling to this state. The clerk was not his usual self, no question. His gaze fixed on one spot, like he looked at something Stanton couldn't see.

The cart neared the smoking, stone-built kiln. High piles of cut wood were nearby, ready to feed the fire. Full sacks of lime were stacked tidily. Mounds of cut limestone awaited burning and it was next to one of these that Stanton could see the slain figure of Eustace on the ground. He could not make out any detail at this distance, for which he was grateful. That gruesome task would come soon enough.

Three people stood grouped around a wooden barrow a good distance away from the body. One – a small, bent old man – he had never seen before. The other two he knew well: Katerine Flocke and Adam Drake.

Stanton had questions, and plenty of them. He tried to catch Barling's eye to judge his reaction to who was present. No luck.

'You can stop here,' said Benedict to the driver, who did so at once.

The three passengers climbed out onto the rutted roadway, the prior first and Stanton helping a silent Barling down.

'May I ask if you'll be long, Prior?' asked the driver.

'That will depend on the so-called wisdom of the King's clerk. Won't it, Barling?'

By all the saints, the prior could be a snappy fellow. Stanton expected a sharp snap from the clerk in return. But no. Barling didn't react.

What on earth was the matter with him?

The prior looked back up at the driver. 'Why do you ask, brother?'

'It's just that I have to collect Brother William as soon as possible this morning,' the man replied. 'I had to bring him over Throwley way last night. An urgent message had come about a great miracle, a noblewoman cured of a crushed foot. William wanted to speak to her, have it recorded in time for Easter and the arrival of the King.'

'Last night?'

Stanton caught the whispered words from Barling, though he knew they weren't for him.

188

The clerk stared up at the driver of the cart, all colour gone from his face.

'You hear that, Barling?' said the prior. 'The arrival of our lord King. I remind you in case it has slipped your mind.'

His blabbing seemed to cut Barling deeper than a knife and the clerk clutched the side of the cart for support.

'Are you feeling all right, Barling?' murmured Stanton.

Barling waved a hand to stop him and let go of the cart.

The prior was replying to the driver. 'I was not aware of that. Give me one moment.' He marched over to where the body lay, took in the scene, and made a noise of disgust. Then he turned on his heel and came straight back.

'You pair.' Benedict called to Katerine and Drake. 'When the King's men have finished, take this wretched man's body in your barrow to the priory. That is an order.'

They gave a silent bow of acknowledgement as the prior kept talking.

'Unless perhaps you and Hugo Stanton could do it, Barling?' He climbed up onto the cart and scowled at the clerk. 'You might as well, for all the good you are doing here. Useless. Useless!'

Stanton steeled himself for Barling's flood of ire. But to his astonishment, the clerk was meekness itself.

'I can only offer my apologies, Prior,' said Barling. 'I accept full responsibility for the continued state of affairs. Should you wish to dismiss us, we shall go from this place.'

Go? Stanton wouldn't. Couldn't. He had to see the necromancer.

'Dismiss you?' said Benedict. 'I wish that I could. But it's the Archbishop that has put you in charge, not me. Make no mistake, I will ask him. Proceed.' Benedict nodded to the driver, and the cart set off at a pace.

'That man's mood is going to be the end of him one of these days,' said Stanton. The end of him, too, if he were sent away before he'd had the chance to speak to Rosamund. 'Eh, Barling?'

Faith, the clerk had gone even paler. 'Stanton,' he said quietly. 'I fear my thoughts are scattered. Can you please start the enquiry? I will examine the body while you do so.'

'Of course I will, Barling. But I'm worried about you. Are you unwell?'

'Rest assured, I am hale.' Barling walked off before Stanton could ask him anything else.

Stanton made his way to the shocked-looking trio before him of Katerine, Drake and the old man. 'I assume that you found the body?'

'It was me, sir.' Katerine looked even more dishevelled and dirty in the bright morning light. 'Oh, it's terrible.'

'And me and all,' said Drake, voice quavering and chins quivering. 'Awful it is. Awful.'

Drake, finder of the first body, the discovery of which had caused him to be sick and wet himself.

From what Stanton could see, the man hadn't had as extreme a reaction this time. Yet he still seemed close to collapse. Katerine didn't appear to be much better.

'Shocking, it is. But nothing to do with me, sir,' said the old man. 'T'were too early for me to start, sir. This pair were already here when I came and Eustace was dead.'

'And who are you, fellow?' said Stanton.

'I'm Venner, the quarrymaster. I work the days. Martin Eustace's only job was to keep the kiln going through the night. If the fire goes out, we're finished.'

'If I could have a word, Venner?'

'Your servant, sir.'

Stanton drew him away so they could not be overheard.

He made sure he asked Venner the right initial questions, though he knew that the small, aged man with his lack of physical prowess could not possibly be the murderer. Venner's answers told Stanton that the quarrymaster had lived and worked in Canterbury his whole life, and folk knew him as an honest, law-abiding man. Besides, he'd been in bed all night with his wife. His eldest daughter, her husband and their six children slept in the house too.

Stanton went on. 'You said that Katerine Flocke and Adam Drake were already present with Eustace's body when you arrived this morning?'

'That's the truth, sir. By the Virgin's blood, they were in a right state, screaming to me about a murder. The lad, Drake, was sat on the ground, pale as anything. To be honest, I weren't that shocked, not at first. I thought Eustace had been overcome by the fumes and fallen into the kiln. It can happen with this job, y'know, and he was the worse for drink all of the time. But when I saw him, with Christ's Cross carved into his forehead?' He spat hard. 'A devil was abroad, no question.'

'What about Katerine?'

'She weren't much better than Drake. Can't blame her. Lost her husband the same way, didn't she?'

'Did you know Peter Flocke?'

Venner shook his head. 'Keep myself to myself out here. I do see Katerine regular as she collects the lime. God didn't give her many brains. Knows her manners, though. No cheek from her.'

'Did you know a pilgrim by the name of Robert Norwood, a loud and unkempt man?'

'No, sir.'

'Do you know of anybody who had disagreements with Martin Eustace or who would've wanted to do him harm?'

'Nobody that would want to harm him, sir. But Eustace hated Lambert Green for sacking him and felt it sorely. It didn't happen often, but they'd run into each other at the kiln when Green would come to sort out my payments with me. The cursing from both sides would fill the air.'

Stanton nodded. 'I know of the strife between them.'

'Thing is, sir, Green had a point. Yes, he's tough on his men. But his job is to get that choir built. He couldn't have the likes of Eustace drunk out of his head up on the scaffolding, or working on stone with sharp blades. Eustace would have killed himself or somebody else. And now?' He pointed over at the body, where Barling bent low in his examination of it. 'God rest his soul.' He made the sign of the cross. 'Don't know what else I can say, sir. Now if you'll pardon me for being so bold, I've got stone to pick.'

'I won't keep you any longer. Thank you, Venner. What you've said has helped me.'

'Don't know how it could, sir. But bless you for doing God's work. Martin Eustace didn't deserve the end he got. Nobody would.' With a last sober look over at the body, Venner went to his work nearby.

Once the rap of metal on stone started up, Stanton walked over to the waiting Katerine and Drake.

'I know it won't be easy,' he said. 'But I have to ask you both about what's happened.'

'Sir.' Katerine's eyes were swollen from crying. 'It was my idea to come to the kiln early, as I needed to get more lime. I was very behind with my work.'

'See, the barrow's heavy,' said Drake. 'So I told Kat I'd give her a push with it, like. That's why I came.'

'But when we got here, we found . . . that.' She nodded in the direction of the corpse, where Barling worked on.

'It's just like Peter Flocke's, sir,' said Drake.

A stifled sob came from Katerine.

'Sorry, Kat. I had to say it.'

'Did you see anybody near the kiln?' said Stanton. 'On the road to the kiln?'

'No, sir.'

'Nobody, sir.' This from Drake. 'When we saw him, Eustace, like, we went back along the road, fast as we could, until we found a lad who could run to the priory. Me and Kat aren't built for running, see.'

'Then we came back and waited and then Quarrymaster Venner came,' said Katerine. 'At least Adam was with me. Because I . . . I keep thinking, I should've been on my own. What if Adam hadn't been with me? I could be lying there too, dead, all cut up. Just like Peter.' She broke down in stifled sobs.

'Don't take on, Kat.' Drake patted her arm like a baker knocking back dough. 'Don't take on.'

'Stanton.' He looked over to see Barling beckoning to him. To his deep relief, Barling appeared more himself.

He joined the clerk. 'Is it as everybody's saying?'

Barling nodded. 'Murder by the same hand. The body slashed in a frenzy. The holy Cross carved into the forehead. Every wound with a sharp blade. See for yourself.'

Stanton did, the horror appalling him afresh.

'I would be certain from my examination of his limbs that he was slain sometime during the night,' said Barling.

'When he was alone at work here,' said Stanton. 'It's such a deserted spot. Even if he had fought back or shouted out, nobody would have heard him.'

'I cannot see that there is anything else to be found,' said Barling. 'You two.' He raised his voice to Katerine and Drake. 'It is time for you to remove this man's body, as directed by the prior.'

'Yes, sir,' they replied in unison.

Drake looked like he might faint, Katerine a mite stronger.

All the same, Stanton couldn't have a woman do this job while he stood idly by. He raised a hand. 'Stay back, Katerine. Drake, you and I can do it.'

Drake gaped but obeyed. 'Sir.'

There wasn't much to the late Martin Eustace, and Drake, whispering frantic prayers, took most of the weight as they lifted him into the barrow.

Stanton would never forget such a hideous task.

'Back to the priory with you,' said Barling to Drake.

'Yes, sir.' The large man complied, Katerine coming to his aid to take the other handle. They trundled off back to the road that led to the city, Venner pausing his work as they passed to lower his head in respect, hands clasped in prayer.

'We should make our way back also,' said Barling. 'I will take our leave of Quarrymaster Venner.'

As he did so, Stanton took a final look around. No, nothing that seemed out of place.

Then he spotted Eustace's bag, the filthy sack that the man had demanded the night he'd been thrown out of the Roulf alehouse, propped up by the side of the kiln.

Stanton picked up the bag. He didn't know what to do with it. Maybe give it to the quarrymaster.

He should check inside, in case it contained anything that somebody closer to Eustace should have, whoever that might be. He doubted it.

Stanton pulled the greasy string closure open and looked in. His stomach lurched at what it contained.

No, he wouldn't be passing this bag on.

Stanton was keeping it. And he had to tell Barling of his discovery. It wasn't going to be easy.

Chapter Thirty-Five

'I usually favour a cart over feet for travel.' Stanton fell into step beside Barling as they started the long walk back to the city. He carried Eustace's bag on his left side where the clerk couldn't see it. 'But I'd rather crawl on my hands and knees than share a cart with the prior again this morning. Eh, Barling?'

'Yes, he is furious,' said Barling quietly. 'But who can blame him?'

The odd meekness from Barling once again. 'I can, for one,' said Stanton. 'It's all very well him shouting and screaming about us not getting any answers. He didn't do any better. He shouldn't have berated you like that. I could see how much it shocked you.'

'His berating of me did not shock me, Stanton. My reaction was to the words of the driver of the cart, not the prior.'

'The cart driver? Barling, have you fallen on your head recently? You're making no sense.'

Barling gave a sharp sigh. 'I am making perfect sense, Stanton. I really thought I had arrived at a credible answer last night. But I did not.'

Stanton's goad had worked. 'Then tell me. I can't know your thoughts.'

He listened as they walked on, the clerk giving his list of reasons for suspecting Brother William. 'They were very solid reasons, Barling,' he said when Barling had finished.

'Yet they disappeared into thin air this morning when I heard the driver say that Brother William had been away from Canterbury all last night, recording a noble woman's miracle. William could not possibly have killed Martin Eustace, whom, as we have established, was killed by the same hand.'

'I see what you mean,' said Stanton. 'It was still a clever line of thinking.'

'Not clever enough,' said Barling. 'Can you imagine the consequences if I had spoken without all the facts?' He shuddered.

'I can,' said Stanton. 'But you didn't. You did right, Barling.'

'I was fortunate. Nothing more. My reputation should not depend on a chance encounter with a cart driver. Prior Benedict is right. I should make my own representation to the Archbishop. Tell him that I have failed. It is only right that I confess to my shortcomings.' He squared his narrow shoulders. 'Even if that means he sends us away.'

'No.' He couldn't leave. His appointment with the necromancer beckoned. 'You must carry on.' It came out more forceful than he intended.

Barling looked at him askance. 'Are you giving me an order, Stanton?'

'It's just that I believe we may be less behind than we think,' said Stanton, dodging the question. 'And what Benedict said to you wasn't fair.'

'He said it to both of us,' said Barling.

Stanton shrugged. 'I get told off all the time.'

His reward was the tiniest twitch up of one corner of Barling's mouth. 'Usually deserved.'

'Maybe.' Stanton knew he was headed for another telling-off from Barling. Barling just didn't know it yet.

'Did you discover anything of note from your questioning of Katerine Flocke and Adam Drake?' said Barling. 'They are too close to this for my liking. Drake finds one body, that of Peter Flocke. He and the grieving widow find another, Martin Eustace. They were watching us from the scaffolding when we were dealing with Robert Norwood's corpse.'

'I wondered about that too,' said Stanton, 'when I first saw them present at the lime kiln earlier. Now that I've spoken to them, I don't believe for a minute they are the culprits. They were both beside themselves with fear, which you and I saw with our own eyes. What's more, the quarrymaster's account matched what we know of them. He's not caught up in any of this and his answers were sound.'

'Always good to have an independent voice in these matters. But it does not help us.'

'Venner might have.' Stanton related the quarrymaster's account of the strife at the kiln between Eustace and Lambert Green. 'I think we need to go back to Green.'

'I will acknowledge,' said Barling, 'that I have been resistant up to now to the idea of Lambert Green being involved. But in the face of such little progress, I agree.' He sighed. 'Yet what of Robert Norwood? He has no links to any of this.'

Stanton chose his next words with care. While his findings were important, they were certain to anger the clerk. 'There could actually be a link from Eustace to Norwood, Barling.' He held up Eustace's sack. 'In here.'

'What is that filthy object?'

'It's Martin Eustace's bag. I found it at the kiln.'

'You simply took it?'

'Listen to me, Barling. You saw when you examined his body that Martin Eustace had his lime-burned hands bandaged?'

'I did,' said the clerk. 'What of it?'

'He had ointment for them too.' Stanton drew it from the sack. 'This ointment.'

'Again, what of it?'

'It's made by Margery Clement, the herbalist that treated pilgrim Robert Norwood.'

Barling's eyebrows went up. 'And how do you know that?'

'I . . . I've been to her house. That's how I know she made this burn ointment. I saw identical pots on her shelves.'

Barling stopped dead.

Stanton braced himself.

'You went to see Margery Clement, Stanton? Went? Even after I expressly told you not to? You took it upon yourself to completely disregard my orders?'

'Barling, I wasn't going against your orders. At least not completely. I went with Elena Whitehand.'

'Who on earth is Elena Whitehand?'

'You've met her. The young woman who stopped us to ask for help in finding her sister, remember?'

'Oh. Her.' Barling gave a brittle laugh. 'I see.'

'No, you don't. She wants nothing to do with me.'

'That is most unusual for a young woman.'

It was, and it bothered him, though he'd never admit that to Barling. 'I felt sorry for her, and I wanted to help her in her search. And I saw it as an ideal opportunity to talk to Margery and her nephew.'

'Her nephew?' Barling looked at him aghast. 'You decided to spread loose talk even further?'

Stanton could have cut his tongue out. 'No, I misspoke. Elena told me there are two Clements, aunt and nephew. That's all.'

'May the Almighty grant me patience.' Barling briefly raised his gaze to the sky. 'Then tell me, Stanton, what you found of relevance on your unofficial visit.'

'Margery confirmed that she treated Norwood, which the physician Gilbert Ordway had already told us. I didn't get a chance to ask her anything more because Nicholas arrived home from the cathedral.'

'The cathedral? What is his business there?'

'He's an exorcist, helps pilgrims to be rid of evil spirits.'

The clerk sniffed. 'I see.'

'Barling, we have a link with Norwood.' Stanton held up the ointment. 'And a link with Eustace. We need to go and see Margery Clement. You and I. Together.'

Barling looked at him for a long moment. 'Loath though I am to admit it, I agree.' The clerk set off walking again. 'But first it is necessary for us to see Lambert Green.'

'Does this mean we're not telling the Archbishop that we're running away?' Unwise as it might be, Stanton couldn't resist a small barb as he followed.

Barling gave him no reply.

Chapter Thirty-Six

'And that is how Martin Eustace died,' concluded Barling, in his account to Lambert Green. 'In exactly the same way as your mason, Peter Flocke, and the pilgrim, Robert Norwood.'

He and Stanton had found the second master mason in the yard of his lodge, marking full sacks of sand with a crude cross in whitewash on each one.

'Did you, by any chance, ever have dealings with Norwood?' asked Stanton, before Green had the opportunity to comment.

Green carried on with his painting. 'Course not.'

Barling shot Stanton a look that warned him not to interrupt further. He said to Green, 'I am sorry that I have had to give you such sad news about Eustace, a man who used to work for you.'

'No loss to me,' said Green. 'Eustace was a waste of time. Loved the bottom of a barrel of ale more than anything. Unreliable. Like so many. Of course I sacked him, and I should've done it long before I actually did. Now if that's all, I'll bid you good day. Sirs. I'm extra busy, because as always, I have workers missing.'

'I can inform you where at least two of them are,' said Barling. 'Katerine Flocke and Adam Drake are taking Eustace's body to the priory for burial.'

Green flung his brush into the bucket of whitewash with a loud splash. 'What in the name of the Martyr are those two doing that for? I need them here!'

'Prior Benedict ordered it,' said Barling. 'It is right that he should have done so.'

'No, it's not right.' Green's face was a contorted mask of fury. 'He has dozens of monks and servants at his disposal, but still he has to take my labour? My hands? My workers?' He booted one of the sacks. 'While all the time we are behind. Behind. It's all fine and good for those at the top. They can present a tale where all is going smoothly, going ahead of our plans. That the magnificence is being restored. Then they will summon me. Why is it so slow? Why are we behind? They never give it a rest. Ever.'

Barling attempted to speak, but Green carried on over him.

'I can only say that Peter bloody Flocke is dead so many times. That I can't find hands like those out of thin air!'

'I can see how it must be a great pressure to do what's been ordered, with no thought for how it might be achieved,' Barling said, trying to mollify him.

'It is a great pressure, and one that gets greater by the day,' said Green. 'Including today. I need to go and go urgently. The latest summons is for me to explain the cost and why it is growing so much.' He flung a hand in the direction of the work. 'Look at the scale of it! It's not like roofing a bloody pig pen, is it? And if you see that pair, Drake and the Flocke slattern, tell them to get themselves back here as soon as possible. There's work to be done. They've already spent half the morning gadding about.' He stomped off.

'Transporting the body of a murdered man is hardly gadding about,' said Stanton. 'Lambert Green is harder than a bag of carpenter's nails.'

'Yet even he is under intense pressure,' said Barling. 'The same as Prior Benedict is.'

201

'Maybe it's true about the cathedral curse. Maybe the curse is to send men mad?'

Barling fixed him with his most stern look. 'Stanton, I do not know whether your words are jest or simply preposterous.'

Stanton shrugged. 'A little of both, perhaps? Nothing else is making sense.'

'None of either, man,' said Barling. 'Put all feeble-minded thought of cursed cathedrals aside. For now, we proceed to the house of Margery Clement. I believe you already know the way?'

Chapter Thirty-Seven

But, much to Barling's ire, there was nobody home at the wretched house of the herbalist woman. Their journey here through stinking, squalid alleyways that had beggars emerge from all sides to pester them had been for nothing.

Margery Clement's door was locked tight, and there was no answer to Stanton's repeated knocks and calls.

He kept close to his assistant. The unsavoury-looking individuals going by dropped their gaze to his purse far too often for his liking.

'I hope nothing has happened to the Clements,' said Stanton, turning to Barling with a worried look in his blue eyes.

'I think it is unlikely,' said Barling. 'Yet we have had experience of locked doors hiding all manner of horrors. If this were a house on a deserted lane, I would suggest that you could force a shutter or perhaps try to pick the lock. But we are already the subject of all sorts of unwanted attention. And if we were to be proved wrong, then such a commotion is bound to reach the ears of Prior Benedict. Try again.'

His assistant redoubled his efforts. 'Margery! Hello!'

A shutter flew open on the house opposite to the sound of wailing and a red-faced woman leaned out. 'Oi!' she shouted. 'Less of your noise. I'm trying to get my baby to sleep.'

'We have no wish to disturb anybody,' said Barling. 'We seek Margery and Nicholas Clement. Do you know where they are?'

'Where they are every morning,' she said. 'She'll be out gathering more of her smelly herbs, and he'll be creeping around at the cathedral, looking for business.'

'Do you know what time they'll be back?' asked Stanton.

'No. But I wish it was never. The stink of the smoke from their thatch. The noises he makes. Both are as bad as each other. Between the pair of them, my life's a misery, so it is.'

The wailing from the unseen baby went up in volume, and the woman slammed the shutter closed again.

'Then all we can do is wait?' said Barling to Stanton, incredulous.

'Unless you have a better idea, yes.' Stanton sat down on the less than clean front step. 'This happens to me all the time when you send me out on court errands. Looking for people can be a frustrating business. Are you not going to join me, Barling?'

'Join you in sitting practically on the ground, like the rest of the beggars we passed? No.' Sometimes, his assistant really did not know the kind of man he was.

After several minutes of standing, then several more, Barling's legs began to ache, and the dirty step began to appeal somewhat. But he could not possibly place himself in such an undignified position. Finally, after what he judged to be over an hour, he heard Stanton say the words which were long overdue.

'Here she is.'

'Finally,' said Barling.

The elderly woman who approached them carried a wide, shallow basket that was full of all manner of greenery. She was just as Stanton had described to him in appearance and stature.

Barling saw the recognition in her face at Stanton, followed by a look of horror when her eyes lit on his own dark clerk's robes.

'Oh, please don't tell me Nicholas is in trouble,' she said to Stanton as she reached her front door. 'He has a gift, a true gift.'

'We are not here because of Nicholas, mistress,' said Stanton. 'Please, may we come in?'

'Of course, sir.' Margery unlocked the door with shaking hands and brought them inside, placing her basket on the table.

The scent of dried herbs was overpowering. Barling would have preferred that she left the door open, but he needed to make sure they would not be overheard and so did not object when she closed it again.

'Mistress Clement,' said Stanton. 'This is Aelred Barling, who is a clerk of the King.'

'Sir.' She gave a deep bow, clearly in equal terror and awe.

'When I came to see you last night with the woman called Elena,' said Stanton, 'you will remember that I asked questions about people you have treated. Barling and I would like to ask you a few more. You are not in trouble. We are just trying to get information on a matter that is most sensitive.'

'Of course, sir. I am your servant.'

'I had mentioned a man by the name of Robert Norwood to you last night,' said Stanton. 'But we were interrupted by Nicholas coming home.'

'It is true, sir, that I treated Robert Norwood. He was a very sick man when I saw him, and a most unhappy one.'

'Did you ever find out the reason for his unhappiness?' said Barling.

'No, sir. He only ever said to me that he had to get well before he could go home. He'd only turned to me because he ran out of money to pay the physician, Gilbert Ordway, and Master Ordway would do no more for him. I treated him anyway, but there was little I could do. I do not expect that he is long for this world.'

Barling exchanged a brief glance with Stanton before he asked, 'And what about Martin Eustace?'

'Yes, sir. I treat Martin's hands.' She sighed. 'Though in truth, I might as well not bother. Burning lime is a dangerous job. With his constant drunkenness and shaking, his flesh is wounded every night. I worry for his safety. But I do what I can, no matter how many times I have to do the same thing.'

'Unfortunately for Eustace,' said Barling, 'your worries for him had foundation, because he has indeed perished at his place of work.'

'Oh, no.' Margery's wrinkled hand went to her mouth. 'What befell him, sir?'

'He was murdered in the same manner as the stonemason, Peter Flocke,' said Stanton. 'As was Robert Norwood.'

Barling's irritation rose at Stanton's disclosure of the details of the men's fate. He, Barling, had not intended to do so. But Stanton's words had an effect, one that Barling was not expecting.

'Oh, no,' she said again. 'No. Then, I must confess to you, sir, about a partial untruth I told you last night,' she said to Stanton.

'Which is, mistress?' he said.

'You asked me last night about Peter Flocke, sir. And I told you that I did not know him. That part is true. I did not know him. But I have treated his wife, Katerine.'

'Katerine was ill?' Barling exchanged a glance with Stanton. The widow Flocke had not mentioned this.

'She thought she was, sir,' said Margery. 'She came to me a couple of months ago, as she was terrified that she had the same wasting sickness as her husband. She did not. She was with child.'

A pregnant widow that never mentioned her state? Barling had very little experience of women who were with child. But from what he had, it appeared that they talked about it without cease.

Margery went on. 'I told her about her baby and gave her a supply of ginger for her sickness. I gave her a potion for her husband as well. The herbs in it are good for regaining vitality and vigour.'

'You gave her your cures,' said Barling, 'but did not charge her?'

'She had barely a coin to her name, sir. A sick husband and a baby growing inside her. She needed her money more than I did.'

'Is there anything else you have not told us?' Barling had not intended to scare her, but his question had made her tremble.

'No, sir, I swear to you.'

'Stanton?'

His assistant shook his head.

'Then we will take our leave,' said Barling.

As Margery showed them back out into the alleyway, a cathedral monk was passing on an errand. What colour the woman had drained from her face, and she ducked back inside, slamming the door behind her.

'You see?' Stanton looked at Barling, eyes rounded. 'She was worth talking to.'

'I will allow you that satisfaction,' said Barling.

'And having done so,' said Stanton, 'it will be equally worth talking to somebody else again. Somebody who has told us an untruth.'

'Stop talking in riddles, Stanton. To whom are you referring?'

'The physician, Master Ordway. He told us that he stopped treating the pilgrim Norwood because the man was seeking Margery's help to cure him. Margery has just told us that Ordway stopped treating Norwood because the man ran out of money. A different story.'

'Oh, Stanton.' Barling could not help his smile at his assistant's naivety. 'I of course noticed the difference in their stories. As I remembered that Ordway said the old woman could not be trusted.'

But Stanton did not back down. 'One of them is lying, Barling. And we have three murders to solve. You can't decide who is telling—'

Barling held a hand up. 'We do not have time to argue. We will spend it better in getting Master Ordway to clear up the matter, once and for all.' He could see another muscular beggar advancing on them. 'And I have no desire to wait around here a minute longer. Let us leave at once.'

Chapter Thirty-Eight

Barling heard the screams from inside the house as they approached Ordway's door.

A group of passing pilgrims heard it too. They stopped dead, exclaiming. Pointing.

'God's eyes.' Stanton's look of horror matched Barling's own.

'Run,' said Barling.

They pushed past the pilgrims to rush through the courtyard, Stanton ahead as another terrifying howl came from within.

'Ordway!' Barling shouted as Stanton flung himself at the handle. It wasn't locked.

With a quick turn, he was in, Barling behind him.

A horrible stench filled Barling's nostrils. Burned flesh.

'What on earth?' A furious Ordway stood over a middle-aged man who sat in a chair. Blood splashed all down the man's naked arm and pooled on the floor. The physician held a cautery iron in one hand.

'Oh.' This, from Stanton.

A hot wave of embarrassment broke through Barling. He knew his face was aflame. 'Master Ordway, please accept my sincerest apologies. I did not mean to interrupt.'

'Yes, you did, Barling. You and your assistant came charging through my door without so much as a knock. How dare you?'

A call from outside from one of the pilgrims. 'What's happening?' 'I'll get rid of them.' Stanton acted on his own words.

'Master Ordway, please accept my sincerest apologies,' said Barling. 'I would humbly request that I could have a word when you have finished.'

'I'm happy to be done for now.' The patient hauled himself to his feet.

'So long as you return tomorrow.' Ordway put the iron down into a waiting bowl and reached for a length of bandage. Another bowl contained a blood-letting knife, and a large glass flask was filled with the dark red liquid that it had released.

'Not sure I want to go through this again, Master Ordway.' The man winced as Ordway dressed his arm.

'Such free-flowing blood tells me of a continued imbalance,' replied Ordway. 'It is imperative that you carry on with my treatment.'

Stanton arrived back in. 'Everyone's moved on.'

The patient grabbed his cloak. 'Good day to you all.' He hurried out as Ordway called after him.

'Tomorrow!' The physician went and shut the door behind him. 'What do you want, Barling?' He took a scoop of sawdust from a pail and threw it on the wet, stained floor. 'I hope you've changed your mind and have come for a bloodletting.' He scowled. 'Thanks to your interruption, I have time free.'

'No, thank you, Master Ordway. I am still as well as before. Stanton and I are here because there has been another murder, in the same manner as Peter Flocke and Robert Norwood.'

'Goodness. Another?' The physician picked up the flask of blood and sniffed it. 'Who was it this time?'

'The dead man's name was Martin Eustace,' said Stanton with a scowl.

'I am most flattered that you think I have information concerning every murdered man in Canterbury at my fingertips.' The physician shook his head and replaced the flask on the table. 'But I am afraid I do not believe I know the name.' He made a note on a piece of parchment. 'Perhaps you could describe him?'

'He was a lime burner,' said Stanton. 'Worked the kiln. Had many injuries because of that work.'

'I have never met the man,' said Ordway. 'Or heard of him.'

'Eustace used to be a stonemason,' said Stanton. 'Perhaps you knew him as that?'

'I can only repeat,' said Ordway, 'I have never heard of this man. I have never met him or seen him, to the best of my knowledge.'

'Are you positive?' said Barling. 'He did visit the Clement house regularly.'

'Oh, did he now?' Ordway laughed. 'Then one could conjecture from dawn until dusk about what he was going there for.'

'Herbal cures from the old woman, I presume,' said Barling. 'What else?'

'You mean you don't know about her nephew, Nicholas?' said Ordway.

Barling tried to catch Stanton's eye, but his assistant was looking at the flask.

'I know that he is an exorcist, Master Ordway,' replied Barling.

'I see.' The physician raised his eyebrows. 'It is true that Nicholas Clement presents himself as an exorcist, offering to cast out the demons of the sick pilgrims outside the cathedral. Naturally, he demands payment.' Ordway's mouth turned down in dissatisfaction. 'I have also heard that he offers to conjure in the dark arts.'

'Necromancy?' Barling's stomach turned over in revolted shock.

'I have heard only rumours about his unholy rituals,' said Ordway. 'But I do know one thing: there are so many strange happenings in that house, it would not surprise me in the least if Beelzebub himself had taken up lodgings in it.'

'How interesting.' Barling again tried and failed to meet Stanton's gaze. 'I have one last thing to clarify, if I may. It is regarding the issue of your stopping the treatment of Robert Norwood for his disease. When Norwood could no longer pay you, did—'

Hurried footsteps came from outside. 'Gilbert?' A woman's voice. Raised. Fearful. 'Are you in there?'

The footsteps loudened, and Mistress Isabel Tyson clattered in through the door without knocking. 'Oh, thank the Virgin. You're here.' She must have left her home in a rush, as she wore no cloak over her flower-embroidered silk dress.

'Good lady,' began Ordway. 'I apologise, but—'

'As do I.' Isabel gave but the barest glance in the direction of Barling and his assistant. 'Gilbert, please come. I beg you. Lucia has had one of her turns, and she is worse than ever. Please, help her. Please.'

Barling raised a hand to Ordway to indicate that the physician should go at once. Barling could never countenance an action of his causing harm to a child, ailing or hale. 'Good lady, your daughter will be in our prayers.'

'Thank you, sir.' Her eyes were only for Ordway, who was quickly selecting a number of jars of medicines and placing them into a large satchel of finely tooled leather.

'Come, Stanton.' Barling led the way outside through the courtyard, out of the gate and onto the street, Stanton with him. They stopped by the wall, the better to keep out of the way of the many people passing back and forth.

Barling watched as Ordway and Isabel came out of the gate and hurried off up the crowded street, the widow holding the physician's arm for support.

'What happens now, Barling?'

Barling resisted the temptation to box his assistant's ears. 'What happens now, Hugo Stanton, is you are going to explain to me why you said nothing to me about Nicholas Clement's necromancy.' He fought to keep his voice low. He could not make a public scene though he was sorely tempted to do so. 'What were you thinking of?'

Stanton frowned. 'It was Elena Whitehand who sought Nicholas out, not me.'

'Then it is as fortuitous as it is unusual that she wants nothing to do with you. She cannot be healthy company for you, or indeed anybody, to keep. Neither she nor anybody else should be frequenting such dangerous houses.'

'She doesn't frequent dangerous houses, Barling. Faith, the inn she's staying at is dedicated to Saint Cuthbert. It's as respectable as ours. She went to Nicholas because she was at her wits' end in her search for her sister, Sybil. I went with her to make sure she came to no harm. She didn't.'

'I am pleased you could find the time to help her. Your energies should have been focused on our enquiries.'

'Barling, you would not allow somebody to walk into danger on their own, either. And as for my energies, as you put it, I won't be spending any more on Elena.'

'I am glad to hear it. But it is best to avoid the danger in the first place. Do you hear me?'

Stanton nodded, a mutinous look on his face. 'As always, Barling.'

'And I refuse to spend any more time on such unsavoury matters. With regard to our murder investigations, going back to Gilbert Ordway has not helped. I did not get the chance for him to clarify why he stopped treating Norwood. But that matters not. We did establish that he did not know Martin Eustace and so it does not fit the pattern.'

'Speaking of patterns,' said Stanton, 'that reminds me. What was the prior on about this morning?'

'To what are you referring?'

'Just before we got on the cart,' said Stanton, 'Benedict was talking about a pattern.'

'I had been trying to explain to him how, in a strange way, murders in a pattern can be easier to solve. Obviously, I could not say too much to him, but once we saw the pattern at Fairmore Abbey last winter, the answer became clear.'

'Then have you seen any pattern here?'

'That is part of my frustration. None that makes sense. Here the only thing that seems to be common to all is that there is much strife. The monks are jealous of each other's status at the tomb and in disagreement over the new choir. We have reports of animosity between Lambert Green and his workers. Those who work in the healing arts resent each other.' Barling looked Stanton right in the eye. 'And in case there is any confusion, Stanton, I do not count necromancy as being a healing art.'

To his irritation, his assistant shrugged. Then a strange look passed across his face. 'I wonder, though.'

'Wonder about necromancy? If you—'

'No, not that.' Stanton raised a conciliatory hand. 'I wonder if there's something in what you say. About a pattern.'

'How do you mean?'

'Listen,' said Stanton. 'We've tried to find one for who the victims were. Nothing. Why they were killed. Nothing. The one pattern is how they were killed.'

'I agree,' said Barling. 'But we have been over this.'

'There is another question: when were they killed?'

Barling thought for a moment. 'All at night-time. That does not help much. Darkness hides abominable deeds with depressing frequency.'

'True.' Stanton nodded hard. 'But there's yet another question: where were they killed?'

Barling looked at him in bewilderment. 'In many places. Unconnected places.'

Now Stanton's eyes lit with excitement. 'Maybe they're not.' He pointed up at the cathedral that soared over every roof in the city. 'We've noticed how the builders have seen what's been going on from their place on the scaffolding. The monks climb up there as well. What if there's a link between the places?'

A tiny flame of hope sprang to life within Barling. Went out again. 'One would not be able to see the lime pit from the cathedral.'

Stanton's face fell. 'You're right.'

'However,' said Barling, 'it is still a useful suggestion and one which had not occurred to me. Though I am loath to have to say it with the crowds as dense as they are, we should revisit every site. Starting now. We may see something different when we look at each location with fresh eyes.'

Stanton gave him a wide grin. 'I'm pleased you think I'm useful.'

'Indeed.' They were clutching at the thinnest of straws, Barling knew that. But it was all they had. 'Then let us proceed.'

They might, by an incredible stroke of luck, find something new, something that would lead them to the killer. With his duty to the Archbishop discharged, Barling would get to stay in Canterbury and make his penance.

He prayed that the flame of hope would ignite within him again.

Barling did not need luck. He needed a miracle.

Chapter Thirty-Nine

'I'm sorry, Barling.' Stanton kept his pace slow so the clerk could keep up. 'I really thought we'd find something.' Their hours and miles along the heaving streets, to the cathedral, the masons' yard, the lime kiln had brought up nothing new.

Barling had become quieter and quieter as they'd gone on, his silence bothering Stanton far more than the clerk's usual testiness. As if to match his mood, the sky had filled with grey clouds from which a number of heavy showers had fallen.

'Your apology is not necessary,' replied the clerk. 'I only wish I had had my pilgrim's staff with me.'

Stanton didn't doubt that. But he did doubt a staff would have mattered to Barling's low mood.

As Stanton approached the door of the Roulf alehouse, he glanced aside to catch Barling's wary look.

'It was worth the attempt, I require no convincing of that,' said Barling. 'Just as I equally require a great deal of convincing that this alehouse is where I should break my fast.'

'Don't fret, Barling. You'll be pleased with what they provide.' Stanton held the door open for Barling to enter with him.

'Afternoon.' Ida greeted Stanton and gave Barling a respectful bow. 'And a good afternoon to you, sir.'

Thank goodness.

'I'll have an ale, Ida,' said Stanton.

'I will not,' said Barling.

Ida just smiled politely.

'Two bowls of your pottage as well, please,' said Stanton.

Barling opened his mouth to speak, but Stanton cut across him.

'You have to eat, Barling. The pottage here is made with the best vegetables, I promise. Now sit down before you fall down, eh?'

They took their seats at a bench that was mercifully free of any other customers.

Stanton noticed that it was the same one he'd sat at with Elena yesterday. He wondered if she'd still refuse to speak to him. He didn't blame her if so. To his relief, Ida brought the pottage straight away. It would be harder for Barling to walk out if he was in the middle of eating.

'There you are, sirs,' she said. 'I heard about poor Martin Eustace. Everybody's talking about it. I could hardly believe my ears. I keep looking over to his corner to see if he wants another ale.' She shook her head. 'An awkward bugger, he was, to be fair. But nobody deserves an end like that, sir, nobody.'

'Aye.' John joined in from his usual seat. 'And I hope the other lads from the cathedral find the swine before you do.'

'Thanks, Ida.' Stanton needed to close off the conversation.

Barling was glaring at him like he had found a rat in his food. 'I see our work is the subject of common gossip in here.'

'It's an alehouse, Barling. People come here to talk to all manner of folk. It's partly why it's so enjoyable.'

'I cannot see the enjoyment in that.' Barling gave him a horrified look and took a spoon of pottage. His expression cleared. 'This is quite palatable.'

'I'm glad you think so.' Stanton tucked into his own meal. 'You looked like you could do with it.'

Barling merely sniffed, then looked over as the door opened. He gave a stiff nod to the two priests who entered. 'I am pleased to see the arrival of a more respectable pair than the rest of the patrons,' he said to Stanton.

But the priests didn't sit down. 'Good day, Ida. We've come to take your latest charge back to his family.'

John Roulf came from the back room, wheeling the sickly pilgrim in the little barrow.

'One out, one in, eh, lads?' said Ida to the priests.

'Not sure when you'll have your next one, Ida,' replied one. 'There's been a miracle at the tomb with your next guest. He rose up from his bier today.'

'Oh?' Ida's eyebrows raised.

The priest snorted. 'That he did. Rose up and ran off with two silver rings and a purse.'

A loud chorus of laughs met his words, Stanton joining in.

Ida clapped her hands. 'Oh, that's a good one.'

'Stanton, this is no laughing matter,' said Barling. 'I am appalled that a theft could be the subject of mirth and not scandal.'

Stanton was about to make the point again about the purpose of an alehouse when a familiar black-robed figure strode in, acknowledging the priests and giving a quick blessing to the sick pilgrim. 'Brother William's here, Barling. And he's headed this way.'

Stanton buried his face in his cup, the better to hide his grin at Barling's disapproving face as the monk and alewife swapped a friendly greeting.

'You're a difficult man to find, Aelred Barling.' William slid onto the bench next to the clerk.

'My apologies, brother.' Barling flushed. 'I do not normally frequent alehouses. I hope you do not believe—'

William raised a broad hand. 'If you will excuse my interruption. I have a matter of urgency that I must address with you.' He glanced at Stanton. 'I think your man should leave us.'

'He can hold his tongue, brother.'

Stanton knew Barling's words to William were aimed at him too.

'If you insist.' William lowered his voice so that only their small group would be able to hear. 'When I returned from Throwley this morning, I heard about the murder of Martin Eustace.' He crossed himself. 'God rest his soul. Prior Benedict summoned me to tell me. He is, as you can imagine, greatly agitated.'

Stanton matched Barling's nod. He, in turn, could imagine the churn of the clerk's thoughts. Here William was again, presenting the prior as somebody not in control of events. But the trip to Throwley ruled William out.

William went on. 'Worse, the Archbishop is disappointed. Extremely disappointed. Prior Benedict was completely direct with him. He told the Archbishop, Barling, that as his Grace is due on the morrow, and we are in a worse position than ever, that you have failed.'

'Failed?' The clerk's word was a faint croak. 'Then I am to be sent away from Canterbury, like he threatened?'

Stanton hoped Barling wouldn't collapse from the seat. He, Stanton, had been told by others all his life when he came up short. For Barling, this must be very new. Yet he shared Barling's fear. Stanton could not, would not leave Canterbury before he'd seen the necromancer.

William sighed. 'Prior Benedict is fond of grand announcements and promises. The trouble is, he does not look ahead to how he is going to fulfil them. Sending you away solves precisely nothing with regard to our immediate problem, which is the visit of his Grace. A visit during which he might get to hear of the murders. I made that point to the Archbishop. I also presented a solution to the Archbishop, one which you can assist with, Barling.'

'I . . . I do not know what to say, brother,' said Barling.

'I have suggested that we – you and I – prepare a story for his Grace,' said William. 'A plausible one. By that, I mean a story of what may have happened, should news of the killings reach his ears. A story such as a group of unknown outlaws, who have fled Canterbury in fear of his Grace's arrival and who are being tracked down as we speak.'

'But that is not the truth, brother.'

If Barling had looked about to faint before, Stanton got ready to catch him now.

William spread his broad hands. 'It is not exactly a lie, either. It could turn out to be true in the end. But what the Archbishop cannot, will not, have is no story at all. Do you understand me, Barling?'

The clerk flinched as if he'd been struck. 'Yes, brother.'

Embellishments. That was one of the reasons that Barling had listed to Stanton for suspecting William, information that the clerk had gleaned from Prior Benedict. Looked like it was true.

'Then come with me.' William stood up. 'There is no time to lose.'

Barling stood up, and Stanton got to his feet as well, praying that this task would be complete in time for him to keep his appointment with the necromancer. He doubted it. But his prayer was answered, just not in the way he expected.

'Not you,' William said to him, pointing at the seat. 'You stay where you are.'

Stanton sat back down in profound relief that his evening would go ahead as planned, along with shame that he hadn't argued harder to stay with Barling.

But as Barling walked out, he didn't even glance back. He was already deep in conversation with Brother William.

Stanton took a large drink of ale to help push away his sadness that Barling didn't need him.

A fat man appeared at the door, banging a small drum. 'Who's for a tune?' called the man.

Cheers from the other patrons answered him as Ida waved him in.

The man launched into a loud, lewd verse that had folk howling.

Stanton smiled and raised his cup to the fellow. 'A fine tune, indeed.'

His spirits were lifting. Good ale, a rude song.

And tonight, this very night, he would speak to his Rosamund again.

Chapter Forty

Margery Clement's cramped house was exactly as it had been when Stanton entered it the previous night with Elena and when he and Barling had visited.

But this time, the elderly herbalist wasn't alone.

Nicholas Clement was waiting for him.

To Stanton's surprise, the man had shaved off his pale hair and eyebrows, and he wore fresh white robes.

'I am glad you have decided to come,' said Nicholas. 'I have been preparing all day.'

'I came because it's urgent,' said Stanton. 'I need help in finding the killer of Peter Flocke. I have the payment.' Stanton went to open his belt purse.

'No.' Nicholas held up a hand to stop him. 'You pay me when it is done. Aunt?'

As before, Margery secured the door and dimmed the light in the room.

'Then we are ready to begin,' said Nicholas. 'I must warn you that you have to stay well back. This is no simple conjuration. I will be summoning the dead. It is dangerous.'

'Very dangerous,' came Margery's fearful whisper.

'I'll take care,' said Stanton, unease prickling at him.

Nicholas went through the same ritual as previously, making a salt circle on the floor. This time, he placed a deep bowl of water and his knife in the centre. He stepped out again. An unknown object, about a foot square, rested on the table, covered with a white cloth.

Nicholas whipped the cloth off, and Stanton caught his breath.

A cage, in which a live bat rustled.

Nicholas opened the cage door and grabbed the creature in one quick movement. He returned to the circle, holding the struggling bat in his left hand. He bent to pick up the knife with his right.

Margery muttered an oath.

Nicholas's hand was a blur.

The bat lay headless on the floor and the bowl of water had turned crimson.

Stanton's unease grew. It was one thing to hear about the art of necromancy. It was another to witness it first-hand.

Nicholas knelt before the bowl, staring into the bloodied water. 'I conjure you, dark angels.' He cupped his palms and splashed the foul liquid over his head, where it ran down his white-robed shoulders in red rivulets. 'Those who fell from heaven, I conjure thee.' He repeated the words and the action three times. Then he fell silent, save for his loud, panting breath.

'The spirits are coming,' whispered Margery to Stanton, 'bearing the dead. Not everything they say may make sense at first. Voices from beyond the grave can be strange to our ears.'

'What do you want of me?'

Stanton started, heart banging.

The voice that had come from Nicholas's mouth was that of another man.

'Peter Flocke?' said Stanton.

'Shh,' hissed Margery. 'You cannot talk to the dead. Only through Nicholas.'

A deep, guttural sigh came from the necromancer. The voice again. 'My life was taken from me, taken by another's hand. A hand without a face. The hand of evil. Stole my life.' A low, keening wail. 'My statues, my flowers. They alone have my life now.'

'Tell him I saw them,' said Stanton. 'Such beautiful stone flowers.'

His words echoed in Nicholas's own voice. Then the necromancer's nostrils opened wide. He inhaled and exhaled loudly, over and over. A sweetness filled the air, more powerful than the other scents in this stuffy room.

The hairs rose on Stanton's neck. 'Roses?' Stanton said to Margery.

'I can smell them too,' she said, eyes wide.

'I don't understand,' said Stanton. 'Flocke's were stone. Not real flowers.'

Nicholas raised his head to look at Stanton. Sweat poured down the man's face, mingling with the wet of the bloodied water. 'I do not understand the spirits. They tell me of roses on a tomb.'

Stanton's mouth dried. Rosamund's burial place was covered with carved roses of stone. 'I have mourned at a tomb like that. When I asked you if you could bring back a woman, I was thinking of the woman who lies there.'

Nicholas dropped his head again. 'So come, sweet lady. Do not be afraid. Oh, she is so, so far away.'

'Rosamund?' Stanton could swear he dreamed. He stepped to the circle.

Margery grabbed him by the sleeve. 'Do not enter, sir. I beg of you.'

'So far away, so dark.' Nicholas's teeth began to chatter hard, so hard that Stanton thought they might break. But the necromancer forced the words out. 'Rosamund wants to tell Hugo . . . tell him that her passing was so painful, so very, very painful.'

Stanton thought his heart might stop. Rosamund had returned to him. She had.

With a cry like a wounded animal, Nicholas slumped to one side on the floor, shaking with a terrifying violence.

'What's happening?' asked Stanton of Margery.

'The spirits are leaving.' She brought her hands to her face. 'Please, let him be spared.'

Nicholas went rigid, then drew in a long, long breath. 'They are gone.' He climbed wearily to his feet. 'The woman by the name of Rosamund as well.'

'But you can get her back?' Stanton opened his purse and tipped out many coins into one palm. 'You must.'

Nicholas shook his head. 'Not tonight. I am overcome as it is. But we can try again tomorrow. She left with these words in the meantime.'

'Words? What words?'

'That she will always love you.'

Stanton swallowed a knot of tears. 'As I will her. Did she say anything else?' He was pleading, he knew he was, he could hear it in his own voice.

Nicholas wiped the sweat and bloodied water from his face with his forearm. 'That while she suffered so much, the end, when it came . . .'

'Yes?'

'Was peaceful.'

Peaceful? Stanton stared at him in disbelief, closing his fist around the coins so hard the metal pushed into his flesh. Rosamund's end had been murder: a violent, savage murder. Maybe, like Margery had warned, he had not fully understood the speech of the dead. But what Nicholas claimed were the words of poor Rosamund seemed devastatingly clear. He would try once more. 'You're telling me that she didn't suffer?'

'Not at all,' said Nicholas with a glowing smile. 'She said to tell you that her slipping into the next world was as easy as falling asleep.'

'A great comfort,' said Margery.

'Comfort? It's no comfort.' Rage surged through Stanton, so violent he thought he might be sick. 'Because it's a lie, damn you.'

Nicholas's expression hardened in an eye-blink. 'You cannot doubt the dark arts. Their ways are always not so clear.'

'What my nephew says is true,' said Margery. She looked frightened half to death. 'It is so dangerous to anger the spirits by questioning them. You should not do so. Not in any way.'

'I don't need to question anything that's going on here.' Stanton marched to the door and wrenched it open. 'It's perfectly clear. You pair are both the worst sort of fakes, preying on people's misery and loss.'

'Before you go.' Nicholas held out his hand. 'My payment.'

Stanton thought for a second about refusing him. Instead, he flung the coins to the floor with a loud rattle. 'Take it.'

'So you do believe?' Nicholas smirked.

All Stanton believed was that he'd been loving a ghost. He could see that now. 'You two have shown me that ghosts don't exist. You can have a reward for that. And nothing else.' He gave a final look of disgust at the mutilated dead bat on the floor, a cruel sacrifice to a lie. 'Shame on you. Shame on you both.'

He walked out without another word, despite Margery's pleading and Nicholas's foul response of a mocking oath.

Stanton had had enough of death. He should care more about the living.

Especially one particular living woman. He owed her an apology.

Chapter Forty-One

Stanton stood in the street below the window he knew belonged to Elena's room. He didn't want to knock on the door and have to explain himself to an innkeeper. He would do what he could to rouse her.

He picked up a couple of muddy pebbles from the street and threw one against the closed shutters. It bounced off with a loud crack and fell back down with a clatter. No answer. He threw another. The shutter opened a little way.

'Begone, ruffian.' The female voice was more annoyed than afraid.

It was definitely her.

'Elena, it's me.' For not the first time in his life, he wondered why he was trying to shout quietly.

'Hugo?' The shutter swung wide. 'What on earth are you doing?'

'I need to speak to you. It's urgent.'

'Is it about Sybil?' Her voice lifted in hope, and he cursed himself for being the source of it.

He could not be so cruel as to pretend he had news, though he knew it would bring her running down to the street. 'No, I'm afraid it's not.'

'Then it is not urgent.' She went to close the window.

'Elena. Please.'

After a long silence, she answered. 'Very well.'

She disappeared from the window and was soon at the open front door. 'Will this take long?' she said, keeping her soft voice even lower. 'I had already gone to bed for the night.' She had a large rough shawl wrapped tight over her shoulders that hung long enough to cover her linen underskirts. Her hood sat loosely on her hair, the strings trailing. 'I do not want to wake the house. I could lose my room if I did so.'

'I have quite a lot to tell you,' he said, 'if you allow me to come upstairs. But even if you don't, I want to tell you I'm sorry. I wasn't using you. I was just being stupid. Blind. Thinking only of myself.'

Elena opened her mouth to say something. Closed it again. Sighed. 'Make sure you're quiet,' she said.

He followed her up the stairs and into her little room.

There was nowhere to sit except on the small bed, the covers rumpled where she'd thrown them back. She did not indicate for him to do so, just folded her arms across her chest and looked at him.

'Tell me what all this is about. When I have heard your explanation, I will tell you if you are forgiven.'

'I had a love,' he said. 'One that I gave my heart to. That I lost.'

'Lost loves are two a penny.' Her dark blue eyes remained unmoved. 'As are broken hearts.'

'No, not like that, Elena. It wasn't like that at all. Her name was Rosamund. And she was beautiful and she was funny and she was impossible. And she was the mistress of a high lord.'

'How exciting for you.' A flush rose in Elena's cheeks. 'Now can you please leave, Hugo? I am but a lowly peasant's daughter, and I am very tired.' She made to go to the door, but he stepped in front of her.

'Hear me out, please.'

'Good night, Hugo.'

'Elena, I lost her because she was murdered!' He didn't mean to shout it out.

'Murdered?' Her eyes opened wide in stunned horror. 'How?'

It was like his shout had breached a dam within him, a dam that broke in a flood of tears and grief. 'She was strangled.' The image of his poor dead Rosamund flashed before him again, one he would never forget until the end of his days. 'It was vicious, savage.'

'In the name of the Virgin.' Elena crossed herself. 'Hugo, it is my turn to be sorry.' She put a gentle hand on his arm. 'Who did this to her, to your Rosamund?'

'The killer is dead.'

'Then you got justice. Good.' Elena gave a firm nod. 'Even better, they will be in hell for it.'

'But it doesn't matter. Because I didn't save her, I couldn't, I didn't know. Didn't know how.' He was making no sense, could only sob. 'And now, my life's work is following the murdered, the dead. Looking for answers, trying to stop it, but it keeps on happening, again and again.'

'Oh, Hugo.' She reached up and pulled him to her. 'Hugo.' Her coif slipped off and her hair swung free.

He buried his face in it, in its softness, its sweetness, its warmth, its life, as she held him and held him.

Chapter Forty-Two

Although the hour was very late, with darkness long fallen, Barling had not prepared for bed. He was exhausted, but he knew he would not close an eye. Instead, he sat at his table. But he was not working. His tablet and stylus sat idle. He could not turn to his usual consolation of his writing, for his most recent work had brought him nothing but distress.

He had completed his account of the murders for Brother William as ordered, the one that spoke of the possibility of unknown outlaws, outlaws who had fled, being responsible. He had done so in the monks' library at the priory, with only him and William present. William had conducted his own business at a carved and polished writing desk, with Barling hunched over the small table the monk assigned to him along with a fresh quill, ink and parchment.

Every stroke of the pen had been like the lash of a whip to Barling's conscience. When he had done, he had read it through from start to finish. It was the poorest work he had ever produced. Even his work from his earliest days as a clerk would have been better.

It lacked precision. Detail. The conclusion was weak. Barling knew that the flaws were not because of his writing skills. The flaw was in the task Brother William had set. The monk was asking the impossible: to make truth where there was none.

It had taken him much longer than expected, with William pushing hard for its completion and interrupting him several times in the abhorrent process.

The monk took the finished account from him and read it quickly. 'Not bad, Barling.' He gave an approving nod. 'Not bad.'

Not bad? Barling thought he might strike the man. Aelred Barling's writing was usually of the highest standard, enjoyed, envied and emulated by many. Yet here was this soft-fleshed monk talking to him like he was a spotty boy in a classroom. 'I am a little concerned about the accuracy, brother.'

William waved a broad hand. 'Oh, do not worry too much about accuracy, Barling. What you have produced is perfectly sufficient. I will be adding to it.'

'I do not understand, brother. Do you have any more facts?'

'No, we have all we require. I will be adding more aspects that appeal to the heart.'

'Such as?'

'Such as the woe of the virtuous people of Canterbury. Such as their fervent belief that their lord King's justice would prevail. Such as his Grace's wisdom and holiness in visiting Canterbury at this great feast of Easter. Such as the Canterbury woman who heard the name of the Martyr in the song of a bird and knew that it was a sign that the men would be caught.'

Barling looked at him in bewilderment. 'What Canterbury woman?'

'Oh, Barling.' William smiled. 'There is always a woman somewhere who hears birds talking of miracles. They tell me so at the tomb every other day. It means nothing. But it means everything. It delivers an assurance that all will be well.'

'I see.' And Barling did see. Could see now why Brother William had been so successful where Prior Benedict was not.

231

'Now, if you'll excuse me, Barling.' William held up his own quill with another smile. 'I have my work to do.'

Barling had been dismissed. He'd come back to the inn, hoping to unburden himself to Stanton about it. But his assistant's room had been empty. Still at the alehouse, no doubt.

And still there even at this late hour. Barling put his head in his hands for a moment. Yes, it was to be hoped that a crisis with his Grace had been averted. But Barling had become tainted in the process. Tainted and alone.

Barling heard rapid creaking on the stairs outside. Stanton was back.

He hurried over to the door and opened it up, ready to launch into his usual speech telling Stanton off, even as his heart gladdened for the first time in many hours. 'What time do—'

But it was not Stanton. It was the innkeeper Derfield, dressed in his nightshirt and carrying a lamp, with the look of a man tried past his patience.

'I've not had a guest like you before, sir. With all these summonses, day and night.'

Barling went cold. Another summons.

Derfield went on. 'A messenger came from Prior Benedict. The prior's at the house of Mistress Isabel Tyson. He says you're to come at once. And that you'll know what it's about.'

Chapter Forty-Three

Barling hurried down the stairs of the inn as fast as he dared and out into the dark street, where the messenger awaited him.

'The house of Mistress Tyson, you say?'

'Yes, sir.'

'What in the name of the Virgin has happened?'

'I do not know, sir. I was only told to fetch you.'

'I want you to do something else. Where can I find this house?'

The man rattled off a set of directions. 'It's made of stone. You can't miss it, sir. What do you want me to do?'

'Go with all haste to the Roulf alehouse and find a man called Hugo Stanton. Tell him I want him at the Tyson house immediately.'

'Right you are, sir.' The man sped off.

Barling's mind raced faster than his feet as he followed the messenger's instructions through the streets. Isabel Tyson did not live alone. She had her young daughter, the sickly Lucia. His heart quailed at what might await him. He could not move quickly enough; it was as if he would never get there. But as he approached the fine stone house, one that told of the widow Isabel's late husband's wealth, it felt far too soon.

He could see the shadowy figures of two cathedral monks at the open front door.

'Brothers! It is I, Aelred Barling.' As he walked up, he heard crying. A woman. No words. Just the low, unceasing lamentation of the utterly bereft. It would appear his worst fears were about to be realised. His courage almost failed him but he willed himself on.

The monks stepped back with a respectful bow to allow him entry, and Barling walked through a generous anteroom and then into the spacious hall, where he was met with a scene that took his breath from his body.

Prior Benedict was with Isabel Tyson. She was slumped on the embroidered settle before the carved stone fireplace, grieving like a wounded animal. Her bloodstained hands to her face glowed deep red in the light from the burning logs and swathes of scarlet stained her fine silk dress. Her eyes looked at nothing.

The prior strode over to Barling, his expression icy and his voice low. 'I think you and Brother William may have to amend your tale. Your disgraceful tale. He showed it to me with unseemly pride.'

Barling knew he deserved the remark, but it still stung. 'What has happened here, Prior?' he whispered. 'Is it the child, Lucia?'

'No,' said Prior Benedict. 'It is Mistress Tyson's servant, Hilde.'

Barling was mortified. The old servant had completely slipped his mind. Relief mingled with his dismay. 'Then the child is safe?'

'We do not know,' said the prior. 'She is missing, and we cannot find her. The good lady is distraught, as you can see.'

'Dear God.'

Voices came from the door. Stanton. Heaven be praised.

But it was not. The messenger entered. 'I have been to the Roulf alehouse as you directed, sir,' he said to Barling. 'But there is no sign of Hugo Stanton. Ida said he left just before sunset.'

Not at their inn. Not at the alehouse. Only one other likely place where Stanton could be found remained. Or rather, one likely person. Somebody that Stanton had assured Barling he would be wasting no further energies on. A clear untruth. 'Do you know Saint Cuthbert's inn?'

'Yes, sir.'

'I believe you will locate him at that establishment. He will be with one of the guests, a woman by the name of Elena Whitehand. Tell him he is to come back here at once. That Hilde, servant of Isabel Tyson, has been murdered and that Mistress Tyson's daughter Lucia is missing. Tell him to look out for any sight or sound of her. Now go.' Barling addressed the prior once more. 'I need to see—'

'The King's man?' Isabel was staring right at him.

'Good lady,' began Barling.

'Find her.' She got up from the settle and rushed over to him. 'You must find Lucia. You must.' She grasped for his hands with her bloodied ones.

His stomach turned over at her viscid touch. But such was her distress, he could not repel her. 'Good lady,' he began again.

Isabel ignored him. 'Come.' She pulled him along to the rear of the house. 'Come and bear witness to what he did to my poor Hilde. Come.' They emerged into the darkness of an extensive, paved yard, the prior with them, holding up a large horn lamp.

The yard was filled with plants and shrubs around the sides and a well-stocked, raised herb bed. A wide stone seat. A neat woodpile. A well in one corner.

A place of peace and tranquillity.

Except that on the ground, in front of a stone statue of the Virgin on a plinth, lay Hilde's corpulent body.

'Look.' Isabel half-dragged Barling over to it as he struggled to keep up. 'Look at her.' She let go of him to clutch at her own throat, as if she could hardly breathe. 'Only a devil from hell would do this.'

'It is as before, Barling.' The prior raised the lamp, the better that Barling could see the body of the servant.

The prior was right. Hilde had a cross carved deep into her forehead. Her body had several stab wounds.

'May I ask who found her?' said Barling.

'I did,' said Isabel.

'Did you hear anything?'

'No.' Isabel choked on a fresh sob. 'I was out.'

'What of your other servants?' An affluent woman like Isabel was bound to have many.

'They come in daytime,' she said. 'Only Hilde lived here.'

'A slightly unusual arrangement, my lady?'

'Edmund, my late husband, was a man of great wealth and traded in all manner of fine goods. He trusted just a handful of people and insisted I do the same. Hilde, who had been in his family's service all his life, was among them. Edmund held the view that a strong stone house with stout locks was far more effective against thieves than any man or woman. But . . .' Another sob.

'You say you were out, good lady?'

She nodded. 'I visit Master Ordway on some evenings. Neither of us has a spouse, so it is welcome company for us both. He would, of course, come to visit me, but as you can imagine, so much of our conversation turns to Lucia and her poor progress. I cannot run the risk of her overhearing. He accompanied me home, as always, and made sure I was safely inside with the door locked before he left. I went to kiss Lucia good night.' Her breathing quickened. 'But she was not in her bed. I could not find Hilde, either. I called and called. Then I noticed the door to the yard was not locked, so I went outside. And then I found Hilde.' Her voice cracked. 'But not my Lucia. The monster must have taken her.' She put her hand to her chest. 'I cannot breathe. I swear to you, I cannot. Please. Help me find her. Please.'

'Barling?'

Isabel cried out, as did the prior.

236

Barling's heart jumped then steadied again. 'We are in here, Stanton.' Thank goodness. 'It is my assistant, good lady,' said Barling to Isabel. 'Fear not.'

Stanton came in through the half-open back gate, breathless from running. But he was not alone.

To Barling's perturbation, Elena Whitehand was with him. Stanton had told Barling he had no ties with her. The realisation of Stanton's lie cut him deeply, even in the midst of the horror he was dealing with.

Stanton's gaze fell on Hilde, and he grimaced, putting a hand out to Elena. 'Don't look.'

But she already had. She did not flinch, instead crossing herself with a steady hand.

A shame. Had she created a fuss, Barling would have had the perfect excuse for banishing her. She had no business being here. He turned back to Isabel. 'Where have you searched for Lucia so far?'

'The house. Three times. All of this yard. I was screaming for her, for somebody to fetch help. A few people heard, came running, called for the prior.'

'When I arrived, a commotion was building, though limited by the late hour,' said the prior. 'I ordered people home to restore order.' He gave Barling a meaningful look.

'Of course.' To try to keep word from spreading, more like.

Prior Benedict went on. 'And to keep people safe, with such a devil roaming the streets. My monks are continuing to look for Lucia.'

'So, good lady, you did not see or hear anything directly?' said Barling.

'Nothing.' Her reply was more sob than speech.

'Mistress Tyson, if I may,' said Stanton. 'Was this gate open when you found Hilde?'

'Yes, it was. And it should not have been.'

'Then perhaps Lucia slipped through it and wandered off?' said Stanton.

'No, that would never have happened.' Isabel shook her head. 'Never.'

'You are so sure?' said Barling. He knew little of children. But what he did know suggested to him that they could be as elusive as mice in a wattle and daub wall.

'Yes, I am sure,' said Isabel. 'The hasp on that gate is not within her reach. She is not tall enough.'

'Then perhaps Hilde left it open before her death?' said Stanton.

'Again, no,' said Isabel. 'The hasp is that high because it was Hilde who made me have it moved up there. She was the one who would harp on about the alleyway at the back. She had a terror of Lucia getting out.' She choked on another sob 'She would never, ever have left that gate open. Whoever killed Hilde will have done that. Done that as they carried off my Lucia.'

Order, Barling reminded himself. They must have order. In any investigation, be it a missing child – or worse. He scanned the shadowed yard once more, his mind made up.

'Mistress Tyson,' he said. 'May I suggest that you and the prior go inside?'

'What good will that do?' asked Isabel.

'I would ask that you search your house again, but this time, look for any sign of the killer in the house. They may have entered. We do not know.'

'And you, Barling?' said the prior. 'What will you do?'

'We will search the yard for the same.'

In truth, they would indeed be searching the shadows of the large yard. But their methodical search might not only yield a clue or a sign of the killer.

Barling knew there was a chance, a very real chance, that it would yield a child's body.

Chapter Forty-Four

'What's going on, Barling?' Stanton kept his voice low as Isabel and the prior went back inside. 'You don't usually ask the relatives of murder victims to look for clues.'

'As we do not usually include others in our enquiries.' The clerk gave Elena an ill-tempered look. 'Perhaps she should remove herself.'

'Or perhaps I could be of help.' Elena didn't budge.

The clerk ignored her, speaking to Stanton alone. 'I sent them in there so that we could conduct a full and proper search of the yard. A search that may not only turn up clues, but another body.'

Stanton muttered an oath and dragged his hands through his hair. 'Oh. I see.'

Elena blanched but still stayed where she was.

'I have a very real fear,' said Barling, 'that whoever murdered Hilde will have killed Lucia as well. This killer has no mercy. Look at what they have done to an old woman.'

Stanton nodded. It was hard to find words for such a coward.

Barling went on. 'I know Isabel says that she searched this yard. But it is large and dark, with many corners and shadows. She was looking for her live daughter. We are looking for a body. It is not the same thing.'

'Do you have any advice for me, sir?' said Elena to Barling.

'None other than you could sit on that seat and stay out of the way.'

Stanton's own ire rose at the clerk's rudeness. 'Even better, that you join us, Elena. We can split into three. It will make the search faster, whatever we find.'

Barling drew breath, but Stanton carried on talking over him. 'And with a search, try to start from one spot and work your way back around to it, so you don't miss anything. If anything, even the smallest thing, looks out of place, trust your instincts. Don't ignore anything.'

'I will not.' Elena's jaw set in her resolve.

'I would also say,' said Barling, 'though Stanton and I already know it, that if there is a body, do not call out in a fuss. I want to be able to view it before her mother does and to have a chance to prepare for her reaction. Now, we cannot delay any more. I shall search the herb beds and bushes. Stanton, you take that corner, where the well is. You, girl, that other corner. Pay particular attention to the woodpile.' The clerk set off.

'Sorry about him,' muttered Stanton to Elena. 'You're trying to help. He should be grateful.'

'It does not matter. What matters is Lucia.'

They parted, Elena heading off to her area and Stanton to his, the darkest part of the yard.

An eerie quiet fell, the sounds of their searching like that of night creatures in the bushes.

Stanton bent low under a large evergreen shrub, the ground underneath dry and covered with hard, dead leaves and spiky twigs. He raked his hands through. Nothing. He moved to the next one. Did the same. Then his fingers met something soft. He closed his hand on it and peered in, heart pounding. But it was just a pile of old feathers.

A sudden rattling and a cry from Elena made him start. 'Elena?' He stood up, trying to make out what was happening in the gloom.

'What in the name of the Virgin are you doing, girl?' Barling. Furious.

240

'I'm sorry,' came Elena's calm reply. 'I disturbed a rats' nest in the woodpile.'

Stanton braced for a tirade at her, but the clerk just made a disgusted noise and was silent again.

His own search moved on. Another bush. Nothing.

Then he was at the well, its low walls and the ground around it covered in damp moss. He peered in. And then his heart really did almost stop. For in the darkness below, he made out a flash of something pale. Pale hair?

Jesu Christus. Forget quiet.

'Over here.' Stanton turned and ran for the lamp that the prior had left, arriving back at the well at the same moment as Barling and Elena.

'Is it Lucia?' Barling's drawn face was shadowed in dread in the light.

Elena's face could be stone, her lips moving in quiet prayer.

Stanton held the lamp up over the well. The pale object became even clearer. It was the top of a little round head, one with pale blonde hair.

Stanton wanted time to stop. Wanted to never have another moment pass, so he would never have to tell a mother that her only child was dead. Would never have to draw that little body from the well. Would never have to see what it was that the depraved monster on the loose had done to Lucia Tyson.

But time did move on.

Moved on to the next beat of his heart.

And the next.

And at the third, the blonde head moved.

And a filthy, terrified small face looked up at him from the darkness of the well.

A weak cry that he could swear came from heaven. 'Mama?'

Chapter Forty-Five

'Your master is still angry with you, isn't he?'

'He's not my master,' replied Stanton to Elena. 'He's just Barling. But yes, he's in a foul temper.'

They made their way through the dark streets on their return to Elena's inn, streets where Stanton saw every shadow as the murderer stalking their next prey.

'But even he was happy that Lucia was found alive.' Elena gave a long, contented sigh. 'It really was a miracle, wasn't it, Hugo?'

'It was.' His own heart still sang. 'She was a quick thinker, wasn't she, for one so young? Hiding in the well like that.' He'd only been able to marvel as he'd heard Lucia's account as she clung to her mother and her mother to her.

Hilde, out in the yard to fetch some firewood. Slow.

Stanton could imagine, Hilde taking ponderous steps in the dark.

Lucia, following her out, unseen. Trotting over to hide next to the well, so she could startle Hilde by jumping out in jest.

Then the bad ghost in the yard. A figure without a face, concealed in a robe or a cloak.

That was all they'd been able to get from the child, who had been rigid and barely able to speak with terror.

They were no further along with the identity of the murderer.

'It must have been the Virgin's hand that guided her over to the well in the first place,' said Elena. 'Because it spared her seeing the killing too. The sounds must have been terrible enough.'

Stanton grimaced. 'They were certainly enough for her to hide herself.'

'Do you honestly think the killer would have murdered her too, Hugo?'

'Yes, I do. Believe me, Elena, I've seen the evil that takes hold of those who kill. That's why I'm making sure you get to your inn in one piece.'

'Barling did not see it that way.'

Stanton shook his head, his jaw set. 'No, he didn't.'

Outside the Tyson home, after making sure that the stone house was locked and secure, the prior and monks rushing off to inform the Archbishop, a furious Barling had given him a tongue-lashing that was as quiet as it was full of venom.

'You mean to tell me, Hugo Stanton, that instead of coming with me to carry on with our enquiry, now that it has reached new heights of urgency, you are insisting on wasting time in walking this girl through the streets of Canterbury?'

'Yes, I am, Barling. Those streets are too dangerous for her to be out on her own.'

'But she is only out on them because she came traipsing along with you. She should not be here in the first place. This delay is all your doing.'

'Whether you like it or not, she is here, so that's that. I'll catch up with you and the enquiry as soon as Elena is safe in her inn.'

Barling had given him a long, long look. 'I suppose,' he finally said, 'that at least she has shown me what you truly are. A selfish, lazy good-for-nothing who is interested only in himself. Do not trouble yourself with coming back. I can manage perfectly well on my own.' With that, he'd stalked off.

243

Stanton and Elena arrived outside her inn.

'Safe and sound,' said Stanton. 'At least I got something right tonight.'

'Safe, yes.' She held up her right hand. 'But not completely sound.' Her first and second fingers were at an eye-watering angle and wore the dark stains of angry bruises.

'What have you done?' he said, aghast.

'The woodpile,' she said. 'There was no rats' nest. I sent logs rolling with my own clumsiness and crushed these. I said about the rats so Barling wouldn't get even angrier.'

'I reckon I'd have yelled my head off.' He sucked his teeth. 'You need to get those bandaged up as soon as you can. Do you want me to help you?'

'Do not worry about me, Hugo Stanton. You are very sweet, but I can manage by myself. Thank you for seeing me back.' Elena stood on her tiptoes and gave him a quick peck on the cheek. 'Now go and find your master.' The inn door opened at her knock, and she was gone.

Stanton set off to his next destination, remaining alert for anyone suspicious.

A plague on Aelred Barling. Let him stew in his own fury for a couple of hours.

Stanton would take the edge off his own ire with a few good ales.

Never mind Barling and his lack of thanks.

Lucia Tyson was still alive, and he had found her.

That was thanks enough for Hugo Stanton.

Chapter Forty-Six

Despair brought so many souls to the tomb of the Martyr.

Aelred Barling knew that.

In the two thousand, three hundred and three days since Thomas Becket was murdered and the miracles had begun, thousands had flocked to Canterbury, seeking his aid in desperate pleas. Pleas silent, whispered, prayed aloud: a chorus as constant as the waves of the ocean washing onto the shore.

And here Barling was, lost in his own despair, with his mute appeals, among the multitude of those seeking help from the saint.

The King would arrive tomorrow, and Barling was no nearer to finding who this savage killer was. His hope that had risen when Stanton had arrived tonight, the hope that Barling would not be on his own with this task, was dashed. His own wrathful, sinful jealousy had driven Stanton away.

Four people had lost their lives, one after another, in a relentless horror that Barling was powerless to stop. He had a sickening terror that this killer would not stop, either. Anybody who would slay a defenceless, sick old woman like poor Hilde had been sent straight from hell itself.

Sweet holy and blessed Martyr, I implore you to intercede for me, a poor sinner. Grant me the grace to follow in your wisdom and mercy. Sweet blessed Martyr, I implore you.

He would stay here as long as he could tonight, pray on and on until the guardian monks allowed him no more time.

Sweet blessed Martyr, I implore you.

And he would keep returning and returning until he got an answer. He would not be like those who, if their prayers were not immediately answered, turned elsewhere.

Sweet blessed Martyr, I implore you.

He would not turn elsewhere, like Isabel Tyson had, to try to save the life of her sick child. Though a monster would have taken little Lucia tonight. Perhaps the Martyr had been watching over her. Saint Thomas had already granted the miracle of saving the life of a girl who had almost perished in a well. This could be another.

But the Martyr still had not cured the child's sickness. Gilbert Ordway was the child's last hope.

Barling believed it to be a forlorn one, but at least the mother had the means to keep paying Ordway.

Not so Katerine Flocke, for her sick husband, Peter. Nor Robert Norwood.

Barling's heart began to beat a little faster.

As for Martin Eustace . . . No. His heart calmed again. Ordway had never had any dealings with Eustace. Unless the man was a consummate liar. Barling had met one or two of those in his past.

And now there was Hilde. Poor old, slow, breathless Hilde. Slow and ill from her dropsy. But killed by a vicious hand.

Hilde, who was also in charge of the sick Lucia. The child was being treated by Ordway. Could the physician also been ministering to the servant?

Barling crossed himself and rose to his feet. It could be nothing. It could be everything.

He had to ask Isabel Tyson if her murdered servant's sickness had been treated by Ordway. It could, finally, be a way into the truth. The truth of somebody with the blackest of hearts.

He made his way back along the dark streets to Isabel's house, his pulse racing, aware of the echo of every footstep and the glimpse of every shadow.

He knocked on the door.

Nothing.

He knocked again. And again. The widow must sleep very soundly, though who could sleep after the night's terrors, he did not know.

Then Isabel's voice came from within, her words choking on a terrified sob. 'Who . . . who's there?'

'It is Aelred Barling, mistress. My apologies at having to disturb you again at so late an hour and in the midst of your grief.'

'One moment.' He heard a key in the lock, followed by bolts being drawn back, and the door opened.

The tear-stained Mistress Tyson had not been sleeping. She had cleansed herself of the horrific bloodstains but was still fully dressed in fresh clothes and held a large fire iron in one shaking hand. 'Come in, sir, quickly, quickly.' She slammed the door after him, snapping the bolts shut with her free hand and locking the door. 'What are you thinking of? You should not be abroad. There is a devil still loose on the streets.' She gestured at the door with the fire iron, her eyes wild in fear. 'We do not know their face. It could be anybody who passes us.'

'I came because it was imperative that I do so. I have to ask you a couple of questions about Hilde. But first, how is Lucia?'

'Sleeping, thank the Virgin.' The woman trembled like she had the worst ague and slow tears still rolled down her cheeks. 'But I fear I will never close an eye again.'

'I do not wish to cause you any further anguish, but I must ask you about Hilde. Hilde was unwell with dropsy, was she not?'

'Yes, she had been for a couple of years.'

'Did Ordway treat her?'

247

'Gilbert Ordway?' She palmed the tears from her face with her free hand. 'No. I did try to persuade her. I tried to reassure her that I would her pay for everything. I know how costly he is. But she would not have it. I like the old ways, my lady, she would say. It didn't do her any good. And now . . .' She choked on another sob. 'This hell has befallen us.'

'May God grant us mercy, it has.' He could almost taste his disappointment. Ordway had not been involved. He, Barling, had been wrong. Again. 'I will not take any more of your time, good lady. If you could allow me out?'

'Of course, sir.' Isabel set to unlocking and unbolting the door.

As Barling went to step out into the night, the faint echo of something she had said claimed his full attention. He paused. 'Good lady, when you told me that Hilde said she liked the old ways, what did you mean?'

'She insisted on seeing that herbalist woman.'

Barling's stomach lurched. 'Which one?'

'Margery Clement. Hilde had done so for years. One old woman with another. Hilde would come back with the most appalling-smelling ointments and poultices. I doubt if they did the slightest bit of good. But she swore by them.'

Now his breath came fast in his chest. *One old woman.* Yes, that was the tiny, aged Margery.

His own thought back at the tomb, just a short time ago: *A consummate liar. Barling had met one or two of those in his past.*

One or two. One or two consummate liars. Two. Two of them.

Margery, the trusted healer, the woman who would waive costs in an outward show of virtue. A lure to ensnare people. To ensnare Peter Flocke through his wife, Katerine. Robert Norwood. Martin Eustace. And Hilde.

But such aged and frail hands could not have slain her prey.

Other hands could.

248

Both are as bad as each other.

The words of their neighbour to Barling and Stanton as they had been waiting outside the house.

The hands of Margery's nephew, Nicholas.

Nicholas Clement, the necromancer. The man who profited from the dead. The man whose hands had performed unholy rituals, over and over. Whose hands had the strength to stab and stab every one of his victims. And who would have revelled in the sinful sacrilege of carving the sacred Cross into their foreheads.

'Oh, dear God.' Barling's words came out as a low moan.

'Are you feeling unwell, sir?' Isabel's brow furrowed in concern.

'No, good lady,' replied Barling. 'But I must go. Immediately.' He gestured to the door. 'Make sure you lock up. Tight. Open to nobody. Do you understand?'

Her petrified nod and slam of the door told him she did.

Barling fought down his own terror as he set off into the night again.

Help. He had to get help.

Chapter Forty-Seven

'I pray both of those devils are home, Barling.' Brother William hurried alongside Barling as they made their way through the reeking alleys that led to the house of Margery and Nicholas Clement.

Two other cathedral monks were with them. The number of their group, along with Brother William's furious demeanour, meant that the few beggars who continued to slink along these streets at the late hour stayed away.

'As do I, brother.' In truth, Barling was shaking, not just from his panicked rush from the Tyson house to the cathedral, but with trepidation at what was to come. The last time he had faced a murderer, it had almost cost him his life.

He thanked God for Brother William's reaction when he had sought out the monk at the tomb. The man had listened closely to what Barling had said. Even better, his reaction to Barling's words had been swift and decisive.

The Clement house was in sight, smoke curling from the thatch.

William waved a hand to slow their pace and ensure a quiet approach. 'I can see cracks of light through the shutters. At least one of them is in there.'

Barling willed his steps forward, resisting the urge to flee that flowed within him.

They reached the door.

William looked around at the other monks. 'Are you ready?' he said.

Both men nodded yes.

William pounded on the door. 'Nicholas and Margery Clement! Open up in the name of Christ Church.'

The door opened a crack, and Margery's tremulous voice sounded through it. 'Good night to you, brother. What can I do for you?'

To Barling's shock, William kicked the door hard in response, and Margery fell back with a cry.

'Confess to your murders, you witch.' William marched in, Barling behind him with the other two monks to see Margery trying to stand, shrieking for mercy. But there was no sign of Nicholas in the small room.

'You'll cast no more spells.' William yanked Margery upright and shoved her into the hold of the monks. 'Where is he?' he bellowed. 'Where's Nicholas?'

A scuffling noise. From behind the door.

Barling whipped around to see a white-robed man scramble out, knife aloft in one hand.

Margery screamed. 'Nicholas, no!'

'Get him!' shouted William.

Nearest to Nicholas, the first monk dropped his hold on Margery to grab for him.

The blade landed deep in the monk's arm.

As the monk staggered away with a roar of pain, Nicholas shoved past him and was out of the door, half-falling on the muddy step.

William lunged after him but the necromancer got to his feet, William's clutch slipping from his sleeve.

'Stop, you devil.' William went for him again.

Nicholas slashed at him with the knife.

251

Barling pulled William back and the blade missed by a hair's breadth.

Nicholas's gaze met Barling's for an instant. 'Curse you.' Then he jumped from the step and was off.

William followed. 'Barling, with me.'

Barling acted, matching William's pace. But neither he nor the soft-bodied monk had the necromancer's speed.

'Nicholas Clement!' came William's panted shout. 'Stop!'

No response. The gap between them began to open up.

The necromancer was getting away.

Then further up the street came a slow-moving cart, rumbling towards them, the lamp-lit driver hunched low in the front seat as he steered his horses with care through the street that was barely wide enough to fit through.

Nicholas skidded to a halt with an oath and ducked down a side alley.

'We've got him.' William sped up, Barling falling a few strides behind.

He rounded the corner to see William advance on Nicholas, the necromancer with his back to the dead end of a stone wall.

Nicholas waved his blade from side to side. 'Stay away from me. Do you hear?'

'I hear nothing except the voice of a murderer.' William, still moving forward.

'Brother, don't.' Barling tried to catch him up, breath searing his chest. 'He's going to kill you.'

'Death doesn't scare me.' William launched for Nicholas as the necromancer swung his weapon, ducking back at the last second.

'Nor me.' Nicholas swiped again in a wide arc.

Barling searched around in the filth for anything, anything at all, that he could use as weapon. He had to help William. And if William were to be cut down, he, Barling, would be no match for the savage necromancer.

William rushed Nicholas with a yell and the blade grazed the monk's cheek.

But the blow didn't land.

William was too fast. He grabbed the man's thin wrist and twisted it hard, a twist that ended in a sickening crunch.

'Dark spirits, come to my aid!' howled Nicholas.

'No, they won't.' William forced the necromancer's arm up behind his back.

The clatter of the knife on the ground had Barling dart forward and scoop it up.

'Get going.' William twisted his captive's arm further, leading to fresh howls of pain but no resistance.

Barling followed along as they hastened back to the house, sickened by the bloodied weapon he held in one hand.

'We have them both,' said William as they walked in. 'Despite this one—'

'I wanted to help,' said Margery, voice trembling. She stood in the corner, her stick-like arms secured in front of her and her hands tied.

'Shut your noise, woman.' The first monk squatted down next to the one who had taken a stab to the arm. 'Thank goodness you're back, Brother William.'

The wounded man sat on the floor, breathing heavily, with one hand clapped over a wad of linen that he held to his arm. Blood ran freely down the sleeve of his habit and onto the floor.

'May the saints preserve us.' Barling put the knife on the table and grabbed another piece of linen so he could take over the staunching of the flow.

William frowned. 'We have to get you to the priory infirmary, brother. That wound needs sealing and quickly.' He shoved the whimpering, moaning Nicholas over to the firm hold of the second monk. 'Tie a strap around that broken wrist. You'll have no bother controlling the man if you do. Just pull on it if he gives you trouble.'

He turned to the monk on the floor. 'Let's get you going. Barling, bring some more of that cloth.'

They set off, William half-carrying the injured man.

As they passed through Newingate, Barling could see the bandage was already soaked with blood.

The monk was ghostly white. 'I don't know if I can make the infirmary, Brother William.' Sweat pebbled his forehead.

William's expression lost its usual certainty. 'You will, of course you will.'

Barling cast around in desperation. He recognised the street they were on. 'Brother William,' he said. 'The physician Gilbert Ordway lives close by. I know he has cautery irons.'

'Good thinking.' William lifted the monk almost off his feet as they made for the Ordway house.

As they approached it, Barling frowned to himself. The physician's courtyard gate was ajar and through the gap he could see that the front door stood wide open. 'Ordway! We need your help.'

He did not stop to wonder, yanking the gate wide for William and the monk and running in ahead to alert Ordway.

But no Ordway appeared. No greeting came. Only silence.

For Gilbert Ordway lay dead on the floor of his home, stabbed to death, blood in a wide pool around him, a pool in which the knife lay.

And a crude Cross was gouged deep, deep into his forehead.

Chapter Forty-Eight

'Another ale, Ida,' called Stanton over the hubbub of voices in full throat in the Roulf alehouse.

'Give me a minute, flower.' She hurried past with two armfuls of cups, headed for a table packed with excited carpenters.

Customers had been coming and going, many staying, and all full of gossip and rumours about the events of the night.

Stanton drank alone. He didn't mind sharing his table, but he'd no wish to join a group or for a group to join him.

It wasn't like him.

Usually, that was the first thing he'd do: make a quick friendship, swap tales tall and bawdy and funny.

But tonight, there was a very select list of topics on people's lips. The arrest of Margery and Nicholas Clement. The murder of physician Gilbert Ordway.

And widespread praise for the man responsible for bringing the pair to justice, Aelred Barling, and his cleverness in doing so.

Stanton listened to it all without saying a word as he drank steadily and swiftly, hardly tasting John's good ale.

'I've heard that this man Barling can see into the future. A bit, like.'

'Hard work, y'know, finding criminals. Good on the man. We had our henhouse raided every week for a year. Never caught 'em.'

'My wife's been asking if we can get that man Barling to look into a forged coin that she got.'

Yes, Aelred Barling was the hero of the hour, though the clerk would faint if he thought he was being talked about so freely in an alehouse.

Margery and Nicholas Clement.

Barling the hero had only thought of them because he, Hugo Stanton, had pushed him into the idea.

Stanton took another drink. Yes, his pride was sore wounded.

But it didn't hurt as much as his feelings. Barling's last tirade at him had cut deep, especially his last words. *Do not trouble yourself with coming back. I can manage perfectly well on my own.*

It looked like Stanton's fears over the last few months had finally been realised.

Aelred Barling didn't want or need him any more.

It would take more than a night on the ale to get over that.

But a night on the ale would surely help.

Chapter Forty-Nine

Barling walked along the almost deserted streets, exhausted and alone.

It had taken some time for him to explain all to Prior Benedict and then for Barling and Prior Benedict to explain all to Archbishop Richard in turn.

Barling had not expected the Archbishop to have left his bed to hear the account. But Richard had listened intently, jubilant that the killers had been found. The man had even thrown Brother William's account of outlaws on the fire. What was more, Richard had cared not when he'd heard that Margery and Nicholas Clement were protesting their innocence. The audacity. Barling and Brother William had been attacked by the knife-wielding Nicholas, not to mention the man's collection of objects for the unholy rituals.

It was fortunate and a credit to William that he had managed to seal the injured monk's arm with one of the dead physician's cautery irons. Otherwise, there would have been yet more blood on the Clements' hands. Richard proclaimed that they would face their punishment in the court of King Henry and that they would hang. If there had only been a little more time, Richard could have arranged for their execution in front of the King. But tomorrow, Maundy Thursday, was already a very busy day for his Grace.

Exhausted as he was, though, Barling knew he wouldn't sleep.

He wanted, no, he needed to talk to somebody about all that had happened. And the only person he had was Hugo Stanton.

Stanton had been right. Right about pursuing enquiries into Margery Clement.

Barling should not have dismissed his suggestions. He should have listened. He had to find his friend and apologise.

He climbed the stairs at their inn, but Stanton's room was empty, the bed neat and unoccupied despite the late hour.

Then his assistant would still be at the Roulf alehouse. He made his way back out and to the alehouse.

The door was closed, but that could mean nothing. Alehouses seemed to keep the strangest hours.

Barling knocked hard on the door. 'Hello? Open up, can't you?'

Nothing.

He knocked again, harder this time. 'Mistress Roulf, are you within?'

Still silence and a closed door.

Barling knocked so hard and long, he hurt his knuckles. 'It is I, Aelred Barling. I am trying to establish the whereabouts of Hugo Stanton.'

No response. The house was shut for the night.

Barling walked away, his pride a hard lump in his throat.

That left only one place.

Stanton would be with Elena Whitehand.

It mattered not. Barling would go there anyway, seek Stanton's forgiveness for his behaviour, which had for some time been as bad as, if not worse than, that of the worst sort of churl.

Even if Stanton sent him away, at least Barling would have tried.

Chapter Fifty

'God alive, Ida, don't let Barling in.' Stanton's words sounded hollow in his ears, head down as he was in a large pail, emptying his guts of most of the ale he'd drunk tonight. 'He'll string me up if he sees me in this state in public. Can't face him and his fuss right now.'

Another series of hard raps on the door. Barling's peeved voice. 'Mistress Roulf, are you within?'

Stanton raised his head, clutching on to the bench table for support. Helped to keep the room from spinning too. 'He's very presis . . . Pers . . . He hates being told no, y'know.'

'Don't worry, flower,' Ida said to Stanton as she damped down the fire for the night. 'I'm not opening the door for no one.'

'You can say that again.' John Roulf swore under his breath as he cleaned his carving tools. 'The second I did, there'd be people in that door, shouting for more ale. It never ends, no matter what time we close.'

'It never does.' Ida sighed, dusting off her hands. 'We'll slip you out the back when you're a bit more restored.'

Another volley of knocks from Barling. 'It is I, Aelred Barling. I am trying to establish the whereabouts of Hugo Stanton.'

'Are you sure?' Ida jerked a thumb at the door, even as Stanton nodded, grabbing for the table once more.

The Roulfs carried on with their tasks, tidying, cleaning, putting everything in order.

Meanwhile, all was quiet from the door.

'Think he's gone.' Stanton gave a loud hiccup.

'Sounds like it.' Ida came over, wiping her hands on her apron. 'You finished with that bucket?'

Stanton hiccupped again. 'Yeh. Think so.'

'Good.' She picked it up and took it to the back room where he heard the slosh of her emptying it out into the yard.

John grinned his gap-toothed grin at Stanton. 'Waste of good ale, son.'

'I know,' said Stanton. 'Breaks my heart.'

'You'll just have to do it again tomorrow night, flower.' Ida had returned, this time with a broom.

'Maybe not as much.' Stanton got to his feet, swaying. He gave a sour belch. Curse it. He still wasn't done being sick. 'Bucket.' He clapped a hand over his mouth, took two steps, and threw up. His legs gave as well, and he plonked down hard on his backside.

'Oh, for the love of God.' She sucked her teeth. 'John. Fetch a cloth, will you? He's got it all down himself as well as on my floor. And me nearly done with this.' She went on sweeping.

'Aye, some folk really can't hold their drink.' John lumbered off to the room at the rear, returning with a bucket of water, in which a grubby cloth floated. He put it on the ground next to Stanton.

'I'm very sorry.' Stanton thought about trying to stand up, then thought again. He looked up at John. 'Honest.'

'It happens, son. Just clean it up as soon as you've got yourself straight, eh?'

'I will.' Stanton squeezed out the bunched linen cloth and washed his hands first.

The Roulfs carried on with their work, she gathering up cups and taking them through to the kitchen at the back, he moving an empty barrel, picking it up with ease in his huge hands and rolling it through after her.

Stanton dipped the cloth in again. Now for his mouth. It wasn't too bad, but it felt sticky. He tried to unfurl the cloth to give his whole face a good wipe at the same time. But the cloth stayed scrunched up. He peered at it more closely. It must be tangled or something.

But it wasn't. It had a whole lot of stitching holding it together. He pulled at it and it fell into the right shape. He held up a dirty woman's embroidered hood. One identical to the spotless white hood Elena Whitehand wore. He'd seen it with his own eyes.

Elena's words to Stanton about her sister, Sybil, said to him in this very alehouse.

'*She was furious. She had to wear a rough pilgrim's tunic, which she hated, and a full hood over her hair, which she hated even more.*'

'*Like yours?*'

'*Exactly like mine. Our mother sewed them for us, embroidered the name and the symbols of the Martyr on them.*'

Stanton fought the ale fog in his head. This didn't make sense. The hood should be covering the missing Sybil's hair. Not floating in a smelly bucket in an alehouse.

The Roulfs were still busy in the back.

He couldn't leave it. He had to show it to Elena. He needed to go now, while he still had the chance to take it with him.

Stanton cleared his throat. 'Thanks, my friends,' he called. 'I'm done, and I'll get out of your way.'

They didn't answer him. Some sort of argument seemed to have broken out.

Stanton reached for the bench, hauled himself up. Damn it to hell, he was still without proper use of his legs. Never mind. The front door wasn't far. He could do it. Linen cap shoved into his belt, he made a staggering scramble that knocked over a stool. He didn't care, he was at the door, his numb hands pulling, pushing at the handle. It wouldn't budge. It was locked. Of course it was. The key, he needed the key.

A huge hand grabbed the scruff of his neck and lifted him off his feet.

'Going somewhere, son?' John flung him on his back on the floor, winding him hard.

Stanton looked up, trying to get a breath.

The Roulfs stood there, side by side. No smile.

'It's in his belt, John.' Ida was on Stanton in one movement, her hips over his thighs, powerful in her long skirts. She ripped the cloth from his belt. 'There you go.' She held it up with one hand and John took it from her. 'And ask me the next time you want a cloth, you silly bugger.' She pressed her hands flat on Stanton's shoulders, pinning him down and crushing her full weight hard on him. 'Now, what are we going to do with you?' She sucked on her bottom lip and looked up at her husband. 'Can we bring him below to the cellar? I wouldn't take long with him, I swear. He'd be a real treat.'

Stanton got a breath in. Just. 'Off.' The only sound he could make, even as his mind yelled for help.

'You know I'd like to watch that, Ida.' John grinned. 'But no. Not this time.'

'Why can't I, John?' Ida let go of one shoulder to grip Stanton hard by the face, her strong fingers digging into his cheeks. 'And when I'd finished, handsome boy, you could lie with the rest.'

'The rest?' It came out as a gurgle.

'We could put you next to Sybil Whitehand, Hugo. She doesn't smell too bad, either, with all the quicklime. Looks a bit off, though.'

John grunted a laugh. 'That's a good one, Ida.'

Stanton fought for air, fought for sanity. He was drunk, so drunk he wasn't understanding. The Roulfs were having fun, that was all. Sybil Whitehand was sleeping downstairs. Sleeping. Safe. Alive.

But John's next words tipped Stanton into the hell of the truth.

'Gorgeous, was Sybil. Shame Peter Flocke thought so too.'

Over John's shoulder, Stanton saw the neatly arranged carved candles and votive offerings for sale. The badges made from intricately carved moulds. Made by John Roulf, the expert carver.

'No, no.' Stanton tried to shout, could hardly make a sound. Ida's grip was iron.

'A real shame.' She sighed. 'You could say it was a cross we had to bear.' She winked at her husband.

'Another good one, Ida.' John squatted down beside her, the sharp blade he used for carving in his hand, inches from Stanton's face. 'Now, hold him steady, Ida. I've got work to do.'

Chapter Fifty-One

If the innkeeper at Saint Cuthbert's was put out by Barling's arrival at midnight asking to speak to Elena Whitehand, he did not show it.

Barling was not sure if it was his announcing himself as the King's man in such a modest house. It did not matter what thoughts the innkeeper had, even impure ones. Barling had not come to speak to Elena. Only Hugo Stanton.

But it was a puzzled-looking Elena that came down to the hallway, a concealing cloak over equally concealing linens.

'Aelred Barling.' A deep frown dented her brow. 'What brings you here, sir? I trust it is not to berate me further.'

'I apologise that I did so. No, it is not that.'

Her frown lifted. 'Unless we have another miracle and you have news of Sybil?'

'No, I am afraid I have no news of your sister. That is not why I am here. I am here because I am looking for Hugo Stanton. Can you send him down to me, please?'

'Hugo?' She shook her head. 'He is not here. He should be with you. That was where I told him he should go.'

Now it was Barling's turn to frown. 'When?'

'When he brought me back from the Tyson house,' she said. 'He wanted to make sure I was safe from the killer.' She pursed her lips. 'Which was very good of him.'

'There is no more risk,' said Barling. 'The killer has been caught. Or rather, killers. Two of them.'

'Two?' She blessed herself, her fingers strapped up in a tight bandage. 'By the blood of the Virgin.'

'And they are known to you: Margery and Nicholas Clement. But only after they killed again, murdering physician Gilbert Ordway.'

She paled. 'Hugo and I were in that house. It could have been us.'

'I know,' Barling said. 'And I hold myself accountable that you and he were exposed to such danger. I want to talk to Stanton about it all. To ask his forgiveness for my dismissal of his suspicion that they were involved. Had I listened to him, lives might have been saved.'

To Barling's surprise, Elena gave him a small smile. 'Then you have got a heart, sir.' Her smile went again. 'But where is Hugo?'

'He has not been in his room at the inn,' said Barling. 'I have tried the Roulf alehouse, but it is closed for the night. Which is why I came here.'

'I think we should go and have a look for him,' said Elena. 'In my time in this city, I have seen many souls who decide that an alleyway or haystack is a good bed, particularly when they have had a bellyful of ale. And we know how much Hugo likes his ale.'

'That he does.'

'Give me a moment,' said Elena. 'I will dress properly and come with you.'

She was back down in an efficient few minutes, neat and modest as always.

As they set off, Elena said, 'Let us take opposite sides of each street, the better to look down side streets and dead ends.'

'A sensible suggestion,' said Barling.

Elena was more pleasant company then he'd expected. She had an economy of speech that was unusual in a woman, and she did not waste time on idle drivel, focusing on the task in hand.

They came upon a number of those in slumber outside, several drunks but many more pilgrims, too poor or too tired to find a bed for the night.

His own bed began to call him.

'I regret to say this,' he said to Elena. 'But I am not sure that we are going to find Stanton tonight.'

Elena was crossing in front of an alleyway as he spoke. She raised her hand in a wave to somebody along it.

'You have found him?' Barling's voice lifted in hope.

'No. It's only John and Ida Roulf. That explains why you could not get an answer from their alehouse. The two of them are bringing their latest pilgrim guest to the cathedral.'

Barling frowned. 'But they have no pilgrim tonight. I witnessed that exchange myself.' He crossed the road, to see them disappear around a corner, wheeling a figure covered with blankets in a barrow.

Two of them.

As Barling had realised when trying to identify the killer. His reasoning had brought him to Margery and Nicholas Clement. Two who nevertheless proclaimed their innocence.

Sweat washed over Barling.

Stanton's exchange with Barling, when they arrived in Canterbury on Palm Sunday evening. Barling insisting to Stanton that there should be order in any investigation.

Stanton's reply. *Unless the killer has a very different story. Then it's not much help to you, is it?*

It was not. Barling had accused the wrong two.

Chapter Fifty-Two

'Are you all right, sir?' said Elena to Barling. 'You look quite unwell all of a sudden.'

'Indeed, I am not well.' Barling had trouble speaking coherently in his terror. 'Because I am wrong. Was wrong. Wrong about the killers. By the blood of the Martyr, I had the wrong two.'

Elena stared at him in shock. 'Are you saying that Margery and Nicholas are not the killers?'

'Yes, I am. I am saying that it is Ida and John Roulf.' Barling set off at a run down the alleyway, not caring if Elena came with him, though her rapid footsteps told him she did.

'If there is no pilgrim on that barrow, who is it?'

Barling would not answer.

'It's Hugo on there, isn't it?'

'I don't know,' panted Barling. But he did. Of course he did. And Stanton might be dead already. Barling could not look at her. 'Just pray. And even better, run faster.'

They were soon at the cathedral. A few souls milled around as always, no matter what time it was. But of the Roulfs, there was no sign.

'I can't see them.' Her voice rose in panic. 'I can't see them.'

'There's the barrow,' said Barling. 'Over there, at the base of the scaffolding.'

They ran to it. It was empty.

Barling's stomach turned over, and Elena gave a horrified gasp.

'The blankets,' she said. 'They're covered in blood. What have they done to him?'

Barling could not, would not think about it. 'We need to consider what they have done with him instead. Where have they gone?' He scanned the expanse of open space around this part of the cathedral. Nothing. He was failing. Exactly as the prior had accused him.

Elena bent to the barrow, hauling the blankets out. 'There must be something in here, something that will tell us.' She sat back on her haunches, defeated. 'Nothing. It is like they have disappeared into thin air.'

Barling looked at her. Looked at the ladder she stood next to, which led up to the first layer of scaffolding.

'No,' he said. 'Not thin air. Just air.' He pointed with a trembling finger. 'They've gone up.'

Elena stared up too.

Barling could barely make out the hulking form of John Roulf and the movement of Ida's skirts. 'They have got something with them, but it cannot be Stanton, surely?'

'It could,' she said. 'John Roulf is as powerful as an ox. I have seen him carry a full barrel of ale as easily as a basket of flowers. We have to see. I'm going up.' She put one foot on the ladder and brought her hands to the rungs above. Then stopped with a suppressed cry of pain.

'What is it?' said Barling.

She stepped back down. 'It's my hand. I broke two fingers earlier. In the yard.'

Barling looked up again. The movement carried on.

He knew what he had to do. No matter how much it terrified him. For losing Hugo Stanton terrified him even more.

'Listen to me, Elena. I am going to do what I can to save Stanton. If I still can. You must go now and summon the prior, summon the monks. Get help and get as much of it as you can. Do you hear me?'

Her eyes met his, and she gave a firm nod. 'Be careful, Barling.' She ran off.

Barling put his hands on the ladder. He wished they weren't shaking so much. He wished he had strength in his legs as well.

He began to climb, hand over hand, up the ladder, his sweat-coated palms grabbing for the next rough rung, then the next and the next. Up, up the scaffolding. Up the scaffolding that soared a hundred feet up the walls of Canterbury Cathedral.

Barling's hold grew more and more slippery in his terror, his breath deep gasps that burned his chest. His arms ached. His knees would hardly work his numb legs and feet.

As he climbed higher, the breeze strengthened. It tugged at his clothing, whistled in his ears, reminded him that there was nothing at his back except emptiness and the long, long fall down. He could not, would not look around.

He was on the third ladder. The third platform. Where he saw the movement of the Roulfs further up again.

And then he knew.

They were heading for the roof of the choir. They would dump Stanton up there, another body for the so-called cathedral curse.

Stanton's body. A rage tore through Barling, hotter than the cathedral fire.

They would not get away with this outrage. He would see to that.

He made his way carefully along the platform, searching for some items that he prayed would be there. God answered his plea. It took Barling a short while to make sure he had everything.

He climbed on.

When he stepped onto the roof, his legs would hardly support him. The night wind buffeted loud and strong up here. Good. It would mask his movements.

Barling bent low, scanning for the Roulfs. Then he saw them.

Off to one side of the roof to the choir. The temporary roof.

269

John hauled Stanton's body from his shoulders and lowered it down.

The roof planks creaked and shook in response.

'Careful, John.' Ida's voice floated over on the wind.

'Don't fret, woman, it's all right,' said John. 'And look, he's losing lots of blood. That's good, isn't it?'

'It is.' She put her arm around her husband and kissed him. 'We'll get a good pool of it, make it a good show. Then you can finish him off.'

Losing blood. It was like lightning passing through Barling. That meant Stanton was still alive.

Barling made his preparations, his hands shaking. He hadn't much time. And he did not know if his plan would work.

He got to his feet. Started running across the roof towards the Roulfs. Towards Stanton. Holding a stonemason's pickaxe aloft.

The Roulfs looked up.

'What the devil?' John's jaw dropped.

Barling stopped, out of their reach. 'I will have you brought to justice,' he said.

Ida smiled. 'Oh, for the love of God. Snap his neck, John.'

John went to grab for him, but Barling moved closer to the middle of the roof.

John stepped towards him. 'No, you won't.'

'Yes, I will. Justice for Peter Flocke.' Barling brought the pickaxe down hard on the roof plank under his feet. 'Robert Norwood.' It shook. Trembled. But held, curse it.

John grinned. 'Come here, little man.' He flexed his powerful shoulders.

'Martin Eustace.' He stepped to another one. Soft under his feet.

'Don't let him get away.' Ida stood up to step after John.

Barling brought the pickaxe down again. 'Hilde.' The head went straight through the plank. The plank started to split. Crack.

'John, stop him. He knows about them all!'

'Gilbert Ordway.' Barling gave it one final blow.

John reached for Barling. And the section of roof gave beneath them.

Barling fell first.

John yelled and grasped for the splintering wood even as Ida screamed and flung herself at him to save him. Their double weight crashed through the roof, through the soft, half-rotten planks that Prior Benedict had complained of so bitterly.

But Barling swung safe on the scaffolding rope he'd knotted around his waist and secured to a stout upright. Just as Lambert Green had done on the day he showed him and Stanton the pillar carved by Peter Flocke.

Though he still had no head for heights, Barling forced himself to look down.

The bodies of John and Ida Roulf lay on the floor of the cathedral choir far below, their blood staining the new stone that had been laid that very day by the stonemasons of Canterbury.

Chapter Fifty-Three

One week later

Barling entered the prior's solar, where Benedict and the Archbishop were sitting at the long table, deep in conversation. What looked like the plan of a large building was spread out before them.

The Archbishop looked up. 'Ah. Barling.'

'I hope you are ready for me, my lord. The monk outside told me to come in.'

'Indeed, we are.' Archbishop Richard indicated a seat at the table as Benedict nodded. 'Sit. I am looking forward to hearing this account in full. I see you have many notes with you.'

'I do, my lord.' Barling placed them on a free corner as he sat down. 'Though I could tell you the story without them.'

'As you told us the story on the night you concluded the murderers were Margery and Nicholas Clement?' This from the prior.

Barling flushed.

'Benedict.' The Archbishop's voice held a warning. 'An error was made but no bad came of it. Margery Clement has been released. I have granted Nicholas clemency for his violent acts. But he still has to account for his sinful dealing in the dark arts. He has many years of penance ahead of him.' He nodded to Barling. 'Proceed.'

'The story of John and Ida Roulf's evil will be burned into my soul for the rest of my days.' Barling put a hand on his notes. 'I have pieced my account together from a number of sources, including what John and Ida said to the captive Hugo Stanton. They told him much, believing their secrets would die with him.'

'How is young Stanton?' asked the Archbishop.

'Improving, my lord,' said Barling. 'Though I have been very busy, so I am not sure from day to day.' His heart saddened as he said the words.

'Good progress is always good news,' said the Archbishop. 'Go on.'

'Ida and John had been preying on vulnerable young pilgrims for some time,' said Barling. 'Ever since they arrived to live in Canterbury.'

'They took advantage of the numbers who come and go here, my lord,' said Benedict. 'We have a high turnover of tenants.'

'As they equally took advantage of the coming and going of so many pilgrims,' said Barling. 'Ida and John would befriend them, take them in, make sure they were alone and lost, then savagely murder them and bury the bodies in the cellar beneath their home. We found a total of six victims in there, all at different stages of decay.'

Both the Archbishop and the prior crossed themselves, with expressions of utter revulsion.

'One of these victims was the young pilgrim Sybil Whitehand, sister to Elena. The Roulfs had believed Sybil to be alone and killed her for their depraved pleasure, as they had with the other victims in the cellar. Their evil knew no bounds. But they did not know that the stonemason Peter Flocke had seen Sybil outside the cathedral on the day she arrived, from his perch high on the scaffolding. He had been having an affair with her, an affair that he had had to keep secret from his wife, Katerine, who is a mason's servant. He would meet Sybil at night and sneak her to the attic in the masons' lodge.'

'Adultery,' said the prior solemnly. 'A grave sin.'

'Indeed,' said Barling.

'A question, Barling.'

'Yes, my lord Archbishop?'

'If Sybil Whitehand was staying with the Roulfs, how is it that nobody saw her there?'

'Ida made sure that Sybil, and all of their pilgrim victims, only ever used the back entrance to the alehouse,' replied Barling. 'They also made a public display of taking pilgrims in for charity, as the priory rental agreement stipulated. These would always be infirm or have lost their wits. Either way, they would not have been able to report on anybody they saw in the upper rooms. They were simply not able.'

The Archbishop nodded. 'Then the Roulfs thought they had everything covered off, except that Peter Flocke had seen Sybil?'

'Yes, my lord. And Peter Flocke paid dearly for his adultery with Sybil. On the day Ida and John murdered Sybil, Flocke showed up at their alehouse, asking Ida about her. Flocke had been expecting Sybil at their usual time. When she hadn't arrived, he decided to come and look for her there, as it was where she had told him she was staying.'

The Archbishop sat forward. 'But Sybil was already dead.'

'Yes, my lord,' said Barling. 'Ida and John claimed to Flocke that Sybil had gone back home, which seemed to puzzle Flocke, as Sybil had said nothing about leaving to him. Flocke left the Roulfs, saying perhaps she's gone to the lodge and he'd missed her. Ida and John could tell that Flocke was not at all sure about their story. They couldn't risk anything that might link them to Sybil, the young woman they'd murdered thinking she was completely alone and without friends in Canterbury. They had to act at once.'

'Dear God,' said Prior Benedict. 'They were without a soul.'

Barling went on. 'John followed Flocke to the masons' yard and stabbed him many times. As he stood up from his evil work, he came face to face with the carved stone ready for placement in the

274

cathedral. A carver himself, of badges and votive offerings, John was inspired, if that is the right word in such evil circumstances, to therefore carve the symbol of the holy Cross onto Flocke's forehead. John hoped his sacrilegious act would direct attention elsewhere. All was well for a week. Nobody had any idea who killed Peter Flocke.'

'Including me,' said Prior Benedict, sadly.

'I cannot see how you would have found the truth at that stage, Prior,' said Barling. 'Stanton and I were equally lost when we first started out in this enquiry.'

'Go on, Barling,' said the Archbishop.

He did so. 'Ida and John listened in on Stanton's clever questioning of roughmason Adam Drake in their alehouse. If the focus stayed on Flocke only, then it could lead to Sybil eventually. Ida and John could not take that risk, however slight. They had to muddy the waters. The pilgrim Robert Norwood was an easy target and a very public one. Everybody had seen and heard the man rave around the cathedral and the streets.'

'That we had,' said the prior. 'For many a year.'

'The problem now for Ida and John,' said Barling, 'was the lime burner, Martin Eustace. He had been providing them with quicklime, which they needed to mask the dead bodies they buried in their cellar. He was a drunk and so was happy to be paid handsomely in drink. But with us, the King's men, asking so many questions, they reckoned it would not be long before we asked him a few. We would certainly have been curious as to why an alewife and her husband required large supplies of quicklime.'

'I cannot countenance the depths of their evil,' said Archbishop Richard. 'It is matched only by their cunning.'

'It was the quicklime that caused poor servant Hilde's death. John had gone to the deserted kiln to get what quicklime he could before somebody else took over the work. He ducked into Isabel Tyson's yard to avoid a group of pilgrims on the streets. Hilde saw him and started shrieking. He had to silence her.' Barling drew a hand across his forehead. 'But there is one happy part to the story. John did not realise that Isabel Tyson's nine-year-old daughter was in the yard with Hilde. The child hid in a well.'

The Archbishop gave a long, contented sigh. 'I believe God was watching over her.'

Barling inclined his head in agreement. 'Physician Gilbert Ordway must have seen John make his escape, and so John silenced him. Hugo Stanton came very close to being their victim as well. They had already carved a cross in his forehead while he was still alive. Their torture of him was for their own entertainment. Though it will fade in time, Stanton will bear the scar forever.' Barling folded his hands. 'That concludes this account of my investigation, my lord.'

'Well done, Aelred Barling.' The Archbishop gave him the broadest smile. 'I can see why my lord de Glanville praises you. It is well deserved.'

'Yes, well done.' The prior's smile was less broad.

'You may go.' The Archbishop waved him to his feet.

'Thank you, my lord. I will be going to the tomb of the Martyr to offer up my prayers of gratitude.' And indeed Barling was.

But before he did so, there remained one last task in this investigation. One that he had to carry out, no matter how much he wished otherwise.

For it was a task that involved confronting a killer.

Chapter Fifty-Four

Barling's knock on the door of Isabel Tyson's house was answered by a young female servant he did not recognise. 'Is your mistress at home, girl?'

'She is, sir.' The girl wore the recent brutal loss of her fellow servant on her face, as easy to read as one of Barling's manuscripts.

'I wish to speak to her.'

A call came from within before the servant could respond.

'Is that Aelred Barling?'

Barling raised his voice in turn. 'It is, my lady.'

Another call. 'Show him in. At once.'

'Sir.' The servant bowed and escorted Barling through to the hall.

The scene that met him could not be more different from the last time he had entered. Instead of the horror of a bloodstained, grief-stricken Isabel and a missing Lucia, mother and daughter sat in comfort on the settle before the fire, the child playing with a brightly painted wooden puppet.

Barling allowed himself a modicum of satisfaction but no more. His visit would shatter the peace of this house forever. He could not let that deter him. He had his duty to perform.

'The King's man. The man who brought Hilde's killer to justice.' Isabel rose, giving him a warm, gracious smile. 'Welcome, sir. To what do I owe the honour?'

'I would first like to enquire about Lucia, mistress.'

'She is recovering steadily. Isn't that right, Lucia?' said Isabel.

'Yes, Mama.' She gave a firm nod.

'I am pleased to hear it,' said Barling. 'Mistress Tyson, I would like to have a word with you about another matter.'

'Certainly. I am at your disposal, sir.' Another beguiling smile.

'In private.'

'Of course.' She addressed the servant girl. 'Take Lucia to my solar and wait there until I summon you.'

'May I please take my puppet?' asked the child of her mother.

'You may.' Isabel ushered her solemn little daughter out with the servant, then closed the door behind them. 'Now, sir, what is it you would like to speak to me about?'

Barling did not alter his polite tone. 'I want to know, mistress, why you murdered the physician, Gilbert Ordway.'

The colour left her face. 'I think you should leave. Immediately.'

She had given Barling his answer. But he needed to hear the words from her lips. 'Mistress, the usual reaction when I accuse somebody of murder is for them to deny it. You have not.'

'If you do not leave, I will call my manservants and have you removed by force.'

'As you wish.' Barling inclined his head. 'But mark this: if I walk out that door now, I will return shortly with help in removing you to the city prison to await trial by the King's justices for murder.'

'If you really believe I killed Master Ordway, why did you not bring such help with you?' Her voice trembled. 'After all, I...I might attempt to kill you also.'

'There are day servants in the house, as I have seen and as you had informed me on the night of Hilde's murder. I did not feel under threat in coming to see you by myself.'

She folded her hands together and went over to the fire. 'I still do not quite understand why you came alone.'

'Because I do not think that entering your house with a group of strange men and dragging you out would benefit the cause of justice in the least. Moreover, Lucia has been through more than any child should. I do not want to further add to her distress. You can choose to tell me here or tell the King's justices in the court. But either way, you need to tell the truth.'

She was silent for a few moments before she said quietly, 'The truth is: yes, I killed Gilbert Ordway.'

Barling had obtained her admission of guilt. He had been correct in this course of action.

The silence grew, Isabel twisting her hands, one around the other. Barling waited.

When her question came, she asked it without looking at him. 'How did you guess?'

'I knew when I saw his body that another hand had done it, although I did not know at the time who that was. The cross made on Ordway's forehead was jagged and clumsy, whereas those made by John Roulf were perfectly carved. I thought perhaps Ida had had a turn. But when I listed those they had killed along with Peter Flocke, it was clear from Ida's words that Hilde was the last. When I called out Ordway's name, they looked blank. Finally, John never left a weapon. You used one of Ordway's own bloodletting knives and left it by his body.'

'But how did you know it was me?'

'When I returned that night to question you about Gilbert Ordway,' said Barling, 'I had to knock for some time to gain entry. It struck me as odd at the time that you would take so long to answer, given the horrors of the night. You would hardly have been asleep. When you did answer, you were fully dressed, albeit not in the clothes you had been wearing earlier. Now, I can understand that, given the blood and spoil that stained those clothes from Hilde's body and from Lucia when she emerged from the well, you would have wanted to change them. But considering the lateness of the hour, I could not understand why you would change into outdoor clothes. Furthermore, you mentioned your terror of a killer on the streets. I realised your terror was real, for you went abroad to Ordway's house knowing that a brutal murderer was on the loose. And I cannot be certain, but I would guess that your outer cloak is badly stained with blood and hidden from sight. For Hilde is not here to clean it for you.'

'You are most perceptive, sir.'

'But perceptive as I am, Mistress Tyson, what I cannot imagine, is what would drive you to such an act? You appear to be a woman of compassion. I witnessed your grief at the death of Hilde. It was clear that you cared deeply for her. You love your child without end. What on earth could have driven you to murder Gilbert Ordway?'

'You said you wanted the truth, sir?'

'I do.'

So Isabel Tyson gave it.

And what she told him would never, ever leave him.

Chapter Fifty-Five

Isabel could not stop weeping, weeping for poor, dead Hilde. Weeping for joy and relief too, that Lucia had somehow miraculously been spared this night.

She could not release Lucia from her arms, either, uncaring that her child was still covered in mud from the well. They sat together on the settle before the fire, the flames of the thick logs burning low, logs which Hilde had laid earlier in the day. Their lives had been changed forever in less time than it took a fire to burn through its load of wood.

'Oh, my sweetest girl, my sweetest one. You are safe, thank the Virgin you are safe.'

Lucia clung to her, her small hands tight, tight, tight around Isabel's neck. 'Will the bad ghost come back, Mama?'

Isabel could not answer at first. 'Oh, my sweet one.' She fought to control her sobbing. Because the bad ghost was still out there. 'I will make sure that the bad ghost can never hurt you, my sweet. I promise you that. Mama will fight him off, I promise. Do you hear me?'

Then the world changed again, in a single, crushing thud of Isabel's heart.

Lucia nodded. 'Can you fight Master Ordway off too?'

She moved her daughter's little face so she could look straight into it. 'Lucia, what are you talking about?'

'Gilbert Ordway had whispered words of love to her, sir,' said Isabel to Barling. 'Words that a husband would say to a wife.'

Barling's stomach constricted at such repellent behaviour from the physician. But he could tell from Isabel's demeanour there was more. Much more.

She went on. 'It happened when Lucia was alone with him. Ordway would tell me that it was necessary for him to do some of Lucia's treatments in private. Worse, the monster kissed her with his filthy mouth agape. Sir, she is nine years old.'

'Dear God.' Barling's revulsion deepened. 'So you went to confront him?'

'Yes. I should have waited, but I could not. I got Lucia off to sleep but I could not close an eye. I wanted to give him the chance to confess. To admit what he had done.' She briefly met his gaze. 'To somehow explain the horror of what Lucia told me, though it defies explanation.' Her mouth curled in disgust. 'But he denied and denied and denied it.'

Ordway gave a condescending smile. 'My dear lady, I think Lucia's mind must be addled after her ordeal.'

'No, Gilbert. It is perfectly sound. She told me everything.'

'Yet I am her physician. If I say her mind is unsound, then it is I who will be believed.' His voice hardened. 'Not some little whore.'

'What did you call her?' whispered Isabel.

'You heard. Like mother, like daughter.'

'What a fool I am to never have seen your wickedness. You must never, ever come near her again. Do you hear me?'

'I do,' said Ordway. 'You can rest assured she will no longer be my patient. A shame. But there are plenty more like her. Weak little girls, who I can keep weak with the right combination of' – he smirked – *'medicines.'*

'They were the last words he spoke, sir,' said Isabel. 'I grabbed one of his bloodletting knives and drove it straight into his chest. He collapsed, and I knelt over him, cutting into him again and again and again.' She swallowed hard. 'It was as if, sir, I was possessed.'

'Possessed by a demon?' said Barling.

'No. Possessed with a rage so pure that I was completely calm. I knew the greatest truth: that such a man should never walk the face of this earth for another second.'

Barling was loath to press her. But he must have the full picture. Line, by line, by line. 'So pure that you arranged it so that another would take the blame for your actions?'

'Another who would take so many lives. I am happy to face my God with that.'

'You did not know that at the time.'

'I knew enough. I knew that whoever it was, that person was happy to take the life of a kind, defenceless, old woman. And would have taken the life of my sweet, defenceless child, had she not had the cleverness and courage to hide herself away.' She shook her head. 'The terror of which gave her the courage to tell me about what else was going on. All of it.' She put her hands to her face.

Barling waited for her to compose herself once more.

Isabel dropped her hands. 'Can you believe, sir, that Ordway told Lucia that she was ill because she was a sinner? That she would only get better if she kept what he did to her a secret? And that if she told anybody, God would see to it that she would sicken and die, without ever seeing her mother again?'

Barling tried and failed to provide a response. In truth, he could find no words to express the depths of his revulsion.

'When I heard those words from my innocent daughter's mouth, I knew I had to deal with him, and deal with him quickly. For I knew it was only a matter of time before you and Hugo Stanton found out the answers.'

'You could have told somebody about what was happening.'

'Told them what? That a noted physician was a depraved monster? Who would believe a woman and a little girl against such an esteemed man?'

Barling could not reply. His conscience reminded him how quick he had been to dismiss Stanton's doubts about Ordway.

'I realise my killing of Gilbert Ordway may mean I never see heaven. But dwelling in Paradise would be no bliss if I had allowed that man to continue to walk the earth. And if I go to hell, I look forward to finding him there. Witnessing his eternal torment would be a salve to mine own.' She was quiet again for a moment.

Then, 'May I ask you this one thing, sir?'

'What is that?'

'When they take me to the hill to hang me, can you ensure that Lucia does not see it? She will know of it, know what happened to her mother. What her mother did.' She bit her lip. 'When she becomes a mother herself, perhaps she will understand.'

'I will make sure she does not see it.'

'Thank you, from the bottom of my heart. And there is one more thing.' Her hands shook as she fumbled for her purse, and she took out a shiny silver coin. She placed it on the table, where it gleamed like an accusing eye.

'What is that for, mistress?'

'I know that it takes some time before the rope around my neck finally robs the last breath from me. I have heard that one can pay for a man to haul on one's legs. His breaking my neck will finish it sooner.' Her hands had a slight tremor. 'I am afraid that I am not as brave as I thought.'

Barling slid the coin back to her. 'I will pay no such fee.'

'I understand the magnitude of the wrong I have done. My actions have sealed my own fate. You will always have my eternal gratitude for keeping my daughter from such a sight. That is all that matters.'

'She will not see it because it will not take place. Your daughter needs her mother.'

'I do not follow what you mean, sir?'

'I have no wish for Gilbert Ordway to inflict any more suffering. That he should be able to do so from beyond the grave would be obscene.' Barling went to the door.

Bewilderment creased her brow. 'But I have admitted to you that I have killed a man. A mortal sin.'

'That is between you and God, good lady. All I know is that one can ask for His mercy. I have no power in what He decides, only what the decision of the law should be.' He turned the handle and pulled the door open. 'I asked you for the truth and you have given it to me. In the circumstances, I believe the King's justice has been served. You will hear no more from me.'

And with that, Barling bade Isabel Tyson farewell and walked out of her house into the sunlit street.

Chapter Fifty-Six

Katerine Flocke stood in the yard of the masons' lodge, Adam Drake beside her.

All of the workers had been called together unexpectedly by the master mason, the man they called William of Sens.

'Wonder what he wants with us all?' said Drake. 'Hope it's not a telling-off. Mind you, that's usually Green's job.'

Katerine shushed Drake.

A familiar black-robed figure made his way through the parting crowd to join William.

Prior Benedict.

He had a quick word with William, who nodded, then the prior began to speak.

'I will not keep you long,' he said. 'There is much virtuous work to be done, as there is every day. But I wanted to inform you that serious questions have been raised about the accounts kept of the spending on supplies for the holy work with which we have all been engaged. Further questions have been raised about the quantity of said supplies. There appears to be a wide discrepancy between the stores we should have and the stores we actually have.'

'What's he talking about?' whispered Katerine to Drake.

'Sounds to me like somebody's been filling their own purse,' Drake whispered back, eyes round.

Benedict went on. 'But when I sent for my second master mason, Lambert Green, to explain said discrepancies, it turned out that he had fled his lodgings with all his possessions.'

Gasps went through the crowd.

'Make no mistake,' said the prior. 'Flight will not save Green from justice. He will be found, and he will pay for this most heinous theft. In the meantime, I have asked William to appoint a new second master mason. He will be arriving shortly. Now back to work, all of you.'

The crowd broke up at once, with oaths and opinions filling the air.

Drake turned to Katerine, his wide face beaming. 'That's a piece of good news, eh? No more Lambert bloody Green to make our lives a misery.'

Katerine could only nod. She walked away, head whirling, sudden tears a hard sting in her eyes. What was to become of her? Green, her tormentor, was gone. But there was no replacement second master mason that would keep her on, not when she got too big to climb the ladders. Not with a baby strapped to her back.

Drake caught her up, his breath huffing with the effort. 'What's up?'

'Nothing.' Her tears started to fall.

'I could buy you a pie later and all. Would that cheer you up?'

She could only carry on walking, scrubbing at her wet cheeks with her sleeve.

'Kat, wait.' Drake put a gentle hand on her shoulder and turned her to face him. 'I'm no good at knowing what women are thinking. But you're right upset, and I hate to see it.'

'I'll be fine.'

'You could tell me why you're so sad.'

'I couldn't. I can't.'

'Try?'

So she did try. And once she started, she couldn't stop. For months, years, she'd had no one to tell. How Peter treated her. Losing Peter. Green. No money.

Drake did his shocked best to give words of comfort, but he couldn't stop her.

Last of all, she told him about the baby.

He stared at her, open-mouthed.

'Now do you see why I'm sad, Adam?' she said. 'A blasted pie isn't going to solve it. Any of it.'

'But a pie never hurt?'

'Oh, Adam.' She couldn't help a watery smile.

'Me looking out for you won't hurt, neither.' His big face flushed. 'Looking out for the baby and all.'

'You don't have to do any of this, Adam.' She hiccupped, her sobs finished, at least for now.

'I'd like to, though. More than anything. Always thought you were bonny. Right from the first day I saw you. I was right jealous of Peter.' His fists balled. 'Now that I know how he was with you, I wish I'd taught him a lesson.'

'Have sense.' She raised a hand and patted his arm. 'He'd have trounced you.' She kept her hand on his arm.

He nodded. 'You're right. Not really made for fighting, me.' Then he grinned. 'Good at wheeling that barrow together, though, wasn't we?'

'You like wheeling bodies around, do you, Adam?'

He went pale. 'Oh, God forgive me, I didn't mean that, I meant helping you to go for quicklime, not—'

'I'm teasing you.'

'Oh.' His grin returned. 'That's a relief.'

She squeezed his arm. 'And yes, we did work well together.'

'Then how about that pie when we've done our work?' said Adam. 'We could take it down to the river and watch the ducks.'

'Go on. You've won me round,' said Katerine.

Adam beamed. 'Faith, let's make it two.'

Katerine smiled back. She couldn't help it. While inside her, safe inside her, her baby, her precious baby, kicked hard. She knew it leapt for joy.

Chapter Fifty-Seven

Finally, Aelred Barling was at the tomb of the Martyr once more.

Every day since he had set off on pilgrimage from Westminster had required all of his attention and energy. He craved rest, but his body could wait.

He still had his soul to save.

After all that had happened, the Archbishop had granted him access to the watching room over the crypt, so he could pray in peace, for which Barling was truly grateful.

The silent tomb sat below in the pool of glowing light, with the ever-vigilant monks keeping their guard.

The monks allowed no offerings on the tomb's marble lid for now. For on it rested the new charter for Christ Church, Canterbury, granted by the King on Maundy Thursday. Gold coins rested on the lid too, a gift from his Grace.

Another black-robed figure slipped into the watching room, knelt beside Barling and made the sign of the cross.

Prior Benedict.

After a murmured prayer to Saint Thomas, the prior addressed Barling in a hushed tone. 'You can see that the visit from the King has succeeded even beyond the Archbishop's wildest dreams.'

'I am pleased to hear it.' Barling gave Prior Benedict a small smile. 'It would seem that diligence and hard work pay off after all, Prior.'

'Perhaps.' He got a wry smile in return. 'And perhaps not. Archbishop Richard has told me that the King has nominated me to be elected as abbot of Peterborough. I know what the outcome of that election will be.'

'They are sending you from Canterbury?'

'They are. With all honour, I have been told. Archbishop Richard himself will be consecrating my appointment as head of the house of Peterborough.'

'There is no appeal?'

'Barling, for a man of letters, that is a very foolish question.'

'You are right, Prior. Very foolish. It is simply because I am shocked.' He rested his hand briefly on the prior's sleeve. 'And deeply saddened for you. I know how much the cathedral, how much Canterbury, means to you.'

'Thank you, Barling.' The prior's gaze, his face etched in sadness, moved over the tomb. 'In truth, I have not yet found the bottom of the depths of my grief. But I will carry the glorious word of the Martyr with me to Peterborough. The masons are fashioning an altar from two paving stones that were stained with the Martyr's blood. I have possession of a relic also. I saved it from the fire and kept it for my own private worship. I should never have done so, but I can make amends for my sin. I will create a chapel, which will be open to pilgrims.' He nodded to Barling. 'You may want to make your pilgrimage there when it is established.'

'I will do that, Prior.'

A guardian monk gestured from below to Benedict.

'For the next few weeks,' said the prior, 'I am serving the tomb of the Martyr. If you will excuse me.' He rose to his feet and was gone out the door.

Barling began his prayers once again.

'Barling?'

He turned round and his heart leapt to see Stanton enter the watching room, the young man's head still heavily bandaged. Barling got up from his knees and pulled two padded stools side by side.

'You are feeling more restored, Stanton?'

'A lot.' His assistant put his hand to his head. 'Still hurts, mind. And I'll have a scar.'

'But you are alive.'

'I am.' His expression darkened. 'Unlike poor Sybil Whitehand, all the others too. God's eyes.'

'Indeed, John and Ida Roulf's evil was beyond understanding.'

'It was,' said Stanton. 'But we stopped it, didn't we, like I said we would?'

'We did.'

'Or rather you did, Barling. I was too busy with distractions. Like necromancy.'

'It is all in the past, Stanton and—'

'Barling, I had a love who died.'

Barling waited. Sometimes silence was the only correct response.

'Her name was Rosamund. I thought Nicholas Clement would help me to talk to her.'

'I see.'

'It was all foolishness on my part,' said Stanton. 'I wanted too much for it to be real. That want made me lie to you. And that was so wrong. So very, very wrong.' Stanton looked more serious than Barling had ever seen him. 'When I was in the Roulfs' clutches, I promised God that if He let me live, I would tell you the truth. So here I am.'

'Then God has been good.'

'Thing is, Barling, I can tell you a lot of the truth. But not all of it.'

'No?'

'No. But if I tell you that my lord de Glanville has been involved, that might help.'

'Ah.' Finally. Barling had been waiting for this since the first day that Stanton had joined the travelling justices as a messenger. De Glanville had given Barling a terse explanation that Stanton had been a good messenger for the King in the rebellion and so was now joining the ranks of the court messengers with his recommendation. Nothing more, and Barling had been allowed to ask no questions ever since, though he had tried to prise more out of Stanton. 'Then go on.'

'You know I love horses?'

Barling resisted the urge to roll his eyes. 'Yes.'

'Well, that was how it all started. My uncle is a farrier and it was through him, by accident, that I ended up being a monastic post rider for a couple of years. I was faster than almost anybody on the back of a horse by a long way. Word got round about how good I was. Then one day, I got a summons from the abbot. I thought it was the usual, expecting my route to be to another monastery, an abbey in a distant city. But no. The abbot looked deadly serious and I wondered for a second if something had gone wrong, like a girl with child that had come looking for me.'

'Stanton, please do not tell me that you are the father of an abandoned brood.'

'No, no. Nothing like that, Barling. Honest.'

Barling nodded for him to go on.

'It was nothing I'd done. My task was a journey of the utmost secrecy. Such a secret, that if I ever revealed it to anyone, my balls would be removed and fed to me. The abbot blushed when he said this, said that those specific orders had come from the highest authority.'

Barling looked askance at Stanton. 'The highest?'

Stanton nodded. 'It turned out it was from King Henry himself, though I didn't know it at the time. I became one of Henry's small circle of private trusted messengers.'

'You? A secret messenger for his Grace? Are you sure your thoughts are clear after John Roulf cutting your head?'

'Yes. I would say check with my lord de Glanville. But you can't.'

'Proceed,' said Barling with a sigh.

'It was wonderful. I had the best horses, lots of women. My life was perfect. I was allowed to go home to my family from time to time. As for the messages I had to carry and to whom, as God is my witness, Barling, I can't tell you. I took an oath to the King.'

Barling nodded once more. 'I can understand the seriousness of that loyal oath, Stanton.'

'In truth, I'm more worried about my balls.'

'Can I remind you that we sit overlooking the tomb of the Martyr in a house of God?'

'Sorry, Barling.' Stanton raised a hand. 'But everything changed, just over twelve months ago. For that was when I met her.'

'This woman called Rosamund?'

'Yes. Rosamund Clifford.'

Barling opened his mouth to speak. Closed it again. He had no words. He had no breath, either, given what Stanton had just said. Eventually he found some. A little. A whisper. 'You mean to tell me that you, Hugo Stanton, had a love affair with the King's mistress?'

Stanton nodded. 'I did. Henry had locked his Queen, Eleanor, away and rumours swirled that the King had a new young mistress, Rosamund Clifford. I didn't take a lot of notice. Henry's bedchamber was his own business.'

'Precisely, Stanton. As it should have been. What possessed you to do something so dangerous?'

Stanton shrugged. 'The King summoned me to his chamber at Woodstock to deliver an urgent message. And she was with him. Rosamund. The Fair Rosamund. I tried not to stare. I really did. But there she was. Clad in a fur robe that I knew covered nothing except naked flesh. Long, golden hair, tangled from the hours of sex she'd just had with the King, you could smell it in the room. Her beauty was everything that Henry's gnarled face and body wasn't.' He grimaced. 'Then she met my eye as bold as any street whore. Just for a second. But it was enough. The King ordered me to help him with his boots. I was glad to have something to do. Otherwise I'd have kept staring. Henry ordered me to Godstow on his behalf as he'd spent too long abed with Rosamund. He ordered her from the room at the same time as me, so he could get on with penance.'

'My lady.' I beckoned to her to follow me and not try Henry's patience any longer. The door closed behind us as we stood in the empty antechamber. No longer under Henry's eye, I could stare my fill at her. 'I wish you good day.' I bowed and went to move off.

'Wait.' Her order was instant. 'First, you must see me to my chamber.'

I hesitated, glanced at the closed door.

'You would have me wandering the castle unaccompanied like this, Hugo?' She drew her fur cloak tighter around her.

The movement made it clearer that she had nothing on underneath.

I swallowed hard as my groin surged. 'Of course not, my lady.'

'Rosamund.' She held a hand out for me to kiss. Her scent had me surge with want. 'I am not your lady.' Her lips curled in a knowing smile. 'Am I?' Her arm slid though mine and I brought her to her chamber. A few sounds came within.

'That'll be my servant,' she said.

'Then I shall leave you with her service.'

'And what about your service, Hugo?'

'I am loyal to you as his Grace's . . . companion.'

'Loyal? How lovely.' She moved closer. 'A kiss to seal your loyalty?'

'Of course.' I took her hand again. Closer, she was closer.

I bent to kiss her hand once more. Her fingertips glided against my chin, for the briefest moment.

My breath was like I'd run up a steep hill. 'My lady, Rosamund. Your servant is in there and—'

'Is devoted to me, and very discreet.' Her eyes glittered. 'When Henry is away and you have returned, you will come and keep me company.'

'As . . . as your lady wishes.'

'Rosamund does.'

'And that was the start of it. I went to her rooms once, twice. Her servant served smiles, wine and sweetmeats. Rosamund charmed, chatted, sang sweet little songs, her breath warm on my cheek as she sat close to me. She made me tell her all about my riding exploits, thrilling at my stories with wide eyes, clasped hands and moist lips parted. I wanted nothing more than to take hold of her and make her body mine. But I didn't dare, not under the watchful eye of her servant. Then one evening, her servant disappeared, though with a promise she would be nearby.'

Barling waited as Stanton collected his thoughts.

'And that was it. I had her once, twice that evening, her pleasure matching mine. I didn't care that she serviced the King, I put that from my mind. She in turn seemed full of delight with my body. It happened again and again. Rosamund and I would lose ourselves in our lovemaking, then lie for hours after in her big bed, rolling and playing like kittens in a basket. One of her favourite games was to act the King. Though it had shocked me to my core the first time I heard her, she perfectly mimicked Henry's rasping bark. But she would do it with instructions for my hands on her naked body as we lay on and under the finest silk and linen.'

'Put it on my breast, fellow.'

'Rosamund, stop.' I half-laughed, half-gasped in horror. 'It's like the King himself is in here with us.'

'God's eyes, man, have you no fingers for between my thighs?'
Her nose nuzzled my ear, tickling, her small teeth nipping.
'Stop, you're possessed.' I wheezed my hushed, laughing protest.
'Fool. Put your hands on my cheeks, or I'll have your head.'
'Rosamund,' I said, 'you can't do this. We'll lose our heads if we're caught.'

'Hugo,' she said, her hands folded on my naked chest, chin resting on them, her bright hazel gaze boring into mine, 'if we're caught in this bed, we won't lose our heads because I'm laughing at the King. We'll lose them because we have no clothes on and you are pleasuring me.'

'Then I'll plead that I'm not pleasuring you, that I just fell in here.'
Then she slid her hands down. Grasped me by the hips. Moved hers over and on to me with a quickness and ferocity that would make me gasp.

'Oh, but you are pleasuring me,' she whispered before crushing her mouth onto mine. 'You are.'

'Goodness.' Barling had heard rumours around the court of Rosamund Clifford's lust. Stanton would appear to be confirming them. Not that he, Barling, would have fallen prey to it. Ever.

'Then Rosamund was attacked by an unknown assailant,' said Stanton. 'An attempt on her life that failed. The King was furious. He brought in somebody he trusted to investigate. I can't tell you who that was. But the attacks on Rosamund continued.'

'Until one succeeded.' Barling knew. The whole court knew.

Stanton's voice wavered. 'I try to stop the ache in my heart by telling myself that her last time on this earth was one of pleasure, for in many ways it was. She and I, our bodies together, our words soft, our pleasure complete. But that wasn't her last time on earth. No. Her killer didn't allow her the easy passage of a tasteless poison that would let her slip away in her sleep, or even a blow to the head that would take her senses even as it took her life. No, no. They used a thin, vicious leather strap, choking the life out of my beautiful girl even as she fought for breath and for life itself. Rosamund would have known. Known the truth, known it all in her last terrible moments. Did Rosamund think of me at all, I wonder?' He gave a quiet, bitter laugh. 'Hark at me, the fool. If she did think of me, it would be to pray, to beg the Almighty that I, a groom, anybody, enter and stop those murderous hands. But nobody did. Nobody came. I had gone to my bed, would already have been sleeping, my mind and body sated and warm from our lovemaking. I let my Rosamund down. Completely. I failed her.'

'My boy. I cannot imagine.'

Stanton shook his head. 'I don't remember much about the following morning. Well, I do from the point at which the alarm was raised. I ran to her side, to join others. At first glimpse, I saw her rumpled golden hair and pushed my way to her bedside. My call to her died on my lips. Her still, staring eyes, bloodshot and glazed. Her face, usually as clear and flawless as a flower petal, now hideously blotched with pooled blood. The leather so deep in her neck. Her little tongue an obscene slug peeping from between set, swollen lips. Her skin cool and unmoving under my hands even as I shook her, called to her, willed her to wake.'

Barling crossed himself silently. He too had lost a love. But at least they still lived.

'A letter thrust into my hands for the King. *Take it, Stanton. Fast as you can.* I didn't need telling twice. Head down, heartbroken, I kicked that animal like it had killed my Rosamund itself and rode without stopping to Henry. The light had gone from my life. And I couldn't show anything.'

'To keep such pain hidden must have been intolerable.'

'And yet, in all of this, Rosamund was nothing to Henry. A distraction, nothing more. If she had had his heart, I might understand him a bit. But he hadn't loved Rosamund. Once he'd tired of her, she'd have been given away to another lecherous old man. I loved her. But I was nobody. There was me, when I was chosen to be his messenger, proud that I was picked out for being somebody of worth, of regard. But no. I was chosen simply because I was a nobody. I didn't matter, as nobody matters to Henry except a very, very few.'

Barling revered his lord King, but even he would admit the truth of this.

'So you can see why Nicholas Clement tempted me. I had this stupid, impossible hope that he could call Rosamund back. But he's a liar and a cheat. Rosamund is dead and gone. I know that now.' He flushed a little. 'I also have a real woman, a woman who lives, to help me see it.'

'Elena.'

'Yes. I'm going away with her.'

'I see.' Barling would not allow his face to change. Would not allow Stanton to see that his heart was shattering into a thousand pieces at the loss of his friend. Barling knew he had nobody to blame except himself.

'As you can imagine, she is suffering so badly. Not only has she lost her sister, but she has to journey home to tell her parents of Sybil's appalling fate. I don't want her to do that alone. I said I would help her. And so I will.'

'I see.' It was all Barling could say. He feared that if he spoke, he would weep. He was losing the best friend he ever had.

'But first,' said Stanton, 'I have to pray.'

Barling looked at him askance. This was not like Stanton.

'Oh, blessed Martyr,' murmured Stanton, 'I thank thee for a miracle, the miracle of Aelred Barling being able to climb higher than a step or the back of a horse without falling off.'

Barling drew breath to admonish Stanton for blasphemy.

Then the warm weight of Stanton's arm tightened across Barling's shoulder.

'A miracle for which I will be giving thanks every day of my life,' said Stanton. 'As I will for you, Aelred Barling. Henry never thanked me. For anything. It didn't matter. The investigation into Rosamund's murder revealed our affair to the King. The man who found the killer pleaded for mercy for me. Because Henry trusts that man with his life, I kept my head on my shoulders. Then I was handed over to my lord de Glanville for him to decide my future. I was the luckiest man alive that he decided to assign me to his travelling court.' His blue eyes lit with his smile. 'To work alongside the King's clerk.' He got to his feet. 'I shouldn't be gone more than a week. I'm sure you'll be happy waiting for me here.'

'Then I will await your safe return, Hugo Stanton.'

With a final hard squeeze of Barling's shoulder, Stanton left.

And Barling began his prayers.

Not for his soul. His prayers for his soul could wait.

First, he had to give praise to Saint Thomas the Martyr, for his own miracle.

The miracle that he, Aelred Barling, would not have to live his life unloved.

Historical Note

It's always enjoyable to create fictional locations. But some real-life places astound without any elaboration and Canterbury Cathedral is one of them. I had the privilege of visiting when I was researching this book.

There has been a cathedral in Canterbury for more than 1,400 years. Saint Augustine consecrated the first cathedral there not long after his arrival in the year 597. There is no trace of the original building, as a fire in 1067 destroyed it and it had to be completely rebuilt.

Archbishop Lanfranc oversaw much of the construction, but it was his successor, Archbishop – and later Saint – Anselm, who built the 'glorious quire' and the enormous crypt. That choir was destroyed by fire but the atmospheric crypt is still intact.

The cathedral's most famous archbishop is another saint: Thomas Becket, who was murdered there on 29 December 1170. He was slain by four knights acting on one of King Henry II's legendary outbursts of temper. Readers of my Fifth Knight series will know that I took this event and added a fictional extra man to the group.

The knights' original intention may have been to arrest Becket, who had been engaged in a monumental power struggle with the King for several years. But the situation quickly deteriorated, and Becket was hacked to death on one of the altars. The Martyrdom is still maintained in the cathedral and one can stand at the very spot.

Becket's body lay cooling where it fell as the traumatised cathedral monks tried to regroup. Over the next few hours, people converged on the cathedral in horrified disbelief. Those who came dipped their fingers in the blood of their martyred Archbishop, daubed their clothes with it and collected as much as they could. Terror still filled the air, with rumours flying around that the murderers were coming back to take the body, or to slay others. It was feared that the knights would defame Becket's corpse, and pull it across the city behind a horse, or display it on a gibbet. This could not be countenanced. The monks decided to bury Becket in the crypt as quickly as possible.

The miracles began that very night. A man who dipped part of his shirt into Becket's blood went home to his paralysed wife. As he wept in his telling of the murder, she asked to be washed in water containing some of the blood. She was cured immediately. Word quickly spread and the devotion to Becket the Martyr began, with his tomb becoming a major site for pilgrimage. An astonishing 100,000 people came to pray and visit Canterbury Cathedral in 1171 alone. He was canonised in 1173.

It was a huge stroke of good fortune that the monks had chosen to place Becket's body in a stone tomb in the crypt while they set about constructing a shrine. For on 5 September 1174, fire broke out in three cottages near the cathedral. Unknown to everybody before it was too late, the blaze spread to the roof of the cathedral and Anselm's choir was destroyed. A quarter of a century later, a monk, Gervase of Canterbury, wrote a vivid account of the fire and I used this in the novel.

But in a horrible coincidence, I, along with millions of people worldwide, saw a great medieval cathedral burn in real time. On 15 April 2019, fire broke out in the roof of Notre Dame Cathedral in Paris. While it was impossible to look away, the researcher in me partly took over and I made notes from people's real-time reaction on social media and on news reports. Those reactions – almost identical to those reported by Gervase eight centuries ago – found their way onto the page.

Back in twelfth-century Canterbury, the monks were faced with the daunting task of reconstructing their fire-ravaged choir. They commissioned master mason William of Sens, known for his brilliance and technical expertise, who is briefly mentioned in the novel. Unfortunately for him and for future generations, William fell from faulty scaffolding in the choir in 1178. He was badly injured and never recovered. He was replaced and the work was finished by another mason, William the Englishman.

The other characters that are real historical figures are Archbishop Richard, Prior Benedict and Brother William. Archbishop Richard was Becket's successor and understandably, given Becket's fate, was keen to stay on Henry's good side.

Benedict had been a monk at Christ Church Priory for many years and had been present the night Becket was murdered. His tenure as prior was short-lived and he did end up as abbot of Peterborough, with his election following nomination by the King. His devotion to Becket never faltered and he made Peterborough another centre of Becket pilgrimage.

Less is known about William, who may have been Irish. Both men recorded miracles, often the same ones and in different styles. William did replace Benedict as recorder, as the monks preferred William's style. William did claim he had had visions of the Martyr, with Becket telling him that he should take on the task. The Miracle Windows, which are the stunning stained glass windows that one can see today in the cathedral, are based on Benedict and William's records. They date from the late twelfth and early thirteenth centuries.

The remainder of the characters are fictional, though their lives are based on the less elevated in society.

Pilgrimage is of course still done today by millions of people of different faiths across the globe. Every individual will have their own personal reason for embarking on one. For medieval people, going on pilgrimage could be done to show piety or to carry out a penance. The less virtuous went for the rich pickings that could be had or to have a really exciting holiday. The hope of a cure of mental or physical illness brought people to shrines in their droves. The reports of miracles must have given many great solace and comfort, even if they did not get their cure. People also travelled to shrines to give thanks for prayers answered. Pilgrim badges were a common, cheap souvenir of a trip to a shrine, worn either on one's person, clothing or pilgrim staff.

While medieval people sought aid from the saints for illness and disability, they also looked to medical practitioners. The twelfth century had a remarkable selection from which people could choose, from expensive physicians and surgeons to cheaper barber-surgeons and midwives. Herbalists were also much in demand. But, overall, the twelfth-century medical profession was not viewed as a specialism. Practitioners engaged in a wide variety of medical interventions as well as a number of other trades. It was not unusual to find a doctor who was a bailiff, an ale-taster who specialised in fixing people's bad feet, or a practitioner who would treat dogs as well as people.

A further group who could offer help from afflictions were the exorcists. There was a widely held belief that illness could be caused by demonic possession. Exorcism, the casting out of devils, was practised by clergy at all levels. Lay people also performed these rites. Herbs could cure demonic possession too. The important aspect of exorcism was that it was the saints who were invoked.

Necromancy was its sinful cousin. Demonic magic was a perversion of religion, practised it was believed by those who had turned away from God and instead to the devil. It was, like seances and other more recent rituals that claim to summon the dead, or invoke demons or the devil, a sham. The conjurations relied heavily on props, sleight of hand and illusions to convince an audience and to make them part with their money. The realisation of fraud is not a modern one. John of Salisbury, secretary to Thomas Becket, wrote in 1154 of the belief in evil nocturnal assemblies, 'only poor old women and the simpleminded kinds of men who enter into these beliefs'.

It could be said that the real group of miracle workers were those that wielded axes, hammers and chisels, and mixed mortar that is still holding up walls after a thousand years. Using only their hands and the most basic tools and machinery, people raised astounding buildings like Canterbury Cathedral, with its exquisite stonework and carvings. Its height and size are impressive enough today, even surrounded by office and apartment blocks and multistorey car parks. In a twelfth-century setting, it must have truly seemed otherworldly.

Lastly, I hope everyone noticed Stanton and Barling's commitment to the Lenten fast. The consumption of salted herrings and little else for six weeks must have been truly grim. Records exist of medieval people being incredibly short-tempered as well as painfully thirsty by the end of Lent. But there was one detail that I left out, as I didn't believe anybody would believe it was true if it was mentioned in a crime novel. Salted herrings were known as white herrings. Herrings that had been both salted and smoked were called . . . red herrings. Reader, you couldn't make it up.

Acknowledgments

In the popular imagination, novelists beaver away alone in a garret, emerging with a finished manuscript that is ready for publishing. The reality is somewhat different, and this writer has many people to thank for making Stanton and Barling's latest outing the book that it is. My agent, Josh Getzler, can't quit the twelfth century and has brought his hard-working assistant, Jon Cobb, along for the ride. Editor Andrew Noakes at The History Quill provided a wealth of insightful guidance and a huge amount of encouragement. Ian Critchley came on board once again and demonstrated his all-seeing eye. To my eternal shame and to his equally eternal credit, he remembered more details about Aelred Barling than I did. Thanks also to Helen Baggott for her scrupulous attention to detail. Special mention must go to Chris Shamwana at Ghost Design for yet another stunning cover in the series. There are many historians whose excellent work I have consulted and who are mentioned in the bibliography. My readers and reviewers are as wonderful as ever. It's impossible to describe how motivating the steady stream of emails and messages asking for more Stanton and Barling has been. And, as always, my Jon and my Angela are everything. With the pandemic lockdown of 2020, I've been sharing the garret with them. I've loved every second.

List of Characters

Aelred Barling, clerk to King Henry II
Hugo Stanton, his assistant

Clergy of the cathedral
Benedict, prior of Christ Church, Canterbury
Brother William, monk
Richard, Archbishop of Canterbury

Builders of the cathedral
William of Sens, master mason
Lambert Green, second master mason

Peter Flocke, freestone mason
Katerine Flocke, his wife and mason's servant
Adam Drake, roughmason
Martin Eustace, lime burner

Dwellers of the city
Gilbert Ordway, physician
Margery Clement, herbalist

Nicholas Clement, exorcist and necromancer and nephew to Margery

Isabel Tyson, widow of a mercer
Lucia Tyson, her daughter
Hilde, servant to the Tyson family

Osbert Derfield, innkeeper
Ida Roulf, alewife
John Roulf, her husband
Elwin Venner, quarrymaster

Pilgrims to the city
Robert Norwood
Elena Whitehand
Sybil Whitehand, sister to Elena

Bibliography

No historical novelist could do what they do without the sterling work of historians, and I am no exception. For anybody wishing to delve deeper into the real history behind this novel, I can recommend the following:

Abbott, Edwin A., *St. Thomas of Canterbury: His Death and Miracles* (London: Adam and Charles Black, 1898).

Finucane, Ronald C., *Miracles and Pilgrims: Popular Beliefs in Medieval England* (London, Melbourne and Toronto: J.M. Dent & Sons Ltd, 1977).

Foyle, Jonathan, *Architecture of Canterbury Cathedral* (London: Scala Publishers Ltd, 2013).

French, Roger, *Medicine before Science: The Business of Medicine from the Middle Ages to the Enlightenment* (Cambridge: Cambridge University Press, 2003).

Getz, Faye, *Medicine in the English Middle Ages* (Princeton, New Jersey: Princeton University Press, 1998).

Gimpel, Jean, *The Cathedral Builders* (New York: Harper Colophon Press, 1983).

Guy, John, *Thomas Becket* (London: Viking, 2012).

Hartnell, Jack, *Medieval Bodies: Life, Death and Art in the Middle Ages* (London: Profile Books Ltd/Wellcome Collection, 2018).

Henisch, Bridget Ann, *Fast and Feast: Food in Medieval Society* (University Park, Pennsylvania: The Pennsylvania State University Press, 1976).

Keates, Jonathan and Hornak, Angelo, *Canterbury Cathedral* (London: Scala Publications Ltd, 1980).

Kieckhefer, Richard, *Magic in the Middle Ages* (Cambridge: Cambridge University Press, 1989).

Knoop, Douglas and Jones, G.P., *The Mediaeval Mason: An Economic History of English Stone Building in the Later Middle Ages and Early Modern Times* (Manchester: Manchester University Press, 1933).

Urry, William, *Canterbury Under the Angevin Kings* (University of London: The Athlone Press, 1967).

Webb, Diana, *Pilgrimage in Medieval England* (London and New York: Hambledon and London, 2000).

Woodman, Francis, *The Architectural History of Canterbury Cathedral* (London, Boston and Henley: Routledge & Kegan Paul, 1981).

About the Author

E.M. Powell's historical thriller and medieval mystery Fifth Knight and Stanton and Barling novels have been #1 Amazon and *Bild* bestsellers. *The Canterbury Murders* is the third novel in the Stanton and Barling series. Born and raised in the Republic of Ireland into the family of Michael Collins (the legendary revolutionary and founder of the Irish Free State), she lives in northwest England with her husband, daughter and a Facebook-friendly dog. She's represented by Josh Getzler at HG Literary. Find out more by visiting her website www.empowell.com or follow her on Twitter @empowellauthor.